RAVENSONG

CAYLA FAY

SIMON & SCHUSTER BFYR

NEW YORK   LONDON   TORONTO   SYDNEY   NEW DELHI

SIMON & SCHUSTER BFYR

An imprint of Simon & Schuster Children's Publishing Division
1230 Avenue of the Americas, New York, New York 10020
This book is a work of fiction. Any references to historical events, real people,
or real places are used fictitiously. Other names, characters, places, and events are
products of the author's imagination, and any resemblance to actual events or
places or persons, living or dead, is entirely coincidental.
SIMON & SCHUSTER BOOKS FOR YOUNG READERS
and related marks are trademarks of Simon & Schuster, Inc.
For information about special discounts for bulk purchases, please contact Simon & Schuster
Special Sales at 1-866-506-1949 or business@simonandschuster.com.
The Simon & Schuster Speakers Bureau can bring authors to your live event.
For more information or to book an event, contact the Simon & Schuster Speakers Bureau at
1-866-248-3049 or visit our website at www.simonspeakers.com.
Interior design by Hilary Zarycky
The text for this book was set in Bell.
Manufactured in the United States of America
First Edition
2 4 6 8 10 9 7 5 3 1
Library of Congress Cataloging-in-Publication Data
Names: Fay, Cayla, author.
Title: Ravensong / Cayla Fay.
Description: First edition. | New York : Simon & Schuster Books for Young Readers, [2023] |
Audience: Ages 12 up. | Audience: Grades 7–9. | Summary: Stuck in high school until her
eighteenth birthday, demi-god Neve is eager to join her sisters in their fight against evil, but
when she meets Alexandria, a girl with a dark secret, Neve must choose between duty and love.
Identifiers: LCCN 2022020798 (print) | LCCN 2022020799 (ebook) |
ISBN 9781665905299 (hardcover) | ISBN 9781665905312 (ebook)
Subjects: CYAC: Mythology, Celtic—Fiction. | LGBTQ+ people—Fiction. | Sisters—Fiction. |
Fantasy. | LCGFT: Fantasy fiction. | Novels.
Classification: LCC PZ7.1.F388 Rav 2023 (print) |
LCC PZ7.1.F388 (ebook) | DDC [Fic]—dc23
LC record available at https://lccn.loc.gov/2022020798
LC ebook record available at https://lccn.loc.gov/2022020799

For Lauren, first and forever

CHAPTER ONE

The girl with her arm in a sling didn't look like a god. She could have been any other teenager eagerly counting down the days until graduation. The busted arm might've been from a sports injury, or an unlucky fender bender. No one would suspect that she'd hurt herself fighting a demon.

Well. They might start to suspect something when they saw the silver sword held tight in her grip. Newgrange Harbor High School didn't have a fencing team, and even if it did, a blunt fencing foil could never be confused with the weapon Neve Morgan held with practiced grace, like it was an extension of her arm.

The sword's weight was familiar, the leather-wrapped pommel perfectly molded to her grip, and for the hundredth time this week, Neve felt a stab of annoyance that it had been relocated to the armory, instead of being under her bed where it belonged. Besides her bedroom, the armory was where she kept most of her weapons anyway, but it was the *principle* of the thing.

Despite her aggravation, Neve felt the muscles in her neck

loosen the moment her sword was back in her hand. The armory smelled like burnished steel and the oil she and her sisters used to maintain their blades, but more than that, it felt safe. Their weapons were ancient—as old as they were or older—held together by magic and a strict maintenance regimen, but only about a third of the collection was still used in battle. The rest were mementos. Tokens from battles long past, both lost and won. Neve wasn't allowed to know their stories, not yet, but sometimes she liked to imagine the glory of it. Why *that* longsword? Or those arrows? What had been strong enough to chip the blade of the double-bladed axe in the corner?

It was a game she'd played since she was little, one she used to play with her sisters, until they both grew up and left her behind.

Tonight, however, Neve wasn't interested in telling herself war stories.

"Mab's tits, Nee," said a voice at her back. Neve jumped at Mercy's sudden appearance, as if she'd been caught sneaking out past curfew, not handling a blade that had seen more than a thousand years of bloodshed. "If Daughter Aoife finds you in here, she's going to lose her shit."

"I'm bored," Neve complained, her shoulders tensing slightly. Lying to her sisters was always hard, but at least it was Mercy and not Bay. Mercy—the second-oldest and a middle-child stereotype in more ways than one—could often be persuaded to look the other way when Neve broke house rules. Rules that forbade Neve from handling her weapons when she was injured because no one trusted her not to overdo it, even when she was supposed to be on bed rest.

Bay was different, though. Lying to Bay was impossible.

Neve heaved a sigh. *"Mer-cy,"* she whined. "It's been a *week*."

She wasn't the only one hurt in the fight, but she was the only one who'd taken a nasty demon bite to the shoulder and, to add insult to extremely painful injury, the only one still healing. Oh, the joys of being under eighteen in the Morgan household.

"Next time, remember how this feels before you break formation," Mercy said, rolling her eyes. Neve glowered. Right, like she'd *wanted* a demon to turn her shoulder into shredded beef.

"I had an opening," Neve insisted, falling into the argument they'd already had a half-dozen times since last week. "I saw a chance to kill the stupid thing and I took it."

Mercy pinched the bridge of her nose. "Yeah, and how'd that go, genius? You're still seventeen."

You're still seventeen. You're still mostly human. You haven't manifested yet. Neve had heard those excuses hundreds of times, whenever her family needed a reason to leave her behind or keep her in the dark or baby her like she wasn't just as much a part of the triad as Mercy or Bay. Like she wasn't just as much a god.

Except she *wasn't* part of the triad or a fully-fledged god yet, not really. She was still underage, and until her birthday in eight months she was stuck in the bullshit liminal space between humanity and divinity, separated from the memories of her past lives, her powers, and her sisters, who insisted that she needed to be protected.

Neve ground her teeth. She didn't need to be protected. She was Morrigan. She *did* the protecting.

"I can still fight," Neve insisted. She knew she should drop it. This wasn't an argument she could win—history had proved that dozens of times over—but gods, she just wanted someone to listen to her for once.

"You absolutely can," said a new voice from the doorway, and Neve stiffened as Daughter Maeve swept into the armory, her customary black cloak trailing behind her. Maeve was using her High Priestess voice, which was appropriate since she technically was the High Priestess of the Order of Danu, the sect of nuns who had devoted themselves to raising and protecting the Morrigan for lifetimes. Neve straightened her back in anticipation of a lecture.

"No one doubts your ability to fight," Daughter Maeve went on, adjusting her veil. The Daughters never wore them over their faces inside the convent, but it was still part of the daily ensemble. "But we still worry about your safety. If you die before . . ."

Neve stiffened, a chill crawling up the back of her neck. She didn't want to have this conversation anymore, but Daughter Maeve and Mercy were blocking the door. "I'm not going to die."

"No, you're not," Maeve agreed, and for a brief, beautiful moment Neve thought that the conversation was about to turn in her favor. "Because we're going to keep you safe until you turn eighteen. It's only eight more months. Be patient."

I don't need to be kept safe! Neve wanted to scream at both of them. Her arm twinged, a cruel reminder that despite her protestations to the contrary, she was still breakable.

"You know what happens if you die before you manifest," Maeve said, not unkindly.

Neve glared. She did know. Of course she knew—how could she possibly forget, when it was her family's second-favorite reason to treat her with kid gloves.

If she died before turning eighteen, the cycle ended. The magic that brought them back lifetime after lifetime would vanish, and this would be their last life. They would leave the world unguarded, forever, and the monsters they kept at bay would be free to roam. No pressure or anything.

"I'm not going to break the cycle," Neve grumbled after a long minute, looking at the floor. Neve might be a god and technically a thousand years old, but in this lifetime she was only seventeen, and, divine or not, there was no way she could win a staring contest with an immortal Irishwoman.

"Good," Maeve said, nodding. She inclined her head, like that was the end of it, before sweeping out of the armory as silently as she'd arrived.

"Yeesh," Mercy said when Maeve's footsteps had faded. Then, when Neve shot her a dirty look: "Oh, come on, that could've been so much worse. It could've been Aoife."

Fair enough. Neve didn't have a mother, so she didn't know for sure, but of all the Daughters of Danu—Maeve, Aoife, and Clara, the nuns who had given up their mortal lives to protect Neve and her sisters and ensure that the chain remained unbroken—Maeve felt the most like a mom. Aoife was more of an aunt who would hit you with a wooden spoon in one hand and hex you with the other. Quite literally, considering that she was the convent's resident witch.

With her chance to pilfer her sword well and truly blown, Neve stalked out of the armory, shoving past Mercy harder than necessary to get through.

It was bad enough always being babied by the Daughters and Bay, but Mercy was usually on her side in these fights. They all knew the rules—take your shoes off in the house, always make sure to clean the blood from your weapons, and no talking about their past lives with Neve—but Mercy usually at least pretended that Neve was an equal member of the family.

Mercy, who had carried Neve into the convent after the demon attack, screaming for Daughter Clara. Neve had been a little out of it—massive blood loss will do that to you—but she could still hear the panic in her sister's voice.

One of them got her, Mercy said over and over, like she couldn't believe it. *I think she's dying.*

Neve swallowed hard, shoving the memory to the back of her mind and leaving room for irritation to flood forward. She hadn't been dying. Mercy was just being dramatic.

Except, she thought, her hands curling into fists by her sides, it had felt a whole lot like dying at the time.

No. Neve's knuckles were white. She was fine. She was alive and she was *fine.* The cycle wasn't going to end with her, not anytime soon. This wasn't going to be their last lifetime, not on her account.

Her footsteps felt too loud as Neve wandered the halls of the convent. The dark stone walls loomed so high that the light rarely reached all the way to the top, where the ravens roosted. It made Neve feel small, like it had been built for giants. Despite the Gothic architecture, there was no nave or sanctuary. Neve's home had never been for humans holding mass.

The main hallway stretched the length of the convent like a spine, running from the towering double-door entryway to the massive wall of windows in the very back of the building. The view from the windows was uninterrupted, following the cliffs and providing an eyeline to the ocean. And more important, the spit of shoreline below.

Every other room in the convent pulled away from the spine. Most of the lower floor had been split into the kitchen, armory, and massive library. The Daughters' rooms were there as well, nestled in an offshoot that was the closest thing the convent had to a dorter. Twisted spiral steps led to Bay's and Mercy's rooms, each on opposite sides of the spine. The second floor wasn't a floor so much as a series of rooms disconnected from each other. Some had stairs leading to them. Others didn't. Even after seventeen years, Neve was still finding strange chambers and crawl spaces on the second level. Most were impossible to enter except by way of the thin ironwork catwalks that created a crisscross pattern in the empty air above the first floor. None of them crossed the spine, but Neve and her sisters had figured out the fastest ways to get in and out of one another's rooms without ever touching the ground years ago, back when they still had bedtimes.

There was even less space in the attic. Technically, Neve's room was the only one on the third floor, and there was a staircase that led all the way up to it, though Neve preferred her maze of catwalks and ladders. Sleeping so high off the ground made her feel safe. The extra height gave her a better vantage point on anything trying to sneak up on them from the beach, and she knew that if she fell, her sisters would be waiting below to catch her.

Between the ancient stone walls and creaking ironwork, the convent was never quiet. When she was little, Neve liked to imagine that the echoes were ghosts, or memories, whispering the adventures of their past lives just out of earshot. Now the noise was too much like the dull sound of blessed steel through flesh.

There had been an opening, no matter what Mercy said. They'd practiced that formation a thousand times—Neve could've done it in her sleep, blindfolded. Mercy's broadsword and Bay's scythe had moved so fast through the air that they were reduced to silvery streaks in her vision, but through the carnage, Neve saw an opportunity. Bay's last blow had lodged deep in a wolflike demon's shoulder, leaving it hobbling but not dead. It should've been easy to slip out of the protection of her sisters' spinning blades and make short work of the wounded demon. One clean strike and it would've been over.

Except she'd miscalculated, underestimating its speed. It was down a limb; it shouldn't have been able to move so fast, but one second Neve was standing above the wounded monster and the next she was flat on her back. There hadn't been time to raise her blade or even cry out before the demon's full weight pressed against her chest, smothering her.

The bite hurt like fire, serrated teeth tearing into the meat between her shoulder and neck, ripping at muscle and sinew. Blue-gold blood, *her* blood, sprayed like a geyser before running down her back in a grisly torrent. Somewhere, Mercy had screamed her name before Bay broke formation too.

"Neve?"

Blinking back into the present, Neve expected her sister's face to still be covered in blood and ash from the fight, her pupils blown and massive, eating away at the blue of her irises. But Bay had long since cleaned off the reminders of battle, returning to her usual uniform of soft sweaters despite the clinging warmth of summer.

"You okay?" Bay asked. Neve shook herself, pushing the memory as far down as it would go.

Bay's mouth pulled into a gentle frown, as if she knew where Neve's mind had been. The scars she'd earned trying to free Neve from the demon's jaws were faded now, mostly obscured by her freckles, but Neve couldn't help the way her eyes traced the perpendicular lines where claws had slashed through her sister's cheek.

"I'm fine," Neve insisted, harsher than necessary. She wasn't the one who'd nearly gotten her face clawed off. Bay had the worse injury by a mile, but no one was cooing over her.

Neve very specifically did not think about the fact that Bay's face had been messed up for two whole days, the longest time it had taken her to heal from a fight since she turned eighteen. In fact, Neve had put so much effort into not thinking about it that she wasn't really sleeping, all her mental energy devoted to the whole "not thinking about it" thing. Why would she bother thinking about it? Bay had healed; everything was okay.

"I'm fine," Neve said again. Because she was, even if Bay didn't look like she believed it.

"Good," Bay said after a moment, her voice ticking up. "Because I need help during my shift tomorrow. Mercy's got class and I need an extra hand around the shop."

Neve almost smiled, feeling a rush of gratitude toward Bay. It wasn't training, but at least working at the Three Crows— the little store run by her family and Neve's only extra-curricular activity besides demon killing—would get her out of the damn house. After a week of being stuck inside, she was almost looking forward to going back to school.

"Yeah, okay," Neve agreed.

"Perfect." Bay nodded, ruffling Neve's hair before walking away.

"Wait," Neve called after a moment, remembering something. "Don't we open at eight tomorrow?"

"I'll wake you up at six!" Bay replied over her shoulder without turning. "Good night, Neve!"

CHAPTER TWO

If the convent was home, and the rest of the town was unbearably human, the Three Crows was neutral ground. Nestled off Main Street on the quieter but no less nauseatingly quaint Spruce Way, the shop wouldn't have looked out of place in a glossy, autumn-themed catalog or BuzzFeed listicle for "Top 10 Hidden Gems in Coastal Massachusetts."

Newgrange Harbor had, on more than one occasion, been referred to in regional papers as "Secret Salem, the tiny seaside town with just as much atmosphere and a quarter of the tourists." It was a point of town pride. People were really weird about it, actually, and no time of year was worse than autumn, when the temperature started to drop and the days began to shorten. Newgrange Harbor took fall so seriously that it rivaled football for popularity. As soon as the leaves began to turn in September, it was "spooky season" this and "pumpkin spice" that. Neve was always amazed at the thousands of ways to repurpose dead leaves. She always thought that *this* year would be the year the humans ran out of ideas, but they never did.

She always thought that this year would be the year

humans realized the danger that lurked in their backyard, but they never did that, either. It really was amazing how much humans could rationalize.

Bay made idle small talk as they drove out of the convent's shadow and down into Newgrange Harbor proper. Neve barely heard her, staring out the window as she struggled to shake off the nightmare from the night before.

They kept turning to dust in front of her. Bay and Mercy. In her dreams, Neve was too hurt, too slow, to get to them in time. No matter how fast she ran, she never managed to reach her sisters before they exploded into pillars of ash in front of her. The sharp rocks from the beach cut into her knees as she collapsed, her blood mingling with the disintegrated remains of her sisters as the whole world darkened.

They were gone. Her sisters kept dying, leaving Neve completely and utterly alone. High-pitched laughter, a boy's laughter, rang in her ears as the convent came tumbling down around her.

Gods shouldn't get nightmares. Seventeen or not, Neve was a godsdamned Morrigan, and a little bloodshed shouldn't keep her up at night. It never had before.

She'd also never messed up that bad before, and it didn't help that now her subconscious was punishing her on top of everything else. Part of her wanted to sneak into her sisters' rooms, just as a precaution, just to check that they were still there, but stubbornness kept her in her own bed. Besides, if she did that, they would inevitably ask why, and Neve didn't need to add to the ever-growing list of reasons they had to worry about her.

It was fine. She was fine. She'd get over it.

For better or worse, the Three Crows fit in with the town's picturesque aesthetic: old wood, a cobblestone path leading up to the door, green-gray ivy snaking up the walls, the whole nine. The building had been around for ages, and its ancient bones welcomed Neve and Bay as they walked in through the squeaky door that had begun its life as the hull of a trading ship.

Like her family, the Three Crows had adapted to the march of modernity. As far as Neve remembered from Aoife's lessons, it had started out as an apothecary and though the name had survived the centuries, its original purpose was long gone. It was just a metaphysical supply shop now, selling crystals, herb bundles, candles, and other items with negligible magical properties. They also did a booming business in herbalist remedies. That was mostly Clara's work. Despite not having any actual magic, she was a deft hand at healing. Nothing major, of course, nothing that threatened their secret, but enough to earn them a loyal customer base in town.

In spite of Neve's best efforts to beg off doing any actual work—she was *injured* and had been flat-out banned from working in the store on her own after she told one of the locals exactly where she should deposit her complaint about Neve's "customer service"—Bay didn't let her off easy, tasking Neve with unpacking and restocking the shelves. It was tedious and took forever, but at least she was out of the house. The shadow of the convent didn't stretch quite this far into town, with its looming expectations and history she wasn't allowed to learn.

It wasn't so bad when Bay turned eighteen, because at least Neve still had Mercy to lean on as Bay cycled through a thousand years of memories. Those were a rough couple of months, especially when it felt like a stranger was peering out through Bay's eyes. But eventually the memories settled and she returned, more or less, to the person Neve had grown up with. But it had been over a year since Mercy manifested and left Neve in the dark. Alone.

Something sharp pressed against her palm and Neve blinked to see that the crystal she'd been reshelving had cracked in her clenched fist, its edges digging into her skin.

"Shit," Neve swore, peeking over the tops of the shelves to make sure that Bay wasn't watching before crushing the rest of the crystal into a fine powder and letting it drop to the floor. She'd sweep up the shimmery evidence later. Hopefully, Bay wouldn't notice one shiny rock missing from their inventory.

Neve almost wished Bay *had* noticed. Neve was strong enough to crush stone by accident—maybe if her sisters stopped worrying about hurting her all the time and actually let her train, she'd get even stronger and wouldn't have to wait until she turned eighteen. Then she wouldn't have to spend another eight months hiding behind them in fights.

There weren't many customers in the morning, just a few regulars picking up their orders. Bay took care of them, making polite conversation about Ms. Nesbit's horrible dog—the white kind with crusty eyes—and asking about Mr. Johnson's young son, while Neve scowled at anyone who met her gaze.

"What is *wrong* with that girl?" one of the women asked her companion once she was out the door. She probably thought she was out of earshot. "The other two are so pleasant."

"There's one in every family," her friend agreed, shaking her head. "I wonder how she hurt her arm."

"Drunk driving, I bet."

The second woman huffed, scandalized, and Neve couldn't help the laugh that bubbled out of her. She couldn't even *get* drunk.

"It's not funny," Bay said without looking up from the counter. Her hearing was even better than Neve's.

Neve spun on one heel. "Come on, Bee, it's a little funny."

"You could be a little friendlier," Bay said, and Neve's laughter dried up in her throat. "They're our neighbors."

"They're our responsibility," Neve shot back. "We're not like them."

16

"We're close enough."

No, we're not, Neve wanted to argue, but the bell over the door rang as more humans trickled in, and it wasn't as if she was going to win this argument anyway. She never had before. Bay, Mercy, the Daughters, they insisted that staying close to humanity—interacting with them in the Three Crows, going to school with them, all of it—was important. It kept them from getting too distant, from forgetting why they were fighting, or whatever. Allegedly, being enrolled in high school would keep Neve from becoming apathetic and endear her to their human charges.

Right. Because high school would convince her that humanity was worth saving.

Neve didn't realize until after she'd agreed to mind the cash register while Bay took her break that she'd been tricked. It was after two thirty, which meant that her classmates had officially been set loose, and she would be the one who had to deal with them if they came in the shop. The last week had been boring as hell, but Neve appreciated any opportunity to skip school.

She recognized the first customer immediately, a Newgrange Harbor High School sophomore who paled at the sight of her. Patrick . . . something. Neve couldn't be bothered with last names, but his name wasn't as important as *why* she remembered him in particular: he was one of this year's batch of misguided students who thought they could boost their own social status by taking her down a peg. Some combination of her apathy and blatant unfriendliness had given her a reputation.

Patrick's campaign lasted a whole week. Graffiti on her locker, vicious rumors, the kinds of things that Neve easily brushed off. She would've let it go on forever, but then there had been an attack. Unfortunately for him, Patrick had chosen that day to box her car in her parking spot with his massive pickup. So Neve had smashed in the window, thrown the stupid thing into neutral, and moved it herself. Not exactly discreet, but she was in a rush and didn't have a ton of options.

The next day, she told him in no uncertain terms that if he got in her way again, she would shove his gear shift so far up his ass that it would never see the light of day again. They hadn't interacted since.

Neve watched as, back in the Three Crows, Patrick swallowed hard before marching up to the counter and mumbling out the last name for his pickup order. Neve watched him for a moment, head cocked at a slight angle, before she shrugged and went into the back to grab it. She didn't bother with small talk as she rang everything up and put it into a bag.

"How's the truck, Percy?" Neve couldn't help but ask as he left. Patrick's shoulders hunched. "Does the back wheel still stick? You should get that looked at."

"It's Patrick," he muttered before rushing out the door. Neve snorted.

Only two more NHHS students stopped in before Bay returned, girls Neve knew only by virtue of being in the same grade since kindergarten. Despite her best efforts, in a town as small as Newgrange Harbor, it was impossible not to know people.

"I hear she's living with her aunt and uncle," one girl— Bethany—said as she perused the shelves. "The pastors who live down on Littletree Lane."

Neve's ears pricked, anticipating new rumors about her and her family, but the Daughters were nuns, not pastors, and Littletree Lane was an oppressively idyllic neighborhood that could never be confused with the convent.

"Someone told me that her parents died in a fire," Taylor Lynn whispered. "Burned the whole house down."

"I heard she started it," Bethany went on at normal volume, as if suggesting that a stranger had committed arson was as benign a topic as picking out a scarf.

Neve tuned out after that. She didn't care about high school politics, and despite the momentary strangeness of what she could only assume was a new student—gods, alleged arsonist or not, who would move to Newgrange Harbor, of all places?—she let her mind wander again.

There were too many people in the shop for Neve to

confront Bay properly when she returned from her break, bearing coffee and a pleased smile. Neve finished up with her current customer before snatching the proffered cup out of Bay's hands and slinking away.

"You're not subtle," Neve signed where she knew Bay could see her. Neve and her sisters had learned American Sign Language alongside English and half a dozen other languages, many long dead. It was useful when they wanted to talk behind the Daughters' backs or, in this case, when Neve wanted to yell at Bay in a room full of people.

"Whatever you say, little sister," Bay signed back quickly before welcoming the next customer to the counter. Neve couldn't help her snort of laughter and took a sip of coffee to hide it. Everyone thought Bay was the nice one, but she was just as much of a shit as Neve or Mercy.

"The Daughters are going to let you go back to school tomorrow," Bay said as they walked out of the Three Crows at the end of the day.

Neve wheeled on her, clutching her phone so hard that the glass cracked. "What?"

"Easy," Bay said, covering her mouth with one hand and swatting at Neve with the other. "If Maeve hears that you've broken another phone, she's going to have a conniption."

Neve smacked her sister with the offending phone. "Why didn't you tell me?"

"Because you were pouting!" Bay exclaimed, dodging out of the way. "Gods, moping around the convent like the world was coming to an end. It's called not rewarding negative behavior, little sister."

"I was not pouting," Neve replied.

Bay crinkled up her nose to keep from laughing and flicked Neve's bottom lip.

"Ow."

"You're doing it again!"

Halfway home Neve realized how bizarre it was for her to want to go back to school. But she was benched until her shoulder healed completely. It was something to do, at least. Something boring and tedious, sure, but *something.* Maybe she'd get lucky and one of the football kids would pull a Patrick and pick a fight just to spice things up.

"Well, well, someone looks like they're in a better mood," Mercy said when Bay and Neve returned home. Walking back into the convent after spending the day in town always felt like removing the outerwear they all donned to fit in with the humans who lived below, stripping it away to reveal their true selves beneath.

Mercy looked Neve up and down before rolling her eyes. "Bay told you, didn't she?"

"Neve was extremely well-behaved at the shop all day," Bay replied before Neve could answer.

"Clara!" Mercy called into the gloom—any modern aspects

of the convent were only for the sake of appearances, and besides the kitchen, the whole place was frozen, amber-like, in time. Neve didn't mind the relative dark. Her eyes adjusted, and it had always felt cozy and safe to her. "Bay spilled the beans! You owe me twenty dollars."

"Maiden Mother," cried a voice from the kitchen. Neve snickered as Daughter Clara stomped into the main hall, waving a sauce-covered soupspoon. "Bay, I was counting on you!"

"Sorry, old woman," Mercy said smugly. "You don't bet Triad against Triad."

Neve grinned, warmed as always by the casual reference to her sisters' connection. They were Morrigan, the three-in-one, and more than one historian thought that they were three aspects of a single god. Neve had grown up with that connection, spent her whole life learning about it, but it still felt shiny and new every time Mercy or Bay mentioned it in casual conversation. Neve thought she could go on forever on that tiny glow of belonging, forgetting for a moment that she wasn't quite like her sisters. Not yet, at least.

"'Bet Triad against Triad,'" Clara scoffed. "I have raised you three so many . . . Did you just call me old?"

"Oh, shit," Mercy said, scooting around Neve to avoid getting whacked by Clara's spoon.

"Immortal or not, I'm still younger than you!" Clara shouted as Mercy gave chase down the long corridor.

"Not in this lifetime!" Mercy's voice echoed from around the corner, followed by the sound of socks skidding along stone floors and then a wall-shaking crash. "Don't tell Aoife, don't tell Aoife!"

After dinner—where, if Aoife's sour attitude was any indication, she'd been informed of Mercy's assault against the wall—Neve slipped out to watch her sisters train.

The back of the convent faced the ocean, and the cooling September air was tangy with salt water. The grounds sprawled, the gardens and sparring pit all sheltered from view by the massive hedge that lined the property. Trespassers rarely made it up the drive before losing their nerve and turning back, but there were several dozen spells woven into the topiary to shield it from human sight.

Mercy always joked that if someone saw, they could just say that they were practicing for an upcoming LARP, though that excuse would fall apart as soon as someone saw that they bled the wrong color.

Above them, three ravens circled overhead, their sharp little eyes missing nothing as they kept watch over their charges below. Three birds, one for each of the Morrigan. They grew up together, and at the end of this cycle, each raven would die alongside its sister before being reborn as well. Only the Daughters existed on the outskirts of their little dance of life and death. Someone had to keep an eye on things from the outside.

Neve sat on the hill above the training grounds, but even from a distance she could feel the collisions of their weapons in her bones, rattling her heart into a frantic rhythm. She hated being sidelined like this, but even she had to admit that it was amazing to watch her sisters in action. When she was inside it, she was more focused on scrambling out of the way of Mercy's massive broadsword than the force behind it, enough to crack off the top of a mountain. Neve was too preoccupied with keeping Bay in her sight to appreciate how her scythe turned into a disk of pure silver as it whipped through the air without pause.

They didn't spar with her like that. They both insisted that they weren't holding anything back, but Neve knew that they were pulling their punches, just a little. She was just too fragile. She slowed them down.

Not to mention, if one of them accidentally killed her, that was it. No more Morrigan, no more triad. No one to keep monsters from overrunning the world. Neve's jaw clenched as the image of her sisters dissolving into ash flashed behind her eyelids. The clanging of metal against metal suddenly sounded like cold laughter in her ears. None of them could exist without one another, even if all Neve did lately was slow them down.

Her sisters would've been able to get that demon on the beach without her. They would've dispatched it just like all the others, but Bay had gotten hurt because Neve broke formation.

She'd had an opening. She just hadn't been strong enough.

Neve left her sisters in the training pit, the concussive sound of their sparring reminding her what they were capable of without her. With last night's nightmare still crouched low and ready to pounce in the back of her mind, sleep was out of the question. But wandering the halls would only draw attention from the Daughters, so Neve stayed in her attic room on the third floor, feeling like a ghost haunting the convent. Though she did make a quick stop in the armory to reclaim her sword, some of her tension unspooling with the comforting weight in her hand. She'd endure the lecture about rule breaking later.

Her room was small and sparse, the blue walls tall and sloping to accommodate the architecture. Nothing quite fit right or sat flush, which drove Bay to distraction, but Neve didn't mind. Usually, her weapons—daggers, mostly, with the exception of her short-sword—littered every available surface, and one of the walls was full of holes where Neve liked to practice throwing them. The ceiling was too, which was a little more exciting because she never quite knew when one of her knives would give in to gravity and come back to her.

Without training to keep her occupied, Neve's nerves jangled under her skin, making her buzz with the frantic need to *do something*. She closed her eyes, taking a deep breath through her nose before opening them again and trailing her fingers over the knickknacks that sat on a high shelf running the length of the room. She named them each in turn—chipped arrowhead, tattered flag, homemade doll, hag stone—as she went. They were trinkets from past lifetimes, one of the Daughters' few allowances in the "no talking about past lives before eighteen" rule. Neve had made up a thousand stories about them: the antique vase belonged to a woman they'd saved; the little talisman was from one of the last true witches in the world besides Aoife.

Her collection, along with the mismatch of books pilfered from the Three Crows, probably looked like it belonged to some mythology-obsessed nerd, a hobbyist or forever-student with the world's most niche interest. To Neve, every item was another piece of her family's history. The Morrigan weren't the only gods from the old world, not by a long shot, but they were the only ones still around. The rest of the pantheon was gone, and without her memories, Neve didn't know why.

The books helped her imagine what they'd been like. Brigid and the Dagda, Danu and Áine and Aodh and all the others.

They were probably no more accurate than human accounts of the Morrigan, but Neve liked to imagine what it had been like when her family had been together, all of them in the old world before the rest had vanished without a trace.

Despite Neve's best efforts, her stories didn't keep the nightmares away. They'd never needed to before. Injuries were a part of the job, and even if she healed slowly, Neve always healed.

I think she's dying! Neve had never heard Mercy sound so scared, and the high keen of her sister's panicked voice sliced through her like a wound all its own. They'd all had close calls, but nothing like this.

Neve paced the length of her room, agitated. Every time she tried to draw her blankets over her body, she felt the demon's massive weight on her chest again, crushing her ribs while she struggled to breathe through the pulpy viscera filling her lungs. The dark in her room, usually a comfort, was cold, and it felt like she was being watched from all sides. Like *something* was in there with her. The demon from before, maybe, ready for round two. Ready to take her apart for real now that her sisters weren't there to protect her. Neve's hands clenched into fists by her sides, palms itching for the weight of her weapons.

Actually, you know what? Neve thought, snatching her sword out from under her bed. *Fuck this.*

CHAPTER THREE

Neve didn't let herself think as she threw open the window. Poe, her raven, squawked and blinked his beady eyes.

"It's just a walk," Neve said. She needed to get out of the convent. Anxiety hummed in her ears and she gritted her teeth as she clambered down the wall, hitting the slick grass below with a wet thud.

Neve cast furtive glances behind her as she crept down the hill, waiting for someone to catch her on her way to the beach. Most of the Newgrange Harbor coastline was rocky and inhospitable, and none more so than the spit of craggy shore directly beneath the convent. There were signs up every-where, warning passersby to stay away from the cliffside, lest they fall into the ocean and drown. Or worse.

At the boundary line, Neve tapped one of the signs that she and her sisters had put up years before.

DANGER: BEWARE FALLING ROCKS

DANGER: RIPTIDE

DANGER: NO SWIMMING, STRONG CURRENT

She pressed forward, ignoring the embarrassing skip in her

heart when she passed the barrier. It was just a walk. Just a patrol. Just a quick survey of the perimeter, to prove to her family that she was capable of doing this one thing.

To prove to herself that she wasn't scared.

As always, the entrance to Hell didn't look like much. The convent was more noticeable by far, looming above the stretch of cliffside that had a bad habit of spitting out demons. Only centuries-old instincts hinted that something lurked beneath the ordinary exterior. It looked different during an attack— less "rocky cliff face" and more "swirling portal to Hell"—but Neve didn't expect trouble tonight.

Then, as if to prove her wrong, the skin on the back of Neve's neck prickled with the unmistakable feeling of being watched. She spun around, turning her back on the Gate with an excuse already on her lips, certain that one of her sisters had caught her. Only instead of Bay or Mercy, a white girl in a purple hoodie stared back at her from just inside the boundary line. Enormous headphones were clapped over her ears, securing the hood in place, and even from fifty yards away, Neve could hear tinny music blaring. The girl blinked at her—once, then twice—never breaking eye contact, but her eyes widened when she saw the sword in Neve's hand.

Well, shit.

Neve was momentarily grateful she hadn't put on her

armor before sneaking out, though maybe with it on she could've used Mercy's LARP excuse.

"What the hell is that?" The girl broke the silence first, yanking her headphones down around her neck. She was young, about Neve's age, but Neve had never seen her before. Which, in a town as small as Newgrange Harbor, was next to impossible.

Maiden, Mother, and Crone, of all the ways to meet the town's new resident arsonist.

"You shouldn't be here!" Neve shouted to be heard over the wind and waves. "There's a sign."

Well said, Neve.

"You're here," the girl replied, unimpressed. She hopped closer, balancing on the slick rocks.

"I'm—" Neve cast about for an excuse. *I'm trained for this. I'm actually thousands of years old. I'm trespassing too, so please keep your voice down.* "I'm a Morgan. I'm allowed."

That would be enough to send any townie running, but the girl just crossed her arms over her chest and glared.

Neve opened her mouth to speak before something electric sparked in her blood, setting her nerves alight and raising the hair on the back of her neck. In front of her, the girl's gaze shifted over Neve's shoulder and her eyes widened with panic. Neve whirled, her sword rising just in time to wedge between the fangs of something massive and looming before it could bite down on her neck.

Neve swore, immediately recanting her gratitude for forgoing armor as she ripped her sword free.

The demon was enormous and hideous, with a head devoid of features except for a massive, toothy mouth. Neve gagged at the smell of rotting meat that wafted from its jaws.

"What the hell is *that*?" the girl screamed.

Neve didn't bother to answer as she fought to keep her feet. With her left arm in a sling and no dagger to counterbalance her sword, she listed unsteadily to the right, unused to fighting with only one weapon.

Claws stabbed at her midsection and the demon roared its frustration as she scrambled to avoid its attacks. In a panic, Neve spun, sending up a spray of sand as the demon bit at her. Its jaws missed anything vital, but one serrated tooth caught her sling, shredding it instantly.

"What are you waiting for?" Neve shouted to the girl, who was still frozen in place. *"Move!"*

The demon used her distraction, and this time she wasn't fast enough. Gods, she was never fast enough when it mattered. Blood burst in her mouth, and Neve went flying, landing facedown in the rocky shallows. Pain lanced up and down her torso. *Broken rib*, her mind supplied, automatically running a diagnostic. *Maybe two.*

Her lungs burned and Neve jerked her head out of the water, gasping for air and staggering away from a weight on her chest that wasn't there. Water lapped at her booted ankles and blood ran down her legs in slow-moving rivulets. Her ribs groaned, stabbing into her whenever she breathed. She was barely up before the girl screamed again.

Okay, that's enough, Neve thought, tearing away the last scraps of the sling and holding the pommel of her sword with both hands.

Sucking in a breath, and before she could think about what she was doing, Neve launched herself at the demon, screaming wordlessly. Whether from surprise or pure luck, the demon hesitated for a split second, just enough time for Neve to sink her sword into its side. The creature shrieked and black blood spilled over Neve's skin, sizzling wherever it made contact. Their momentum carried them into the water, and once again Neve's breath was forced from her lungs at the shock of sudden cold. The demon roared as they crashed through the surface, swiping with its claws and trying to take a bite out of her.

Somehow, through the chaos of sea spray, blood, and screams, Neve managed to get her head above water. The demon thrashed, equally disoriented, and Neve saw her opening. Taking half a breath to steady her aim, she thrust her sword into its mouth with all her strength. The tip of the blade burst through the back of its throat.

"Eat shit," Neve panted. The air steamed where boiling blood met icy ocean.

The demon burst in a plume of hellfire and ash, and Neve somehow made it to the shore before her legs gave out. She heard a shout of alarm before the ground rose up to meet her. Pain exploded above her left temple, and then there was nothing.

Something rattled beneath her as Neve came to. It took a few long seconds to realize that it was an engine, and Neve blinked back to consciousness to find herself in the backseat of an unfamiliar car. Wheels hit a pothole in the road, and she cursed as her injuries turned the world into a kaleidoscope of pain.

"Oh, thank God, you're alive," said the girl from the beach, wheeling around to face her, which Neve didn't think was very safe driving. "I thought you'd died for a second there, and then you wouldn't wake up and there was that *thing*, and—"

"Stop talking," Neve growled, struggling to sit up. Her clothes were still damp and she was probably ruining the upholstery with seawater and blood. Her vision swam, and she had to grit her teeth against the scream that wanted to rip from her throat. "Stop the car."

"I'm taking you to the hospital. It's a miracle you're still breathing and there was that *monster* and I almost called 911 but they wouldn't believe me even if I did—you know, on account of the monster, and—"

"No hospitals," Neve groaned, cutting off the girl's rambling.

"You hit your head really hard when you passed out. I'm pretty sure you have a concussion. You need a hospital."

"No, I don't."

"Yes, you do." The girl's voice rose in pitch, and Neve winced as the sound momentarily filled her head with painful static.

Movement caught Neve's eye as a dark shape flew toward the car, and metal screeched as Poe's iron-tipped talons found purchase. The girl cried out and yanked the wheel to the right, no doubt thinking the demon was making another appearance.

"Go home," Neve ordered. Her words were a little too slurred to be intimidating. Maybe she did have a concussion.

Poe cawed balefully, glaring at her with inky-black eyes.

"Go *home*, Poe, and if you tell the others, I swear to all the gods I will pluck you. Don't think I won't."

"And now she's talking to a bird," the girl muttered under her breath. "You definitely need a doctor."

"Pass."

Exhaling sharply, Neve opened the door of the car and rolled onto the street. The girl's shout of alarm was drowned out by the crunch of asphalt beneath Neve's bruised skin. She tried to land on her good arm as much as possible, but it still felt like her bones had been ground into a fine powder.

The car had screeched to a halt by the time Neve staggered to her feet, leaning heavily to one side to accommodate the broken ribs. She hugged her left arm with her right to hold it in place.

"What the hell is *wrong* with you?" the girl yelled as she ran across the road to where Neve stood. Her eyes were enormous with panic, her rosebud mouth pressed into a thin line.

"No self-preservation instinct," Neve deadpanned. She wanted this night to be over. She never should have gone down to the Hellgate on her own, and now she was hurting and had to deal with some human who was too new to know to stay out of her way. "Now, don't you have a house to set on fire? Shoo."

The girl's eyes darkened and her lips pressed even thinner. "How do you—I *didn't*! I mean . . ." She cut herself off with an irritated huff and crossed her arms in a mirror of her pose from the beach. "No. You need help. I'm taking you to the hospital, so get your ass back in my car."

On another night, Neve might have laughed. On another night, the novelty of this person, who didn't know Neve or her reputation, might have been charming. Interesting, at the very least. On *this* night, however, she was soaking wet, bloody, and in a considerable amount of pain. So she did not laugh. Instead, she grabbed the girl by her vibrant purple hoodie and dragged her back to the side of the road with her good arm, remembering to modify her strength at the last minute.

"What's your name?" Neve demanded, spinning the new girl so they were face-to-face.

"Alexandria." The girl's voice was quieter now, but no less fierce as she tilted her chin up. Her eyes, so dark that they looked black, met Neve's without blinking.

"Okay, Alexandra—"

"*Alexandria*." The interruption was pointed. "Like the library."

Neve tried again. "Okay, Alexandria, like the library. You're new here, so I'm going to give you a quick introduction to Newgrange Harbor. That stretch of beach is off-limits. The convent on the hill is off-limits. I am off-limits."

Neve waited for some kind of response, anything that indicated understanding, but Alexandria's eyes just flicked to a spot on her forehead.

"You're bleeding." She squinted and Neve turned her face away. This girl had already seen too much, and the last thing Neve needed was for her to notice that Neve's blood was the wrong color. "Also, your whole schtick would work a lot better if you didn't just get your ass kicked by a monster and then knock yourself out."

Alexandria took a breath and Neve was momentarily distracted by the way her mouth twisted in disbelief, as if she couldn't quite believe what she'd just said. Other than that, though, the girl seemed unfazed about what she'd seen. It nagged at Neve, but not enough to pursue it. Not tonight.

I did not get my ass kicked, she thought instead.

"Don't poke your nose where it doesn't belong and don't ask questions, or next time I won't tell you so nicely."

Neve gave Alexandria one final sneering look before stalking onto the road. She wasn't far from home. She could walk from here. Her ribs throbbed at the thought, but she would rather face down another demon than admit to the human that she needed a ride.

"That was you telling me *nicely?*"

Neve was only a few steps away when Alexandria shouted from the side of the road. Neve almost laughed, but the flash of humor was quickly chased away as panic charged through her again. Her stomach clenched. She'd put her entire family in danger tonight. She could've died. The cycle could've ended right then. A thousand years, all undone.

Anger coursed through her veins, sweet and simple and so much easier to manage than guilt. She wanted to hit something. She wanted to *scream.* The nails of her right hand dug into the skin above her left elbow where she held it close to her chest, pressing so deep that she drew blood.

Neve could still feel Alexandria's eyes on her long after she had limped down the road, toward safety, toward home.

CHAPTER FOUR

P oe didn't give her up.

Neve returned to the convent only a few hours before sunrise, which didn't leave much time to sleep or heal before she had to be up again for school. Binding her wounds ate a precious thirty minutes, longer than it should have, but Neve's hands were shaking and soon slick with blood. She was unconscious the moment her head hit the pillow, exhaustion pulling her into a deep sleep not even her nightmares could reach.

It felt like only minutes had passed when her alarm clock chirped on the bedside table, mocking her with the start of a new day. Neve flung her fist out with more force than intended, reducing it to shards of plastic and electric wiring.

The whole night—sneaking out, the demon attack, being *seen*—felt like a nightmare. Only her injuries, exacerbated by the long walk back to the convent and climbing through her third-story window, served as proof that she hadn't dreamed the whole thing.

"Alarm clocks don't grow on trees, dear," Daughter Maeve chided, sweeping into the room like she did every morning.

Neve groaned, burying her head beneath her pillow. Thousand-year-old god or not, she was still stuck in a teenager's body, and waking up before seven in the morning was unacceptable. "I assume you'll pay for a new one?"

"Isn't money supposed to be your job?" Neve groused, still half-asleep. Of all the Daughters of Danu, Daughter Maeve was by far the most fiscally minded. Maybe knowing how to pay taxes and the difference between stocks and bonds was part of High Priestess training. Neve didn't know, but either way, the IRS had never come knocking at their door.

"I believe I'll let you handle this purchase, dear," Maeve said with a small smile. "The value of a dollar and all that. Come on, it's time to get up, or you'll be late to school."

Neve groaned again, any affection for the old woman evaporating. She waited for Maeve to leave the room before sitting up, wincing as her injuries strained. Thankfully, the brief rest was enough to smooth over the surface wounds, though her vision was still a little wobbly and her ribs would take at least another day to heal. In the meantime, she just had to get through the day without her sisters finding out that she'd gotten hurt. Or how.

Her jaw clenched as she peeled away the bandages and redressed them. A quick trip to the bathroom and a glance in the mirror over the sink revealed dark half-moons stamped beneath her eyes and a small mark on her forehead where she'd bled last night. Neve's skin was gray and pale, making her freckles stand out like splattered ink. She poked at the scar, wishing it would just disappear and take the memory of last night with it. It took a little digging, but Neve unearthed some extremely expired concealer from the depths of her bathroom drawer and daubed it onto the remains of the wound.

Her hands trembled, dusting the counter with setting powder, and Neve gripped the edge of the sink to steady them. She had never faced a demon without her sisters before. Gods, Mercy was supposed to *sense* these kinds of things. Mercy should've known that the demon was coming through the Hellgate—she and Bay both should have shown up at the beach, but they weren't there. They didn't *know*. How didn't they know?

It took Neve too long to release her grip on the sink. She ignored the hairline cracks where her fingers had pressed against the porcelain and examined her handiwork. Her makeup application was sloppy, but it would get the job done. She shook her head, letting her hair fall in her face and hoping her combined efforts would conceal the scar until it healed.

"There she is," Daughter Aoife said when Neve finally made it downstairs. "About time you joined us, Sleeping Beauty."

Neve rolled her eyes, tightening her replacement sling with her teeth. She swiped her backpack from one of the stools in the kitchen before rushing out the front door.

"Don't speed!" Maeve called after her.

Neve sped, racing down the road that led from the convent into Newgrange Harbor proper. She couldn't remember the last time she wanted to waste time at school instead of staying home with her sisters, but today she needed the routine. She needed the mind-numbing sameness to smooth away the jagged nerves that hummed beneath her skin.

Freshmen scuttled out of the way as she roared into the school's parking lot, screeching into her spot at the front with the rest of the senior class. As she pulled her bag out of the passenger seat, her phone buzzed.

Bay: Did you take your sword out of the armory? It's not there.

Neve's stomach dropped into her boots. Her sword. In the confusion, she'd forgotten to retrieve her ancient, irreplaceable, incredibly conspicuous *sword*.

Bay and Mercy were going to kill her. The Daughters were going to kill her.

Neve: No. Check again.

Guilt panged in her gut for lying, but she needed to stall until she had time to go back to the beach. The beach where she'd almost died, where she'd been *seen* . . . Neve was breaking every rule in the book. She should have told her family what happened, should have let Aoife handle the human—they had *protocols* for this—but most of all, Neve shouldn't have gone down to the Gate on her own in the first place.

The bell rang, signaling the start of the school day and breaking Neve out of her panicked spiral. She dropped her head against the cool metal of the car's doorframe, trying not to think about the last car she'd ridden in and the girl driving it.

It only took a few minutes into first period to realize that coming to school wasn't the distraction she'd hoped it would be. Sitting still for nearly eight hours at a time was difficult for Neve and her sisters, boring and insufferable when their bodies were built for battle. But the day had barely started and Neve could already feel her skin tightening over her bones with the need to move, to fight. She was wired, even more keyed up than usual. It felt like she was about to vibrate out of her skin.

The day crawled by, a steady march of droning teachers and endless glances at the clock. Everything was the same, but Neve couldn't stop surveying and resurveying her surroundings. Her muscles pulled taut, ready to spring into action at a moment's notice.

Nothing happened. No demons erupted from the supply closet. No students turned to her with featureless faces and a mouthful of teeth sharp enough to shear her skin and sinew into bloody ribbons. They were all just as boring and human as they had been yesterday and the day before and every day before that. Neve needed to get a grip.

At lunch, Neve sat at the table in the back of the cafeteria where she'd eaten alone since Mercy graduated two years ago. The noise wasn't soothing, but it was familiar, and she was halfway to feeling normal when a tray clattered down directly across from her. Neve ripped off her headphones, glaring. Everyone knew better than to come within fifteen feet of her table.

Everyone except a girl in an oversized purple hoodie who clearly had no regard for her own well-being.

"So, I didn't sleep at all last night," said Alexandria, like the library, sitting down across the table from Neve. "For obvious reasons. You don't look too hot either."

For a second all Neve could do was gape at her, which Alexandria seemed to take as an invitation to keep talking.

"So . . . monsters."

"Go away before I make you," Neve said through clenched teeth.

Alexandria didn't seem bothered, continuing through a bite of her apple. "In front of the whole school?" she asked. Neve glowered. "Thought not. So, I have questions. A lot of questions."

I bet you do, Neve thought with no small amount of bitterness.

"Leave me the hell alone," she growled, pushing away from the lunch table. Neve left her tray behind and strode out of the cafeteria without glancing back. Hopefully, Alexandria would get the hint. She would learn the rules of this town soon enough, and Neve prayed she'd do it without telling anyone about what she'd seen. It had been years since Daughter Aoife had erased someone's memory, and Neve would never hear the end of it.

Gods, what a nightmare. Besides giving the Daughters license to ground her until the end of time, it would only serve as more proof that her family was right to keep babying her. Better to keep quiet and hope Alexandria had some sort of latent self-preservation instinct. Neve could handle this on her own.

Neve wandered the empty halls until the end of the lunch period and arrived at her next class early. She slid into the desk in the back-right corner of the classroom, where she could see everything going on around her, every door and window. It was a strategic choice, made at the beginning of the year and one that usually kept her calm and focused. Today, though, Neve laid her head on her desk, forcibly filtering her senses.

"Alexandra Abbott," Mr. Robinson announced at the beginning of roll call.

Neve's head snapped up and she had a moment of premonitory clarity.

"It's Alexandria," said a voice from the desk directly beside Neve's, which had been conspicuously left open in an otherwise packed class. Until now. "Like the library."

Like the godsdamned library.

Neve made it her mission not to glance in Alexandria's direction for the duration of class, which seemed to stretch even longer than normal. Slumped low in her chair, Neve hid her battered face behind her curtain of red hair, absently braiding the strands one after another after another. Having something to do with her hands was usually a good distraction, but now it only served to remind her that Bay was the one who'd taught her how to braid when they were little, twisting the pieces of hair through Neve's tiny fingers. Bay, who she was actively lying to about her missing sword. Neve's stomach soured even further and then growled in protest of her abandoned lunch.

There were only fifteen minutes left in class when a scrap of paper slid onto her desk, directly into her sight line.

The cut on your forehead looks better. Also, what's that blue shit in my backseat? Did you sit on a pen or something? The handwriting on the note was barely legible, written frantically. Neve stared at the paper for a moment too long before crumpling it up and throwing it into her bag.

She was moving the instant the bell rang.

"Miss Morgan, I have not dismissed class yet," Mr. Robinson called after her. Neve ignored him. Her ribs throbbed, objecting to her speed as she put as much distance between her and the classroom as possible.

There was another period left, but Neve was calling it. She was jumpy and overstimulated, and the building around her looked remarkably breakable all of a sudden. She didn't need another black mark on her disciplinary record. Most of the faculty were willing to let her coast until graduation, but she'd already been written up twice this semester.

Of course, there was the issue of where to go. The convent was a nonstarter. Daughter Maeve would scold her for skipping school, and gods help her if Daughter Aoife caught wind that she'd cut class. She *should* go looking for her sword, but the thought of going anywhere near the ocean made Neve's stomach twist and her breath feel like it was caught in her lungs.

That, she decided, was a problem for Future Neve.

"You should be in school, missy," Mercy said as Neve walked through the ancient, creaking door of the Three Crows.

Neve raised an eyebrow at her sister. "Planning on ratting me out?" She tossed her backpack behind the counter, tensed for any indication that Mercy knew about the demon attack, but just like this morning, Mercy didn't say anything.

Somehow, inexplicably, Neve was in the clear—but *how?*

"Smart-ass." Mercy leaned over the counter to ruffle her hair and Neve smiled, the knot in her chest unspooling a little. She might actually get away with this.

"If you're not at school, you're going to help me here," Mercy declared, sweeping her feathered bangs to the side with a shake of her head. "Watch the counter, I need to do inventory."

Neve snapped her sister a two-fingered salute and watched Mercy disappear into the back of the shop, grateful that she wouldn't have to lift boxes of heavy merchandise, even if it meant she had to deal with customers. Neve wished her ribs would just hurry up and heal before they got her caught.

At least she didn't have to make up some excuse to get out of training tonight. She was still benched until tomorrow, and for once Neve was grateful for her family's insistence that she take it easy.

Her mind wandered as she tidied up, dusting counters covered with knickknacks and dark hardwood furniture probably older than the town itself. She watched a woman peer in through the shop's display window. The woman froze as she caught Neve's eye and then bustled away, a little more hurried than before.

Neve wondered if the woman subconsciously sensed something when they made eye contact. Was there a part of her mind that recognized the presence of something old and powerful and not quite human? Would she and the other locals be more or less afraid if they knew the truth about Neve and her family?

Neve imagined the announcement:

Hi, all. So, the entrance to Hell is three miles away from where you and your children sleep, but don't worry, my sisters and I stop the demons before they can escape and eat you. Oh, and by the way, we're not human, either. We're actually gods left over from a pantheon that you and most of the world have forgotten about. Ever hear of the Morrigan? That's us. Also, every time we get killed, we just come back again. Yes, it is like respawning in Fortnite, *you get it. Okay, good talk, now go about your business.*

More afraid, Neve decided. Definitely more afraid, but only the ones who believed them.

Neve ground her teeth with sudden irritation. Mercy and Bay had always been good at blending in, but Neve couldn't understand their human neighbors. She didn't want to understand them. They were so endlessly content to overlook everything and anything they couldn't explain. The truth could saunter up and shake them by the hand and they would find some way to fit it into their own tidy worldview. And if they couldn't, they just ignored it.

Except for Alexandria, *apparently.* She had seen. She had questions.

No one would believe her even if she did say something, Neve told herself, as if she could will it to be true. Gods, she didn't want to imagine what would happen if their secret got out and people *did* believe. There would be a panic. Her mind flashed to half-remembered classes about the Salem witch trials. The town would lose its collective mind and it would make it that much harder to protect the Gate. Chaos and bloodshed, all because one girl saw Neve kill a demon.

Neve shook her head. It wouldn't happen. Alexandria was just another human; she'd learn to leave Neve alone soon enough. It was just a matter of time before everything went back to normal.

Then, as if to prove her wrong, the bell over the door chimed.

CHAPTER FIVE

"Y ou have got to be kidding me," Neve growled, jumping to her feet and crossing the length of the store in two long strides.

"Hi." Alexandria waved, utterly unbothered by the six feet of seething god looming over her. "Neve, right? I didn't catch your name before, but that's what people call you. Actually, they call you a lot of things and most of them are kind of mean." She stood on her tiptoes to peek over Neve's shoulder. "Cool store. Very witchy. Someone told me you work here and I brought you—*hey*!"

Neve grabbed Alexandria by the hood of her too-big sweatshirt and yanked her out the door.

"You are very grabby, has anyone ever told you that?" Alexandria asked as Neve marched her into the empty alley behind the Three Crows.

"Are you insane?" Neve said, her voice low to keep Mercy from hearing.

Alexandria actually seemed to consider the *clearly rhetorical* question before she answered. "I don't think so. I mean, I've got ADHD out the ass and I'm on antidepressants. But monsters are a thing, so. I'm coping. And you're something too, because you're way too strong and I swear you had a cut on your head yesterday that isn't there anymore. Oh yeah and your sword—"

"Stop!" Neve shouted, too loud. Something in her voice shifted, pitching high and dangerous. The words died in Alexandria's mouth like Neve had stolen her breath away, and for the first time, she looked frightened. Gods, where had she come from and why couldn't she just go back there and leave Neve the hell alone?

"Just stop," Neve said, quieter this time but no less urgent. "Stop following me, stop asking questions, just stop it. It's not safe." *For both of us.* "You have to leave me alone. Don't come around here again and don't talk to me at school."

"Or w-wha—" Alexandria mashed her lips together, frustration chasing away the fear in her expression. Her dark eyes blazed, never leaving Neve's face. "Or what?"

Neve didn't answer, just tilted her head down and let Alexandria draw her own conclusions. There was a brief, tense moment before Alexandria visibly wilted, turning her face away. She mumbled something unintelligible, her eyes fixed on the cracked pavement as she backed out of the alley and vanished around the corner.

As soon as she was gone, Neve deflated. She hunched her shoulders, curling away from the sick feeling that churned in her gut. She wanted to leave too, go back to the convent and hide under her covers like she used to when she was little. She shouldn't feel like this; she'd done what she was supposed to do.

Well, not exactly. She *should've* told the Daughters. Mercy and Bay had never made mistakes like this—they'd never endangered the family like this—and Neve had enough of a complex without being the only one in this lifetime to nearly expose them all.

No, she could handle this on her own. She *had* handled it. If Alexandria wanted to tell someone, she would've done it already. She wouldn't be a problem.

Telling herself so didn't soothe the rotten feeling in Neve's stomach.

Maybe, whispered a tiny voice in the back of her head, *that's because you're lying to your family. Maybe it's because you just scared away the one person who actually wanted to talk to you.*

Neve shook her head, shoving those thoughts away. She'd done the right thing. And why should she bother with anyone outside of her family? She had her sisters. She didn't need anyone else.

"Where'd you go?" Mercy asked when Neve finally composed herself enough to go back inside. "Mrs. Tooney came looking for her order of rash cream and you weren't here."

"Well, gods forbid anyone get between Mrs. Tooney and her rash cream," Neve said, dodging the question.

Mercy brandished a bundle of herbs like a sword, which

only served to remind Neve that hers was still MIA. "Do not joke about the plight of the dermatologically challenged."

Mercy snickered, but her mouth pulled into a frown when Neve didn't laugh along.

"You okay, Nee-nee?" Mercy asked. Her head cocked to the side, and Neve wanted to shrink away from her sister's probing gaze. "You've been quiet all afternoon."

"I'm fine," Neve said. The lie was heavy in her mouth. She couldn't stop thinking about the look on Alexandria's face before she'd left. Gods, why did Neve even care? Alexandria was human. She was small and insignificant, and Neve should just forget that she existed.

Neve sighed, running her hands through her hair when Mercy continued to look at her expectantly, waiting for a better answer. "Just stressed about school. All my teachers are piling on homework."

"Ah, senior year," Mercy said, slinging her arm around Neve's shoulders. "No one appreciates how much we don't give a shit. College is better, trust me."

Neve gave a wan smile. Mercy and Bay were enrolled in community college classes, both studying history, which Mercy thought was hysterical considering they'd lived through a decent portion of it. But unlike her sisters, Neve had no plans to keep up the pretense of humanity once she turned eighteen.

Unfortunately, the guidance counselors at Newgrange

Harbor High School didn't accept "killing demons and protecting your sorry asses" as an acceptable answer for what
she planned to do after graduation. Though they had stopped
scheduling her for college prep counseling sessions, which
was better for everyone.

Neve was spacey and distracted for the rest of the shift
and raced home as soon as they closed up shop. She blew past
Clara and Aoife in the kitchen, ignoring their calls to come
and eat something. She didn't know where Maeve was, but
she couldn't be far, and Neve really didn't want to talk to her
either.

"Nee?" Bay's voice came through her door a split second
after Neve locked it. "You okay in there?"

"Fine," Neve replied. The word was starting to lose all
meaning. "Busy."

"Can I come in?"

"Don't you have training?" Neve asked shortly. She
wouldn't be able to lie to Bay's face. Lying to her over text
was already hard enough. The truth would come out and it
would be nothing less than a complete disaster.

The silence before Bay spoke again was heavy. "Let me
know if you need anything." She lingered by the door for a
moment longer before retreating.

Neve was a terrible sister. There was a special place in Hell
for people like her, but since she wouldn't see it anytime soon,

it seemed to have relocated to her stomach. They didn't lie to one another. It wasn't one of the Daughters' rules, or something they'd ever decided. It just *was*. There was a reason that some books on Irish mythology thought that they were the same person. They were a triad, three-in-one, and Neve was already too distant from her sisters without keeping secrets from them.

None of that changed the fact that her sword was still missing. Neve waited in her room for hours, until after Bay and Mercy had returned from training and the convent settled into relative silence for the night, and then another forty-five minutes just in case.

Walking out the front door or taking her car down to the shore was guaranteed to get her caught, so for the second night in a row, climbing out the window was her best option.

"Mab's saggy tits," Neve spat as she landed too hard and fell to one knee. Her ribs groaned and pain scraped down her spine.

It took longer than she would've liked to catch her breath and start toward the beach, but as long as she kept moving and didn't think about the fact that she was returning to the spot where her sisters would have found her body if—

Neve poked at a tender spot on her side, using the pain to keep from spiraling. *Just keep moving. Don't think about it.*

She stayed as far away from the Gate as possible, wading

through the shallows as she searched for her sword. Her blood had washed away with the tide, but she imagined the sand sucking at her boots, trying to keep her in place long enough to finish the job.

Neve walked a mile up and down the shore and went as far out as she dared, but her sword was nowhere to be found. She turned over rocks and dragged her hand through the murky water, holding her phone in the other hand with the flashlight turned to its brightest setting to aid her search, but it didn't do much. Again and again she prayed that her fingers would brush against the familiar metal, fear and cold making her movements stiff as she had to search farther out, but each time she came away with nothing.

"Shit," Neve swore, hurling a chunk of limestone that was definitely not her sword as far as she could. It had been hours, and if anyone went to check on her, her absence would raise more questions than she could answer.

Gods, what was she going to tell her sisters? Her sword had survived centuries and more wars than history cared to remember, and she had lost it in a single, stupid night.

Neve spent the walk back up the hill to the convent trying to come up with a half-decent excuse, anything that might lessen the punishment that was incoming. She was halfway back when Poe swooped overhead, cawing loudly.

"Poe, you asshole, you're going to get me caught," Neve

muttered as he circled above her. He cawed again before veering off toward the front of the convent. Neve toyed with the idea of ignoring him and heading straight back to her room, but there was too much of a chance he'd raise holy hell and wake her family if she didn't follow.

She found him perched on the roof of her car, feathers ruffled.

"Shush," Neve hissed, clamping her hands around his beak when his chest puffed like he was going to caw again. The raven wrenched his head out of her grasp and delivered a vicious peck to the meat above her thumb. Neve swore, sucking on the spot of blue blood. Poe glowered, tilting his head to peer into the back, where a wrapped package lay on the floor, partially concealed by the seat.

You have got to be kidding me, Neve thought as she wrenched the car door open so hard that the metal groaned.

Neve ripped open the paper. Relief rushed through her as she saw her sword inside, and she exhaled in a loud huff.

You dropped this, said a note taped to the package, written in scrawling handwriting that Neve recognized.

Neve blinked, realization dawning after a few long seconds. Alexandria hadn't come to the Three Crows this afternoon to harass Neve with questions. She'd been trying to return Neve's sword.

And Neve had chased her away.

CHAPTER SIX

With her sword safely back in the armory, Neve breathed easier, but the sick feeling lingered when she woke up the next morning. The fact that she was officially free of the sling didn't do nearly enough to boost her mood.

"Good of you to finally join us," Daughter Maeve said when Neve poked her head into the kitchen. Mercy and Bay were both already eating at the island.

Mercy snorted into her cereal. Neve flicked the back of her head.

"Ow!" Mercy complained, pouting.

"Feeling better today?" Bay asked, ignoring them both. Daughter Clara slid her a bowl of fruit and oatmeal.

"Yes," Neve said, taking a bite to disguise the lie. Her ribs were still healing but the rest of her injuries had disappeared. The circles under her eyes, however, had only gotten darker.

"Oh!" Bay said brightly. "You were right about your sword. I must have just not seen it yesterday or something."

"Wait, hold up. Did Saint Bay do something wrong?" Mercy

asked, clapping a hand over her heart. "Someone record the time and date!"

Bay rolled her eyes. Neve threw a blueberry at Mercy's forehead and excused herself before they could read the emotions on her face.

"Aren't you leaving a little early?" Maeve asked as Neve collected her backpack and made for the door.

"Mr. Robinson wants to talk to me," she said quickly, reaching for any reason to get out of the convent. "Apparently I'm *belligerent* and *disrespectful*." She twisted her voice into a nasally impression of Mr. Robinson's.

Daughter Aoife turned sharply. Her dark eyebrows pulled together, making her severe features look even more thunderous than usual. "If we get another call about your behavior problems, young lady—"

Neve was out the door before she could hear the rest of the threat.

She should feel better. Her sword was back and Alexandria hadn't said anything, but the knot of guilt below her breastbone hadn't loosened in the slightest. In fact, it might have gotten bigger, turning into a monster with a viselike grip on her insides.

Neve daydreamed through her morning classes and avoided the cafeteria at lunchtime, choosing instead to eat outside in the small, walled-in courtyard. The school was close enough to the sea that the air was tangy with salt, and the smell made her muscles tense. She wished for her sword. She wished she had someone to watch her back.

Don't be stupid, she thought. Neve didn't mind being alone; she preferred it. As if to prove it to herself, Neve picked a spot far from the other students, keeping her back to the wall and her eyes on the only door in and out of the building.

Mr. Robinson glared but didn't mention her rudeness from yesterday when Neve walked into his classroom twenty-five minutes later. Even with her eyes trained on her desk, Neve was excruciatingly aware of Alexandria as she entered the class with the rest of the students. She didn't claim the empty seat next to Neve, instead choosing an open desk on the opposite side of the room.

"Please go to your seat from yesterday, Alexandra," Mr. Robinson admonished. Neve winced, noting that Alexandria didn't bother to correct him today. She didn't know why that bugged her, but it did.

In an effort not to glance to her left, Neve tried paying attention to the lecture for once, a flat analysis of the themes of the *Divine Comedy*. One hand tapped a tense rhythm against her leg while she fiddled with her pen in the other, flipping it over her thumb again and again.

It didn't take long for her mind to wander again. Dante Alighieri. Did they know him from one of their lifetimes?

Maybe. They'd met all sorts of people. Bay and Mercy would know, though they wouldn't tell her even if she asked. Blah blah, no sharing memories, blah blah. Whatever magic had started the reincarnation cycle, it intended for them to stay as close to humanity as possible to ensure they always knew why they were fighting.

Neve had been told as much her entire life. She understood it in a vacuum, but there was some part of her that chafed against the pretense of humanity. They were *gods*. What was the point of mingling with mortals who could never truly know them?

Sometimes it felt like *Neve* barely even knew them. She was alone in her ignorance, stuck in her frail, mostly human body while her sisters had moved on without her. Manifesting changed them; the weight of so many centuries of memories took its toll. Bay cried for weeks, withdrawing into herself. One moment she was the sister Neve had known her entire life, and the next it was like a complete stranger was wearing Bay's skin.

Mercy just . . . stopped talking for a little while. She bounced back faster than Bay had, but sometimes Neve still saw Mercy's eyes go cold, like she'd crystallized from the inside out. Who had they been in those lifetimes that made Bay and Mercy react like that? What had they seen? What had they *done*?

Neve didn't notice that class had ended until her classmates began to file into the hallway. She ambled through the rest of the day, distracted. At the final bell, she didn't rush to her car. Instead, she rattled around the school until everything echoed and the whole building felt hollow and strange. She waited until the buses had been gone for twenty minutes and the only cars left in the lot belonged to kids in clubs or the athletes with after-school practice before she ventured outside. Neve hated that she was changing her routine to avoid one human, but she really didn't want to see Alexandria again.

"*What* is going on with you?" Daughter Aoife asked later when Neve picked at her dinner without trying to engage her sisters or the Daughters in conversation. The six of them sat at the far end of the massive teak dining table, clustered in their little corner like they had for as long as Neve could remember.

"Be nice to her," Mercy said when Neve didn't answer. "Her teachers are being dicks and I think she's hormonal."

"Language," Daughter Maeve scolded.

At the same time, Neve's head snapped up. Her throat felt hot. "I am *not* hormonal!"

Their plates and cups rattled against the table, and everyone swiveled to stare at her. Neve's cheeks flamed and she pushed back her chair with an earsplitting shriek before vanishing up the stairs to her bedroom.

Without bothering to lock the door behind her, Neve threw herself into bed and pressed her face into a pillow. Gods, she was a wreck. Shouting at her sisters and making a scene in front of the Daughters. She wanted to blame it all on Alexandria, but Neve had been itchy and restless long before she ever showed up. Mercy and Bay had never been like this; they were just so much *better* than her. They'd never acted out. Maybe Neve was broken.

Maybe she was just an asshole. Neve couldn't decide which was worse.

Bay didn't announce herself, just pushed open the unlocked door a few minutes later. The mattress dipped as she sat down on the corner of the bed.

"You don't have to tell me what's going on," Bay said quietly. "But I'm here if you want to."

Neve bit her lip to keep from saying anything. Tears prickled in the corners of her eyes and she pressed her face deeper into the pillow. Bay didn't leave. Instead, she gathered up Neve's long hair and started braiding.

Bay was the best of them; she had been since they were small. While Mercy and Neve ran around the grounds like wild things, pushing and shoving with strength they didn't yet understand, Bay preferred to help the Daughters around the convent. Sometimes Neve wondered if her sister's gentle nature made her ill-suited for their life, but today she was grateful for it. Bay loved her. Neve hadn't ruined that, at least. And if Bay loved her, how bad could she be?

Neve didn't realize that she'd fallen asleep until the sun peeked in through the bedroom window. It was morning, and she'd slept through the night for the first time since Wednesday. Heavy, restful breathing alerted her to the other bodies in her bed. Mercy must have joined them sometime during the night. She lay sprawled on the right edge of the bed, one leg hanging off the side. Her arm was thrown over her head, covering her eyes.

Pressing her lips together to keep from laughing, Neve snuck out from under the covers to close the blinds. They still had a few hours left to sleep.

"Nee?" Bay mumbled, her blue eyes hazy as she lifted her head. Neve put a finger to her lips and pointed to Mercy, who'd begun to snore softly. Bay smiled and Neve climbed back into the bed. She pressed her forehead against her sister's and fell back asleep, utterly certain that they would keep her safe.

Weekends were devoted to work and training, and Neve threw herself into the routine. No one questioned her willingness.

"Mercy, come on," Neve wheedled on Saturday morning. She'd already put on her armor, and her sword was in its rightful place on her back, her daggers slotted into a half-dozen sheaths scattered about her person. "Before we both die of old age."

Mercy swung her two-handed broadsword in a wide, sweeping arc, stripping a few leaves from the hedges. "Someone's pushy this morning."

Neve grinned, pulling her sword free with one hand and gripping a dagger with the other.

They paced around the practice yard for a few moments, matching each other step for step. Neve was at a distinct disadvantage; she knew better than to make the first move and leave herself open to a counterstrike.

A slight shift in the air was all the warning she had before Mercy was almost on top of her. Neve didn't bother trying to block the blow, instead lurching out of the way as Mercy's broadsword came down with incredible force. She landed hard a few feet away, spinning to counterattack and missing by miles. Mercy was halfway across the practice ring by the time Neve finished her swing.

Despite their vastly different physical capabilities and the ever-present fear that Neve would break like fine china, there was a reason she was still allowed to spar with her sisters even after they'd manifested. Neve would never beat Bay or Mercy, but that wasn't the point. She was fighting demons without her full strength or abilities—killing one on her own was supposed to be impossible. Before the beach, Neve would've admitted as much. Even once she turned eighteen, there would always be something stronger, faster, more powerful. Neve had to know how to keep fighting, even if she was destined to lose.

Neve's heart beat a frantic rhythm as she dove and ducked all over the grounds. She was on the defensive, mostly using her blades to deflect. The clash of steel against steel rang through the air and Neve lost herself in the relentless dance of battle, of give and take. And take and take and—

Mercy appeared in front of her and Neve's heart leaped into her throat. Panic spiked as Mercy transformed in Neve's vision, changing into the faceless demon from the beach, mouth agape and tongue lolling as it tried to take a bite out of her. Neve pinwheeled backward without so much as lifting her weapons. Fear turned her blood to ice.

Pain exploded in the corner of her mouth and Neve fell backward, landing gracelessly in the grass.

"Shit, Nee, are you okay?" Mercy swore, throwing her weapons down. Her face was her own again, the vision dispelled, but Neve couldn't force her pulse to calm.

Neve's breathing was labored and her muscles burned from the strain of sparring. The chill in her chest lingered. She pressed the pad of her thumb against the place where her lip had split. Blood dribbled into her mouth and she spat an inky glob onto the lawn. "Ow. Thanks for that."

"Here to help."

Neve threw herself at her sister without warning, half expecting to see the demon again, but Mercy remained.

Mercy blocked the blow, her smile suddenly cold and approving, and they both charged back into the match.

The rest of the weekend was spent splitting her time between the Three Crows and training, and by Sunday night, Neve almost felt like herself again.

Unfortunately, Neve couldn't spend the rest of her life hiding out in the convent with her sisters. Tomorrow she had to go back to school and figure out how to unspool the knot in her chest that tightened every time she thought about seeing Alexandria. Neve shook her head, flicking a balled-up piece of paper at Mercy as they did their homework together in the library. It made Bay giggle.

Neve didn't need to think about school and the girl she was avoiding. Not tonight. Alexandria could wait until the morning.

CHAPTER SEVEN

The next day marked the beginning of a tense routine that persisted throughout the rest of the week. Neve's mornings crawled by and she ate in the courtyard at lunchtime, despite the rapidly dropping temperature. It was unseasonably cold for mid-October, and Neve was the only one willing to brave the biting sea wind that soared over the courtyard walls. The cold didn't bother her as much as the feeling that she was running away from a fight.

Not running away, she rationalized. *Tactical retreat.* The less contact, the better. Alexandria wouldn't be tempted to ask any more dangerous questions, and Neve wouldn't have to think about the expression on her face when she'd fled from the Three Crows. Win-win.

The afternoons were an exercise in avoiding eye contact. Neve didn't know what it was, but something about Alexandria constantly pulled her focus, no matter how hard she tried to yank it away. The more she tried, the more the knot in her chest tightened.

Gods, all this effort to avoid one girl. At this rate, she was going to have a nervous breakdown well before the freedom of graduation, and she doubted the Daughters would accept "hiding from a human" as an excuse to drop out.

The only thing that kept her from cracking completely was that her stupid plan was working. She'd achieved as much distance as was possible in a school—in a town—as small as Newgrange Harbor, which was something. She didn't feel any *worse*, at least, and Neve was beginning to think that was the best she could hope for.

She would've kept it up all month—hell, she would've kept it up until graduation—if scheduled construction in the court-yard didn't force her back inside a little over a week later.

She contemplated breaking the lock on the courtyard door and going out anyway before reluctantly making her way to the cafeteria. There were other places she could eat—the library, if she was careful about being caught with food, or even her car—but something in her balked at those options. There was running away and then there was *running away*, and she refused to let this human turn her into a coward.

Finding that her lunch table was still empty even in her absence was the ego boost she needed. It was a nice reminder that, despite everything, her reputation remained intact.

Neve reveled in the strangeness of being a Morgan, which her sisters had purposely offset by joining human activities and being polite, even friendly, to their classmates. Gods, why bother? Why not lean into it? All Neve had to do was glower at anyone who looked at her sideways and they learned to steer clear. Not that it was hard. Neve's naturally downturned mouth was meant for scowling. It didn't take much effort to look like she was one snide comment away from slashing someone's tires.

The thirty-five minutes of lunch seemed to last much longer. Neve fiddled with her food, and her gaze roamed around the room before settling on the only other empty table in the cafeteria.

Alexandria sat by herself, doodling in a small notebook. Her hood was pulled over her long hair and clasped in place by familiar oversized headphones. Neve forced her eyes away, checking her phone for something else to look at.

Gods bless Mercy. Neve tapped open her messages to find a video of her sister running through the convent like a bat out of Hell with a black veil over her face. Daughter Clara was right behind her, looking murderous as she held a rolling pin aloft like a club. The Daughters never wore their veils over their faces in the convent, but it was the principle of the thing.

Neve smiled and sent the video to Bay.

Bay: Clara is going to draw a mustache on her face while she sleeps

Neve: I will trade my favorite dagger for that to actually happen

The bubble icon indicated that Bay was typing before something diverted Neve's attention. Whispers rustled around the cafeteria, the pointed, nasty kind that could only mean that a rumor was making the rounds.

It didn't take a genius to guess who they were talking about.

"I heard," someone hissed under their breath, "that her parents died in a fire."

"No," contradicted a boy from Neve's health class. "It was a car accident."

"I heard that she lived in, like, seven other towns before here."

"I heard that she's in witness protection. Peter said she lives with her aunt and uncle, but he says they're federal agents."

I heard, I heard, I heard. Neve didn't know why it bothered her, these swirling rumors and vague accusations, but something about them stuck under her skin. Maybe it was because they were usually about her and her family.

Maybe it was because Alexandria's scared look was still seared into Neve's brain, and she suddenly looked very small and very alone at her table. Adrift in a way that Neve recognized.

Neve moved before she could think better of it, crossing the cafeteria in a few long strides. She set her tray on the table across from Alexandria louder than was strictly necessary, before dropping into the adjacent seat.

"What are you doing?" Alexandria demanded, pulling

her headphones down. She snapped her notebook closed and shoved it into her bag.

"Something stupid," Neve replied. Heavy silence stretched between them, and she was all too aware of the eyes on her. Neve didn't inject herself into the muddled, hormone-soaked politics of Newgrange Harbor High School. She didn't join clubs or sports teams or even talk to anyone if she could avoid it. And yet here she was, sitting with the new girl—the one she'd been avoiding for over a week—all because her shithead classmates were spreading rumors.

Neve was an idiot.

Neither of them spoke for the rest of lunch, or as they walked almost side by side to Mr. Robinson's class, but this time the silence wasn't laden with hostility. Neve was grateful for the opportunity to relax a little.

"I still have questions," Alexandria said under her breath in the final minutes before class began.

Neve sighed. Of course she did.

"You might not want the answers," Neve warned. After her little stunt in the lunchroom, Neve had well and truly blown her last chance to pretend that Alexandria didn't exist, and denying everything outright clearly wasn't the solution.

"Yes." Alexandria's voice was unyielding, and something sparked in her dark eyes that Neve couldn't identify. "I do."

"You won't make any friends by hanging around me," Neve

said, a last-ditch effort to spare herself any further entangle-ment. She'd done this; she'd set it in motion, but Neve still had to try.

"Somehow I think I'll manage."

Neve rolled her eyes, but she couldn't deny the tiny part of herself that cheered at Alexandria's refusal to be dissuaded. That was . . . confusing, and she decided it could wait until later. Or never. Preferably never.

Alexandria frowned, gnawing on her lip. "I know you heard what people have said about me. I, um—I live with my aunt and uncle—"

Neve cut her off to spare them both from whatever expla-nation Alexandria thought Neve deserved. "Once you've been raised by nuns, come talk to me about a complicated home life. It's your business, not mine."

She couldn't help shooting Alexandria a significant look, like, *See how easy it is to leave things alone? Now you try.*

Alexandria snorted, rolling her eyes. Her smile soothed some of the ragged guilt in Neve's stomach and replaced it with something else. Something new and warm. Another entry to the growing list of things not to investigate ever.

Mr. Robinson was halfway through his lecture when Neve remembered something.

You broke into my car, she wrote on a piece of paper before sliding it across the desk.

Is that how you say thank you? Alexandria replied. *You should really lock it if you're so worried.*

Neve snorted when she read the message. She hesitated for a second before writing, *Thank you*, and sliding it back.

You're welcome, Alexandria replied. *Also, what was up with the crow?* There was a hasty doodle of Poe on the corner of the paper. It wasn't a bad likeness.

Neve stifled a smile. *That's Poe. He's an asshole. (And a raven, actually.)*

"Is there something you two would like to share with the rest of the class?" Mr. Robinson asked, spying their note passing from the front of the room.

"Just educating the town's newest resident on the unusual migration of corvids in Newgrange Harbor," Neve said lazily, tilting her chin up at him. Mr. Robinson's frown deepened as a few of her classmates snickered, but he didn't push it.

"You have a raven named Poe?" Alexandria asked as soon as class ended. The question sounded as if it had burst out of her, its intensity compounded by almost forty minutes of not being able to ask.

"*That's* your first question?" Neve tried and failed to mask her amusement.

"It seems like the most school-appropriate."

Fair point. "I was going through a phase. Mercy says—"

Mentioning Mercy stopped Neve in her tracks. She wasn't

supposed to talk about any of this. It wasn't a rule she could just bend or break outright; it was *forbidden*. Their lives and the lives of countless others depended on it. She would be putting everyone she loved at risk, all to satisfy the curiosity of one girl.

A girl who had seen a demon in the flesh—had seen Neve kill it with a centuries-old weapon and bleed blue all over her backseat—and hadn't run for the hills. Or to the cops. As far as Neve knew, Alexandria hadn't told a soul about what she'd seen that night on the beach.

"Are your sisters . . ." Alexandria asked, shaking Neve out of her thoughts. She lowered her voice to a whisper. ". . . like you? Strong? What about the convent, because I have heard some *wild* rumors about what goes on in that place. Also, what—"

"Stop," Neve said. Her mind spun with implications, consequences, and doomsday scenarios. And, beneath it all, an unmistakable desire to tell Alexandria everything, which was even more confusing after two weeks of straight-up avoiding her. "I need . . . I need time to think this through. I wasn't lying when I said that it's dangerous. Just give me some time, okay?"

"Dangerous for you?"

Neve blinked. She didn't expect the concern in Alexandria's voice. "Yes. For you, too."

"Okay," Alexandria said after a moment. She hesitated for a

few more seconds, gnawing on her bottom lip again. "Will you still sit with me at lunch?"

The warm feeling expanded into something gloopy and ridiculous.

"Sure."

Alexandria smiled again. She had a dimple, Neve noticed. Only one, pressed into her left cheek. It was distracting.

"Give me your phone," Alexandria demanded cheerfully. The dimple winked again. "I promise I won't read your messages. I'm just adding my number."

After a long moment, Neve extricated her phone from her back pocket and handed it over. Alexandria typed furiously and returned it just as the bell rang to usher them into their next class. She disappeared into Ms. Nichols's classroom without another word, only pausing long enough to toss Neve a wink at the doorway.

Heat rushed into Neve's cheeks and she loitered in the hall for a few more seconds, trying to force the flush to calm and to ease the sudden hitch in her breath. Alexandria was still smiling when Neve finally walked into the class.

Maiden, Mother, and Crone, Neve thought as she slumped in her seat and hid her red face behind her hair. *I think I'm in trouble.*

CHAPTER EIGHT

Like The Library: Guess who?

Like The Library: It's Alexandria. Duh

Like The Library: Don't worry I sent myself a text from your phone I'm not a stalker/psychic

Like The Library: Not to sound like a creep but why do you only have six numbers in your contacts? Isn't that taking the TERRIFYING GINGER LONER GIRL vibe a little far?

Like The Library: Or is it not far enough? A leather jacket would really sell it. Do you have a leather jacket?

Like The Library: You definitely have a leather jacket. You have the aura of a leather-jacket-haver

"What's got you so smiley, Nee-nee?" Mercy asked, peeking over the counter to read the text messages over Neve's shoulder. It had been a slow shift at the Three Crows, and Neve had started messing around with her phone for lack of anything else to do.

"Nothing," she said too quickly, slipping her phone into her pocket.

"Now, little sister, I think I know what this is about," Mercy said. She pushed over the ledger where she'd been doing the accounting and hopped onto the shop counter. "There comes a day in every young god's lifetime when she starts to get some very human urges."

"Mab's tits," Neve swore. Her cheeks flamed and it felt like her face had turned the color of her hair. "Stop."

"Never forget to use protection. Just because we can't get STIs doesn't mean we shouldn't encourage safe sex practices for our human neighbors."

"Oh my *gods*," Neve moaned, hiding her face in her hands as Mercy launched into a delighted lecture about promoting safe sex. They couldn't even *get* pregnant, and Mercy's short-lived relationships had always been with girls, so there was really no reason she should know so much about the proper way to put on a condom. Neve was seriously considering bludgeoning herself with one of the decorative geodes on the shelves when Mercy suddenly stopped mid-sentence.

Anticipation shivered down Neve's spine as she looked at her sister. Mercy's face was blank, scrubbed clean of emotion where she'd been smiling just a moment before. All the color drained from her skin, making her freckles stand out like tiny stars. She looked like a wraith, the effect made complete by the way her pupils expanded, swallowing the gold-brown irises until there was nothing left but inky black.

"Shit," Neve cursed, whipping out her phone again.

Neve: 911

She sent it to the family group chat, the one they only used in emergencies. And then she tapped out a quick message to the newest addition to her contacts.

Neve: Stay inside. Don't go near the beach.

Like The Library: What's going on? Are you okay? Is this one of those things you can't talk about?

Neve: STAY INSIDE. I'll let you know when it's safe.

She'd barely hit send when Mercy's bloodless lips pulled away from her teeth in a snarl.

"They're coming," Mercy said, her voice a shivery approximation of its usual timbre. This was her ability: a connection to the Hellgate that served as their early warning system. She gave them time to prepare, and until two weeks ago, Neve would've said that her ability to sense demons crossing over was infallible.

"How many?" Neve asked, clasping Mercy's arms. Her eyes had returned to normal, but her skin was still ashen.

"Four."

Shit. That was too many for this early in the season. Neve dove into the back to grab the go bags that were stashed in the storeroom while Mercy started the car.

"Drive," Neve said before the passenger door was even closed. The car squealed into motion and Neve began to pass Mercy her weapons, taking the wheel so her sister could strap them on. With Mercy armed and driving like a maniac, Neve unpacked her own armor and pieced it together over her clothes. She wouldn't need it once she was eighteen, but until then, an errant tooth or claw could shear her in two without protection. Magicked steel kept her torso safe, while the sturdy leather around her joints gave her the flexibility to move. The process took less time than normal; being caught unawares with only thin fabric and fragile skin to protect her was not an experience she cared to repeat, so Neve had been wearing bits of her armor under her clothes since the night she met Alexandria. Just in case.

Neve secured the last of her weapons and pulled her hair into a tight ponytail as they reached the beach. The car skidded to a halt, sending sand flying. The barrier was already live, a shimmering, nearly invisible wall passable only by Neve and her sisters. It was the only way Newgrange Harbor hadn't discovered what was going on just miles down the shore. It would be safer to maintain it round the clock, but Aoife didn't have that kind of magic, so unless there was an attack, the signs had to do.

"This is going to be ugly," Mercy said, gripping her broadsword with both hands. An icy smile spread across her face. She looked like herself again.

"It's always ugly," Neve replied. She searched herself for the fire that usually blazed in anticipation of a fight, but it was buried deep somewhere she couldn't find it.

Bay fell into step beside them, silent like always. Her eyebrow arched. "How many?" she signed, long, pale fingers forming the words.

"Four. Humanoid. Claws and teeth," Mercy said. Her ability didn't tell them everything, but it was enough. She roared a battle cry and they charged through the barrier together.

The chaos was instantaneous. Neve's body moved before she could catch up, bending backward to avoid razor-tipped claws angled at her throat. She snarled a curse, letting her momentum propel her onto the sand. She didn't stay down for long, kicking up in a twisting motion. The demon wobbled as she struck its chitinous torso, giving Neve enough time to leap to her feet and slash at its legs.

"Bay!" Neve cried as black blood hit the beach. The demon barely staggered and it pounced before Bay's scythe could shear it in two. Neve threw herself sideways in an attempt to dodge the grasping claws. She wasn't fast enough.

"Where is she?" the demon snarled. Stars burst behind Neve's eyes as it grabbed her by the throat and slammed her against the craggy cliffside. *"Where?"*

Neve spat, reaching for her spare dagger, but the demon caught her hand. It dug its claws into her skin and wrenched her wrist to one side until the small bones shattered. The demon's laugh was a horrifying parody of humor as Neve cried out. It opened its enormous mouth again and Neve froze at the sight of its teeth, all the fight draining out of her at once. She couldn't move, couldn't breathe. It was going to kill her. The last thing she was ever going to see was its gaping mouth.

There was a flash of red hair and the demon exploded in a maelstrom of burning ash. Neve collapsed onto the sand, gasping as oxygen flooded back into her lungs. Her face stung where the fiery bits scorched her skin. She could already feel black bruises forming around her throat.

"Neve!" Mercy shouted, falling onto the sand beside her. Neve blinked, her vision clearing enough to see that her sisters had dispatched the rest of the demons. The air was choked with ash. It fell around them like black snow, settling in their hair and on their clothes. "Gods, Neve, are you okay?"

Bay didn't say anything, her gentle fingers probing Neve's wounds. Unlike Neve and Mercy, Bay was silent in battle. It was her ability. She was a shade that crept up on her enemies and stole their lives without a sound. Some historians speculated that she was the inspiration for the Grim Reaper myth. Neve always got a kick out of that one, though she had to admit the scythe was pretty memorable.

"Okay, we need to get you back home," Mercy said, lifting Neve in a bridal carry that would have been humiliating if Neve wasn't about to collapse. She didn't think her legs could carry her right now, and her hands wouldn't stop shaking.

All three Daughters were waiting for them at home, pale

but prepared as Mercy helped Neve into the room off Clara and Aoife's chambers that served as an infirmary. No one complained that she was tracking blood all over the hardwood.

The Daughters fussed over them all, muttering that it was too soon for an attack like this. They were right, and demon sightings were only going to increase as the season grew colder and darker. There was something about this year, though. It felt different. It felt worse, somehow, and if Neve could sense it, then the Daughters could too.

Every time she and her sisters turned eighteen and fully manifested, some of the ancient magic that sealed the Hellgate wore away. Magic was funny like that; it couldn't last forever. It demanded a weakness, some way to break. The spell held perfectly for the first eighteen years of their lives, until Bay's birthday. By the time Neve turned eighteen, the seal that had held since their rebirth would be at its weakest. Only their combined abilities would be able to hold back the stronger demons from ripping free and bringing death and destruction with them.

Assuming that Neve didn't die first.

The thought stole the breath from her lungs, and Neve heard the boy's high, mocking laughter from her dreams, cackling as the world burned around her. She'd almost died three times in two weeks. Neve had nearly failed statistics, but she was pretty sure her odds of survival were dwindling.

"What did you do, try to shake hands with it?" Daughter Aoife demanded when Mercy set Neve down. Her harsh tone belied how gently she bound Neve's wrist, wrapping it in a cloth layered with healing spells and Neosporin.

Neve's breath hissed through her teeth as the healing concoction stung. "You're the one who tried to teach me manners."

"What the hell even happened out there?" Mercy asked. Her sword was laid across her knees and she tapped a staccato rhythm on the hilt. Demon blood still speckled the blade, and it was a testament to the Daughters' worry that none of them had nagged her to clean it yet. "What did it say to you?"

"Nothing," Neve snapped, deflecting. The demon's voice snarled in the back of her mind. *Where is she?*

Who? Neve asked the figment of her imagination. Who could the demon possibly be looking for? More important, *why?* Why did this feel connected to her disastrous solo patrol somehow?

She batted away the glass of something healthy and disgusting that Daughter Clara tried to force into her hand. She was tired and hurt and embarrassed. She'd frozen in the middle of a fight and it had almost cost her her life. As if her family needed another reason to baby her.

"You're not going to school tomorrow," Daughter Maeve announced.

"I'm *fine*," Neve protested.

"No, you're not," Daughter Maeve replied, glaring down at her with all the ferocity of an immortal Irishwoman. She took the glass from Daughter Clara's hand and held it out, careful to avoid Aoife on Neve's other side. "You're going to drink this and then you are going to march your behind upstairs and get some rest. No arguments."

"But—"

"*No arguments.*"

"Gods, *all right*," Neve grumbled. She downed the revolting liquid in one gulp and stomped up the narrow, winding stairs to her bedroom, muttering under her breath the whole way.

For all her objections, she needed the rest. Neve fell asleep the moment her body hit the bed, the shock and adrenaline of the fight fizzling away and leaving nothing but exhaustion behind.

Neve's dreams were filled with laughing monsters and hissed questions.

Where is she? Where? A furious chorus demanded all around her.

I don't know! Neve tried to shout, but her voice was gone.

Blue and black blood rained from the sky, mingling into something corrosive that burned wherever it touched her. Her wrist tingled and blistered as if she had dipped her arm in acid all the way up to her elbow. She screamed soundlessly, suddenly trapped behind the barrier that kept the demons out of Newgrange Harbor, but no matter how she battered it, she couldn't pass through. Neve swung her sword as if she could hack it down, but the steel only sparked off with a discordant *tap-tap-tap—*

Swords don't make that sound. The thought was muzzy, rising to the surface of the dream and pulling Neve up with it.

Neve woke slower than usual, her senses dampened by whatever Daughter Clara had given her. Poe knocked on her window with his beak again, tapping insistently. There was something clenched in his talons.

"Hey," she said as she let him inside, too tired to even come up with a proper insult. Poe winged toward her, rubbing his feathered head against her cheek. "Aw, were you worried about me?"

Poe puffed out his feathers, looking affronted at the very notion of bothering himself with her well-being. He extended a leg toward her and Neve caught her phone before it hit the floor. She must have dropped it sometime during the fight.

"Thanks, you shitty pigeon."

Poe made a throaty sound and extended his neck, carefully avoiding her bandaged hand to nip at the fingers that remained unscathed. He cawed again, one wing buffing her on the back of the head as he flew out the window.

Her phone was dead, and Neve plugged it into the wall to let it charge. In the aftermath of everything, she'd forgotten to text Alexandria the all clear, not that it would've mattered without her phone.

Neve checked the clock on her bedside table. Four a.m. Well. Better late than never. It took a few moments for her phone to blink back to life and once it did, it began to buzz. And buzz. And buzz.

Like The Library: Is everything okay? I haven't heard from you in hours. . . .

Like The Library: Hello?

Like The Library: I'm trying not to freak out but it's not working and I am definitely freaking out.

Like The Library: I am about 3 hours away from calling hospitals and morgues looking for a scowly redhead who definitely has a leather jacket.

The texts rolled in one after another, growing more and more frantic until the very last one, delivered almost an hour ago.

Like The Library: Please be okay. Please text me back.

Neve: I'm fine. Sorry. Lost my phone.

Satisfied, Neve laid back down, meaning to go back to sleep. Only about a minute passed before her phone rang shrilly.

"What the hell is *wrong* with you?" Alexandria's voice was slightly warped through the receiver, but the volume more than made up the difference. "Do you know how stressed I've been for the past"—a pause as she checked the time—"*twelve hours?* I think I have gray hair. If I have gray hair, I am going to sneak into your super-secret convent clubhouse and shave you bald."

"Why are you even awake?" Neve asked, trying to process everything else through the exhausted, post-battle haze. "It's almost sunrise."

"What's wrong with your voice?" Alexandria asked, side-stepping the question. "You sound all loopy."

"Got hurt."

"What?" she demanded, her voice dropping to an urgent whisper. Neve winced. She should have lied. "Are you okay?"

"I'm fine now," Neve said, which was true. She should be all healed up in a day or so. "I won't be in school tomorrow, though."

"Okay. I'm glad you're all right. You should get some sleep."

Neither of them hung up.

"Sorry if I worried you," Neve said after a minute when it became clear that the silence might stretch forever if she didn't break it.

Alexandria made a soft sound that might have been a laugh, and Neve wished she could do something to make her feel better. "Just don't die or I'll be really pissed."

"I'll try my best. Good night."

"Good night."

CHAPTER NINE

Neve didn't wake up until almost noon the next day. Between her own abilities and the Daughters' ministrations, her wrist felt mostly normal. She should be fully healed by tomorrow, thank the gods. Her family had enough to deal with without Neve being even more useless than usual.

"And where are you going?" Daughter Aoife asked when Neve padded downstairs, hunger finally driving her out of bed. Her metabolism was already insane, and healing took a ton of calories.

"You look better," Clara said softly, her fingers clasped with Aoife's.

"I am," Neve assured them, waving her hand as proof. She'd removed the bandage earlier and the punctures had already sealed, leaving only a black bruise behind. The scars would fade within a week.

"I hope you're not trying to overextend yourself, young lady," Aoife said severely. Clara just smiled and shook her head before laying it on Aoife's shoulder.

"I'm not, old lady," Neve replied.

Aoife's mouth puckered and Clara made a small sound under her breath, nudging Aoife in the ribs.

"All right, all right, fine. Take this. To speed along the healing, obviously."

Aoife pulled a chocolate bar out of a pocket of her black dress and handed it over. Neve grinned at the two of them, pocketing the candy, and Aoife nodded, her customary frown returning. Neve's smile remained as she watched them go, still hand in hand. Aoife and Clara had been together for as long as Neve could remember. She'd been the flower girl in their small, wonderful wedding ceremony. Neve suspected that they celebrated every lifetime, renewing their vows when Neve and her sisters were still young. It was a good memory. One of the best.

Chocolate in hand, Neve raided the fridge and puttered around the convent for a few hours, wandering through the grounds that Daughter Clara worked so hard to keep tidy before poking around the library. With a single shelf as an exception, none of the titles were published later than the nineteenth century—it was a hang-up of Daughter Maeve's, who considered the library her personal domain—but it was quiet, and the dusty smell of the books was calming.

Neve was snuggled in an overstuffed armchair, flicking through a four-hundred-year-old demonology book, when Bay arrived.

"Hey, you're up."

"Hey, you're talking."

Bay rolled her eyes. She always got a little insecure about the creepy silence that overcame her during battle, but Neve would so much rather turn into a mime than have Mercy's connection to the Gate. Sometimes she wondered what she would be able to do once she manifested, but it was useless to speculate. Bay and Mercy already knew—their abilities were the same in every lifetime—but they wouldn't tell her even if she asked. Too much information, the danger of further distancing them from humanity, blah blah blah.

"How are you feeling?"

"Like I had a bite taken out of my hand," Neve replied without thinking. Bay winced, and Neve immediately wished she could take the words back. She didn't want Bay feeling guilty on top of anything else, especially when Neve was already practically healed.

"Can we talk about something?" Bay asked. She perched on the armrest of Neve's chair. "What happened down there? I've never seen you scared like that."

Neve wanted to argue, but she knew that it was no good. Bay could smell fear like a shark smelled blood. They all could, to some degree, but Bay was damn near infallible.

"I don't know what you want me to say," Neve said after several long seconds of expectant silence. "You guys are always reminding me that I'm basically a squishy human. It's always scary for me."

That wasn't quite true and they both knew it. Since the time she could hold a sword, Neve had craved battle. She and Mercy were alike that way, always eager to train and spar. Even once demons started coming through the Gate, Neve always charged headfirst into the fray. She was fearless.

She used to be, at least. Before she started having nightmares. Before she met Alexandria. Before she faced a demon alone and it nearly killed her.

"It's never been like that," Bay probed gently. "Neve. Talk to me."

"There's nothing to talk about."

Bay didn't accuse her of lying, but the hurt that flashed in her eyes was clear enough.

Neve bit her lip against the instinct to tell Bay everything. She hated the look on her sister's face, but if she started talking, everything would tumble out and Neve wasn't ready to face the consequences of . . . whatever was going on with Alexandria. Aoife would insist on taking her memories and then Neve would be back where she'd started, young and powerless and alone.

"Okay," Bay said finally. She stood, leaning down to press a kiss to Neve's hair. "Love you, Nee."

"Love you too," Neve replied, as if it made any difference at all against the secrets she was holding so close to her chest.

Neve watched her sister leave the library, her stomach squirming. Humming tension crawled under her skin, eventually driving her outside onto the training grounds. So high above the ocean, the sea air bit at her skin and whipped color into her cheeks. Neve embraced the cold, inviting the way it made her blood run quick in her veins.

She gripped her sword and dagger tight in her hands, hyperaware of their uneven weight. Neve ran through the training exercises she'd learned before she was even allowed to use proper weapons, back when she and her sisters had been given wooden practice swords to keep them from hurting each other. Her body flowed from one stance to the next without pause, smooth, fluid movements that belied the power behind them. Without meaning to, she began picturing the demon from the attack, the one that was looking for someone.

Who? Neve thought as she slashed at the invisible target. *Who*—she stabbed her dagger upward in an underhand thrust—*are you*—her sword swung in a tight arc—*looking for?*—another swing, fast enough that her blade blurred in the air.

She practiced the motions over and over, picking up speed until her muscles burned and her breath came in harsh gasps.

"Mother's love, Neve, there you are!" Daughter Clara said, bursting into the training yard. She looked frantic, and Neve's heart leaped into her throat. "Give me those, give me those,"

Clara ordered, reaching for her weapons. "Get inside right this instant."

"What's going on?" It couldn't be an attack, not if Clara was asking for Neve's weapons.

"Just get," Clara said. "Aoife has a change of clothes for you."

Why did she need a change of clothes?

Daughter Clara didn't stick around long enough for Neve to ask, rushing back inside and leaving Neve no choice but to follow.

Aoife pressed a pile of clean civilian clothes into her hands the second she walked in the back door and then shoved her toward one of the tiny downstairs bathrooms. Neve changed quickly, still fiddling with her messy, sweat-drenched ponytail as she emerged.

"—Clara, and Daughter Aoife," Neve overheard Bay say as she walked toward the kitchen. It sounded like she was making an introduction. "*Super* obscure denomination."

"You can thank the British imperials for that," Maeve muttered primly.

Mercy was waiting for Neve by the door, looking delighted in a way that made Neve's little sister instincts tingle.

"Look who we found," Mercy said, slinging her arm around Neve's shoulders and leading her into the kitchen, where Bay and Alexandria were chatting at the island, looking like they'd known each other for years.

"Oh, hey, you're back from your run," Bay said, smiling around the lie. Neve barely looked at her, wholly focused on Alexandria. Alexandria, who was here, in the convent—in her *kitchen*—talking to one of her sisters while Daughter Aoife prepared a mid-afternoon snack as if they entertained guests every day. Bay and Mercy had friends, sure, but Neve couldn't remember any of them being invited back to the convent.

"What are you doing here?" Neve demanded, shock making her voice go flat. Bay frowned, and Daughter Aoife glared daggers.

"Alexandra—" Bay started.

"Alexandria," Neve and Alexandria corrected in unison. Neve ducked her head, but not fast enough to hide her blush.

"Like the library," Alexandria said. Even without looking up, Neve knew that she was grinning.

"Sorry," Bay said quickly, her eyes darting between the two of them. "*Alexandria* came by the shop and she mentioned that you two were friends and that she very kindly gathered the homework you missed today."

"And *I* thought," Mercy said, visibly thrilled with herself, "that she could deliver them in person."

Neve just stared, still unable to process the cognitive dissonance of seeing Alexandria in the convent, dwarfed by both Mercy and Bay, who towered over her by almost a foot each.

They didn't even look like the same species. They *weren't* the same species.

"Well, I think it was very considerate," Daughter Aoife said, breaking through the tension. She shoved a platter of meat, cheese, and grapes into Neve's hands. "Why don't you show your guest up to your room, Neve?"

"Sure," Neve said automatically. She turned on her heel and marched out of the kitchen and up the three flights of stairs, her heart feeling like it was going to beat out of her chest.

"What the hell is wrong with you?" she hissed, spinning to face Alexandria as soon as her bedroom door closed behind them. Neve had told her a dozen times not to come to the convent. Her family would ask too many questions, none of which Neve could answer without admitting everything.

Alexandria's dimple flashed, which was just distracting and unfair. "I get that you're mad, but I cannot take you seriously while you're holding charcuterie."

It took all Neve's willpower not to bend the platter in half, and by the time she reined in her temper and put it down, Alexandria was already wandering around her bedroom.

"So this is where you sleep. It's not how I imagined."

Neve choked, damn near swallowing her tongue. What was she supposed to *say* to that?

Alexandria continued, tapping the blueish-gold walls that were almost, but not quite, the color of Neve's blood. Maeve had objected to the color choice—she thought it was garish—but Neve had insisted. "I recognize this. It's all over my car's upholstery."

Neve fussed with the hem of her shirt as Alexandria continued her lap around the room, looking at the shelves that ran across all four sloping walls and examining the mementos Neve kept there.

She poked at Poe's cage, which hung from the ceiling in its corner, though he hadn't used it in years, preferring to sleep outside. The weapons that were usually strewn about the floor or stacked on the chair in the corner were gone. No doubt one of the Daughters had whisked them away upon Alexandria's arrival.

"Big mythology fan, huh?" Alexandria asked, making her way to the bookshelf. She tilted her head to peer at the titles. "I guess your family does have the whole Irish-as-a-personality-trait thing going on. I was more of a Greek myths kid, myself. The Percy Jackson books were literally my entire childhood and I'm pretty sure they made me gay, but Jesus Christ, the movies were awf—"

"I thought we agreed that the convent was off-limits," Neve interrupted before this could get any more out of hand. She felt very warm all of a sudden.

Alexandria paused and then held up three fingers, flopping down onto Neve's bed like it was the most natural thing in the world. Neve felt like she was seconds away from sponta-neously getting a nosebleed.

"One, we didn't agree on anything. You put on your snarly face and told me that I wasn't allowed," Alexandria said, put-ting down one finger. "Two, I was only at the shop that's *also* off-limits because my aunt is on an herbalist kick. I thought I would just give your sisters the homework and then I was kidnapped by the one with the bangs because pushiness runs in your family, *apparently.*"

Neve winced. She almost felt bad for Alexandria for com-ing up against the unstoppable force that was Mercy with an idea in her head. "Mercy is . . . a lot."

"I'll say," Alexandria said. "Your family is weird."

She had no idea.

"And three, if you don't stop being mean to me, I'm not going to give you your present." Alexandria put down the last finger triumphantly, her dimple reappearing.

"You got me a present?"

"Yes, I got you a present. It was tricky, though, I won't lie. What do you give the vampire who has everything?"

Neve blinked. "I'm not a vampire."

"That was just my first guess." Alexandria shrugged. "I've got more."

That, Neve didn't doubt for a second. Alexandria dug around in her backpack, retrieving a small gift bag that was done up with a bright blue bow. Inside was a stuffed crow with a ribbon tied around its neck.

Glad you didn't get murdered, Alexandria had written in her scrawling script. Neve must have stared at it for too long because Alexandria began to fidget, shifting from foot to foot.

"I know Poe is technically a raven, but you know . . . there are still a lot of crows in town and a group of crows is called a murder . . . and because I thought you died." Alexandria bit her lip, twisting the strands of black hair that had escaped her ponytail. "I'm sorry. Sometimes I think I'm funnier than I am and it's a bad joke so—"

"It's nice," Neve said. That weird warm, gloopy feeling was back. "Thank you."

"You're welcome."

"I was never dying," Neve said. "For the record."

"I have an active imagination," Alexandria replied. "Was this . . . ?" She trailed off, her eyes dropping to Neve's bedspread. She looked like she was steeling herself for something. "Was it another monster? That hurt you?"

"Yes," Neve said, trying to ignore the tiny part of her brain that screamed at her not to say anything. But, she rationalized, she wasn't talking about her sisters, or the Daughters, or the Hellgate. Only things that Alexandria had already seen. "One of them thought I'd make a good snack." She extended her wrist, showing the mostly healed puncture wounds.

"This is what you do?" Alexandria whispered, paling at the sight of the scars, and Neve realized that she'd messed up again. Without the benefit of makeup, the black bruising did look kind of horrifying. "Fight monsters and try not to die, like some kind of superhero?"

"I'm not a superhero," Neve said, because it had made Alexandria smile before, but Alexandria's gaze only intensified. She reached for Neve's hand, threading their fingers together and stroking her thumb over the healed punctures. Neve's heart pounded so loudly that Alexandria could probably hear it.

"I don't want you to get hurt," Alexandria murmured.

"Next time I won't shake hands with a monster before I kill it," Neve said. She didn't like the soft, scared look that had stolen over Alexandria's face. She wanted to wipe it away with a gentle press of her thumb. She wanted to earn back that flashing dimple.

She'd never wanted anything like that before.

That night, even long after Alexandria had left, Neve could still feel the phantom pressure of their clasped hands. Neve didn't know what to do with the strange feelings in her chest, which were new and weird and kind of ridiculous, but she didn't want them to go away.

CHAPTER TEN

Things had shifted. It felt as if Neve's world had tilted on its axis, suddenly spinning toward a new source of light, and she wondered how everyone else was walking around without stumbling in the new gravity. Neve found herself looking forward to passing periods, to lunchtime, even to Mr. Robinson's class, because they were opportunities to see Alexandria.

Alexandria, who was in the middle of a full-throated rant about why Pablo Picasso was an asshole of the highest order when her head snapped up, her attention abruptly diverted.

Neve looked up too, already glaring, as a junior—a Black girl named Tameka—walked up to them. "What are you doing?" Neve snapped.

"Eating my lunch. That okay with you?" Tameka said.

"Sure!" Alexandria said cheerfully. "I'm Alexandria, by the way."

"Go away," Neve growled. "Sit somewhere else."

Tameka looked between the two of them before sitting down next to Alexandria.

"I *said*—" Neve started, not quite raising her voice. Her

throat scratched as though she were shouting and her lunch tray rattled against the table.

The vicious dismissal on her lips was silenced by Alexandria's hand on hers. Neve swallowed her words at the pleading look on Alexandria's face. The tray stilled.

"Look," Tameka said, her eyes flitting to their joined hands for a moment. Neve pulled away, curling her fists underneath the lunch table. "I just need a new place to sit without worrying about my douchebag ex-boyfriend hassling me." She nodded at Neve without making eye contact. "And everyone's scared of Morgan."

Neve had thought so too, but the two exceptions were right in front of her. Finally, Neve just scowled and decided to ignore them both. Alexandria continued with her passionate anti-Picasso tirade, effortlessly folding Tameka into the conversation.

Neve's phone pinged halfway through the lunch period.

Like The Library: Don't worry. You're still my favorite ;)

Neve rolled her eyes, ducking her head against the ridiculous blush that rushed to her cheeks.

Over the course of the next few weeks, and against her explicit wishes, Neve's empty lunch table gained four more occupants: Michael and Simon, the only two openly gay boys at the school who everyone assumed were dating but weren't; Ilma, who had been the new kid before Alexandria and always matched her makeup to her hijab; and Puck, who didn't say much but would probably follow Ilma over a cliff.

"Why the frowny face?" Alexandria asked a few days after it was clear that Neve wasn't going to be able to scare away Alexandria's new friends. Neve recognized them all, obviously; she'd been in school with most of them since kindergarten, but she didn't think she'd spoken to any of them before. "You're going to get crow's feet."

Three, two . . .

Neve couldn't help but smile as Alexandria burst into giggles at her own terrible joke.

"I don't get wrinkles," Neve said imperiously. It was probably true.

"Perks of being a werewolf?"

"Not even close."

Alexandria shrugged. "I'll figure it out eventually."

The thought of Alexandria finding out the truth made Neve's stomach squirm, but there was no harm in letting her guess. Neve still had no idea how she could answer her questions without putting Mercy, Bay, and the Daughters at risk, but Alexandria deserved an explanation. A severely edited explanation, maybe, but something.

Unfortunately, the privacy of their table had been summarily invaded, and Alexandria was doing nothing to discourage the sudden lack of personal space. She even went so far as to collect everyone's phone number and put them into a group chat. A chat that Neve had tried to take herself out of no fewer than ten times, but every time, someone (usually Alexandria, but sometimes Puck) just added her back in again. Neve didn't get the appeal. No one even talked to each other, just sent links and GIFs and memes that Neve didn't understand and refused to learn. Somehow, she'd find the strength to carry on without knowing who Duke Nukem was.

Eventually, and with no small amount of protest, Neve accepted that this was her life now, though looking down at her phone to see that she had thirty-seven unread messages made her want to crush the stupid thing in her fist and be done with it.

"Well, aren't we popular," Mercy commented one night at dinner. Her pale eyebrows vanished into her bangs as Neve's phone buzzed incessantly. "Has it finally happened? Has Neenee made friends?"

"Shut up," Neve said. Why did it matter if she had? Bay and Mercy had plenty of friends for the three of them. She put her phone on silent and stared at her plate for the rest of the meal, fighting the urge to check the chat every ten seconds.

"Don't you have homework to do?" Bay asked when Neve followed her into the armory after dinner, looking for a distraction.

"Right, because I do homework."

"Neve."

"I do enough to pass, don't worry. Gods, it's like you *want* me to unseat you as the family nerd."

"I'm glad you've found people to talk to at school," Bay said, ignoring Neve's snideness. Seventeen years and Neve still didn't know how to deal with Bay sometimes. She was so heart-wrenchingly earnest. Mercy she could handle all day, but Bay was *nice*. "You've always been so solitary."

There it was again, that undercurrent of sadness that had lived in Bay since she turned eighteen. It wasn't always so close to the surface, but seeing the quiet, faraway look in Bay's eyes always made Neve twitchy and restless. But there was nothing to fight, no monster to rage against, just the cold certainty that Bay was hurting and there was nothing Neve could do about it. Gnawing on her lip, Neve settled on squeezing her sister's hand before they both lapsed into silence, settling into the practiced routine of cleaning their weapons side by side.

That night, Neve dreamed that the convent was burning. She couldn't find Mercy or Bay no matter how hard she searched for them. Through the roar of the flames, Neve heard laughter as the Hellgate opened and demons poured through.

She was still exhausted and shaken the next morning, and nearly walked past Alexandria altogether in her sleep-deprived haze.

"Good morning, sleepyhead," Alexandria said, waving her arms wildly to catch Neve's attention. She was perched on the hood of her car with her notebook on one knee, doodling with a charcoal pencil. Alexandria squinted as Neve approached, taking in the dark circles under Neve's eyes.

Alexandria grabbed the Dunkin' cup beside her and held it out. "You look like you need this."

"What is it?" Neve asked, taking it automatically.

Before Neve could get a look at whatever Alexandria was drawing, she shoved the notebook into her bag and hopped off her car.

"Just trust me," Alexandria said, leaning forward to take a sip of the drink. Neve's jaw snapped closed with an audible click. "See? Not poisoned."

Poison was the last thing on Neve's mind as she took a hesitant sip, tasting Alexandria's strawberry ChapStick on the straw. Neve felt herself flush before the drink hit her tongue and she gagged on sugar. It was so concentrated that the individual granules coated her tongue and stuck to the back of her throat.

"What is *wrong* with you?" Neve demanded, spitting the sugary garbage into one of the bushes that lined the parking lot.

Alexandria snickered. "What? It's good!" She plucked the drink out of Neve's hands and took an enormous, satisfied gulp, happily crunching on sugar.

"That is absolutely vile."

"To each their own. Next time I'll bring you a black coffee."

"That was supposed to be *coffee?*"

"You're the one who looks like you haven't slept in a week. Who needs sleep when you've got sweet, sweet caffeine?" Alexandria waffled for a moment, shuffling her feet. Neve braced herself for the inevitable question. "You okay?"

For a split second, Neve considered telling her about the dream, before deciding against it. She was fine. It was just a nightmare. Nothing she couldn't handle.

"I'm good," she said. Alexandria didn't look anywhere near convinced, but she didn't push, continuing to rhapsodize about coffee so sugary that Neve's teeth hurt just listening to her.

"You're a menace," Neve said, smiling a little when Alexandria rounded on her. Her expression was so affronted that Neve couldn't help but laugh.

"I am a *pioneer,*" Alexandria argued, gesturing emphatically with her coffee cup. It was a wonder it didn't fly out of her hand. "Many brilliant minds were unappreciated in their time. Van Gogh, Jonathan Larson—"

"Picasso?" Neve suggested.

Alexandria brandished the to-go cup menacingly. "Don't you start. I am *right* and you will not use my hatred of the cubism dickhead against me."

They bickered about what did and did not qualify as coffee

all the way into the building. Neve was halfway to feeling normal when suddenly her vision was obscured by a riot of black and orange streamers. Colored sunglasses and bell-bottoms accosted her from every angle.

"Gods damn it," Neve muttered.

With the demon attack pulling her focus, she'd totally forgotten that Spirit Week was coming up. Beside her, Alexandria looked delighted, and Neve groaned to see that she had removed her hoodie to reveal a spangly green top and was arranging her black hair into high pigtails.

"My old school didn't take this kind of stuff half so seriously," Alexandria said. "And Friday is Halloween! Great timing, right?"

Halloween. Neve and her sisters knew it by a different name, and it didn't involve candy or costumes. In the back of her mind, the boy's laughter from her dream echoed.

"Come on, you can't tell me that this isn't fun," Alexandria said, adding a pair of circular, pink-tinted glasses to her ensemble and securing a flower crown in her hair.

"You look ridiculous," Neve said, deflecting. Alexandria looked like someone who should be protesting the Vietnam War and riding around in a van with a peace sign decal on its side. She looked beautiful.

Alexandria fished around in her bag before withdrawing a flowy floral top and another crown woven with purple and yellow flowers. "For you."

"No."

"You just said my outfit was dumb. That hurts my feelings." She stuck her lip out in an exaggerated pout. "Make it up to me?"

Neve sighed. "I'm pretty sure this counts as bullying."

The pout was replaced by a blinding smile as Neve let Alexandria press the clothes into her hands. "I prefer 'compulsory character development.'"

Neve's costume was an enormous hit at lunch. Puck and Ilma both laughed so hard that they had to cling to one another to stay in their seats. Tameka left the table altogether, claiming that she needed to "take a lap," whatever that meant. Simon and Michael started whispering to each other and quickly brought Puck and Ilma into their little circle of secrets.

As if they could talk. Ilma's hijab was patterned with psychedelic colors, and Tameka had traded in her usual braids for a full '70s Afro. They looked like they'd stepped straight out of one of those glossy coffee-table books about hippies.

"Ignore them," Alexandria said, turning in her seat so she could fix Neve's crown. Neve held perfectly still, hoping no one would notice the goose bumps that appeared where Alexandria's fingertips trailed over her skin.

"You got it bad," Tameka said when she returned to the table.

Neve glowered but Tameka only winked, her lips twisting into a knowing smile. Cursing under her breath, Neve ducked her head as a blush crawled up her neck. All the while, under the table, Alexandria's knee pressed against hers.

If any of her other classmates had comments about her abrupt shift in style choices, they were wise enough to keep them to themselves. Her sisters, on the other hand, would be utterly unbearable, so Neve was halfway out of the floral top as she walked to her car at the end of the day. She was fairly certain that Michael, and possibly Puck, had taken photos of her, but Neve had no social media to speak of and could only pray that none of the evidence got back to Bay or Mercy. Mercy especially; gods, she would be a nightmare.

"What do you think you're doing?" Alexandria asked, hopping into step beside Neve.

"Putting my clothes back on," Neve said, dropping the top over Alexandria's head.

Alexandria shook it off. "No, no, no, what about the bonfire? You have to stay in costume until then."

"The what?"

"Bonfire," Ilma said as she and the rest of the group began to congregate around Neve's car. "It's a tradition, apparently. We're all going."

Puck nodded and the others murmured their agreement. Neve looked at all of them, her head dropping slightly to one side. She knew about the senior Spirit Week bonfire through osmosis. It was a massive party on the beach that kicked off the beginning of the most annoying week at school, but she didn't know what it had to do with her.

"Oh," she said slowly, looking to Alexandria for some cue to follow. Why were they telling her this? "That sounds . . . fun? Uh. Have a good time, I guess?"

It sounded like a nightmare, actually, but sometime between them invading her lunch table and now, Neve had lost the urge to snap at these humans in particular.

"*Wo-ow*," Michael said.

"You weren't kidding, Xan," Simon added, shooting Alexandria a meaningful look that made Neve want to shake him and demand what he meant.

Alexandria poked Neve in the stomach before she could act on that impulse. "*We* means all of us, genius. Including you."

"I've, um, I've got work," Neve said after a beat of silence that stretched out way too long. Her voice sounded a little too strangled to be casual, but in a million years she wouldn't have predicted this. She didn't get invited to things. She didn't *want* to get invited to things.

So why was there a tiny ember glowing in her chest?

Neve cleared her throat, too loud. "Yeah. Gotta go. I have to cover my sister's shift, so. Bye."

Without waiting for any of them to reply, Neve yanked

open her car door harder than necessary and sped out of the parking lot like she could outrun the overwhelming pressure of all their eyes on her. Expectant, like they'd assumed that she would join them. Like they *wanted* her to.

Neve rolled down all the windows as she drove way too fast into town. She was being stupid. Of course they didn't want her to come, why would they? And it wasn't like *Neve* wanted to go to some crowded human event, in any case. No, she was overreacting, probably feeling some latent effect of not sleeping last night.

She'd nearly convinced herself of that by the time she made it to the Three Crows. Being inside the shop was grounding; the antique interior, eclectic inventory, and smell of dried herbs were familiar and comforting. *This* was where she belonged, and it wasn't as if she'd lied, anyway. Despite the longstanding rule that Neve wasn't allowed to work alone, sometimes exceptions had to be made. Like when Bay was cramming for midterms, for example.

The feeling of relative calm lasted all of twenty-seven minutes and a single transaction (Mrs. Tooney was picking up rash cream for a similarly afflicted friend of hers, information Neve absolutely did not need) before a gaggle of humans thoroughly disturbed her fragile sense of peace. Puck waved as Tameka, Michael, Simon, and Ilma spilled through the door in a riot of color, all still bedecked in their '70s costumes.

"What are you doing here?" Neve demanded, staring at them from where she'd frozen in one of the aisles with a chunk of amethyst in her hand.

"There's the signature Morgan customer service this town has come to expect," Tameka said.

There was a squeal of tires from the parking lot outside before Alexandria burst into the shop as though she'd been shot from a cannon.

"Hi!" she said brightly, beelining to Neve's aisle with a fresh Dunkin' cup in her outstretched hand. "It's black this time, don't worry."

Neve blinked before accepting the coffee-that-was-clearly-a-peace-offering.

"What about the bonfire?" she asked after a moment, surreptitiously sniffing the top of the coffee cup before taking a sip. Black, thank gods. In this particular moment, Neve thought that a single granule of sugar might send her over the edge.

"Eh," Alexandria said, shrugging. "It sounded overrated anyway."

"My ex is definitely there," Tameka added, rolling her eyes. "And I'd rather not."

"Besides," Simon said, standing on his tiptoes to look at the impressive array of multicolored candles on one shelf, "I've always wanted to snoop around in here."

Neve only watched, nonplussed, as the humans spread out, combing every inch of the shop. Michael even tried to sneak behind the counter, but Neve saw him coming a mile off and stopped him with a look. Puck's attempt was much sneakier, but they just shrugged when Neve not-so-subtly placed her hand on the door to the stockroom to keep them from slipping inside.

Alexandria mostly hung around the counter, making increasingly one-sided conversation as Neve watched the rest of her classmates. She expected them to leave once they'd left no geode unturned, but they . . . didn't. They stayed, chatting among themselves like they did at lunch.

"I thought you were excited about Spirit Week," Neve said to Alexandria, pitching her voice low so the others wouldn't hear.

"Maybe I'm more excited to hang out with my favorite vampire," Alexandria replied. Her smile was slightly exasperated, like Neve was missing something obvious. That was fair, she supposed. It felt like Neve hadn't understood much of anything since Alexandria crash-landed into her life.

Alexandria nodded her head to the rest of the group, who were laughing at something Ilma had said, Puck most of all.

"Besides," she said. "I don't see any of them complaining."

Neve chewed on that for the rest of her shift. There weren't many customers, and besides Alexandria trying and failing to convince Neve to let her make a sale, and Michael and Simon loudly proclaiming the quality of the store's wares whenever a customer was within earshot—"it's called 'guerilla marketing' and *you're welcome*"—nothing unusual happened.

They were just there, in the shop, chatting and telling stories like it was something they did every day. Like it was *normal*. And Neve didn't hate it. She kept waiting for the impulse to shoo them out the front door, to scowl until they left, but it never came. All the while, she felt that tiny ember in her chest. It was strange.

Strange, but not bad. Not bad at all.

CHAPTER ELEVEN

Neve's bizarre contentment lasted until the end of lunch the next day, bolstered by the fact that Tuesday's Spirit Week theme—Twin Day—didn't require a costume. Not for her, at least. Alexandria, on the other hand, had shown up to school in all black, a red wig, and platform shoes, which she couldn't walk in but thought were hilarious.

"I can't even tell who's who," Tameka said when the bell rang to signal the end of lunch period. Alexandria was a few inches shy of true Morgan height, even with the heels, but she was barely making do as it was. Neve didn't complain, privately pleased to have an excuse to hold Alexandria's hand.

Alexandria's exaggerated slowness left them trailing behind their little group, not that she seemed to mind. Their distance gave Neve the opportunity to see a boy in a letterman jacket—Cameron, some part of her brain supplied, Tameka's ex—charging down the hallway with three other football players in tow.

"The hell, Tammy?" Cameron bellowed, effectively catching the attention of every student in the hallway. Neve pushed forward without thinking, dragging Alexandria with her. "You think you can go around talking shit and I wouldn't hear about it?"

Tameka stood her ground, glaring at the red-faced linebacker like he was three feet tall. "It's not talking shit if it's true," she replied, supremely unimpressed.

"Bitch," Cameron spat.

Neve shoved closer, but a crowd had formed already, obstructing her path. By her side, Alexandria very deliberately dropped her hand. The message was clear: *get his ass.*

Neve didn't need to be told twice. She made a beeline for Cameron, but before she got there, Ilma, Puck, Simon, and Michael arranged themselves around Tameka, creating a barrier between her and the football players.

"Back off," Simon snapped, his usually friendly face pinched with anger.

If possible, Cameron's face got even redder. "Go blow your boyfriend, you f—"

The word wasn't fully out of his mouth when Neve finally pushed through the throng of students. She grabbed Cameron's jacket and spun him so that he was facing her. The crowd scrambled to get out of her way as Neve pressed both hands against Cameron's chest and pushed him against an adjacent locker, *hard.*

"What the hell are you *on*, Morgan?" Cameron demanded,

his eyes widening with disbelief. He was only a few inches taller, but he easily outweighed her by fifty pounds. Neve didn't respond, anger coursing through her like poison. She didn't question it. Instead, she increased the pressure on Cameron's chest until she could hear his breath straining in his lungs.

Above them, the bell rang, the sound chasing away some of Neve's sudden rage. The lockers groaned when she finally let go. Cameron folded in on himself with his hands on his knees, sucking in greedy gulps of air.

"Come on," Neve said, shifting her backpack between her shoulder blades. She turned her head, catching Tameka's eye. Tameka just nodded, and Neve turned her attention to the rest of the assembled students. No one else spoke, the crowd perfectly still as if the entire hallway was holding its breath.

"Anyone *else* have something they want to say?" Neve shouted. Her voice echoed in the soundless hall, bouncing strangely off the locker-lined walls and making the metal doors rattle. All at once, the crowd dispersed as everyone fled into their respective classrooms.

"That was—" Alexandria started when they dropped into their seats in Mr. Robinson's class.

"Reckless," Neve finished for her. Throwing Cameron across the hallway like a rag doll in front of half the school. What was she *thinking*?

She wasn't, obviously. She'd just acted, and despite breaking one of her family's most important rules, she didn't regret it. Outside of battle, outside of her sisters, Neve had never felt that furious desire to *protect, defend* before. She wondered if it meant something was wrong with her, or that she was getting too distracted, or—

"It was hot as hell," Alexandria corrected. Neve's brain short-circuited, cutting through the spiral. "You were like Xena! Or Carmilla, even though you *insist* you're not a vampire."

Neve was spared from coming up with a coherent response by the phone ringing at the front of the classroom. Mr. Robinson answered it, his head bobbing as if it was on a spring before his eyes found her in the back row.

"Miss Morgan," he said. "You're wanted in the principal's office." If she were anyone else, a chorus of "oohs" would have followed the announcement, but the class remained completely silent. Most of them had witnessed her little temper tantrum firsthand, and anyone who hadn't would know by the end of the class period.

Cameron was already in the office by the time Neve pushed the door open. Neve glared at him and he quickly averted his gaze, slinking lower in his chair.

"So," Principal O'Neil said from behind her desk, steepling her fingers. "I heard that you two had a bit of an altercation after lunch." She looked at them expectantly. "Well? Do either of you have anything to say for yourselves?"

"Not really," Neve said. "Although I do appreciate the break from fifth period."

"Your attitude is not helping, Miss Morgan. Especially since I heard that you were the one who got physical."

Neve started to protest when the door was thrown open, and suddenly the office was much more crowded.

"Neve didn't do anything!" Ilma said.

Michael crossed his arms over his chest. "She was defending Tameka and Simon."

"Cam started the whole thing," Tameka added, shooting Cameron a look so scathing that it would've made Daughter Aoife proud.

"Also, he's a massive dick."

Everyone's heads swiveled to stare at Puck, who rarely spoke, let alone swore. They shrugged. "What? He is."

"Seconded," Alexandria said, obviously trying to hold back a laugh.

"Language aside," Principal O'Neil said, looking a little overwhelmed. "Considering this is Neve's first *major* behavior problem, I'm going to let you both off with a warning. But if I hear so much as a peep out of either of you, I will be taking severe action. Understood?"

"Understood," Cameron said immediately.

Neve just nodded, snapping Principal O'Neil a lazy salute on her way out of the office. Everyone maintained a stony silence until Cameron disappeared around the corner.

"How—" Neve started to ask once he was out of earshot. Alexandria pulled out her phone and waved it, looking supremely pleased with herself. She was still in her all-black outfit for Twin Day, but somewhere in the last few minutes she'd ditched the ginger wig and traded in the platform heels for her usual pair of sneakers.

"Xan put out the all-call," Michael specified. He still looked furious, his heavy eyebrows drawn together.

"You didn't need to do that," Neve said. She slouched, avoiding eye contact with any of them. Why would they do that? They weren't—she wasn't—

Tameka smacked her on the arm. "Yes, we did."

"We weren't going to let you go down like that," Simon added.

"All right, this day is shot," Alexandria announced to murmurs of agreement. "Let's get out of here."

"Puck and I know a place," Ilma volunteered. Puck blushed.

Fighting the urge to fidget but never one to pass up the opportunity to cut school, Neve let herself be carried along with the current as they made their way out of one of the side doors that wasn't monitored. There were half a dozen ways out of the school that didn't involve passing the school secretaries, though Neve was fairly confident that she could out-glare Ms. Higgins and Mr. Andrews any day of the week.

"You're with me, Xena," Alexandria said when they made it to the parking lot.

"And how am I supposed to get home?" Neve asked.

"I'll drop you off tonight and pick you up in the morning," Alexandria replied like it was obvious. She spun her keys around one finger. "I was *invited* to the convent. That gives me special permission. I'm pretty sure it makes me an honorary Morgan or something."

Neve rolled her eyes but got into Alexandria's car without complaint.

"Grow ten inches and we'll see about being an honorary Morgan," she said as they pulled out of the lot. The engine rattled and wheezed as they drove, and Neve had a vivid flashback of coming to consciousness in the backseat. "You need to get your engine looked at."

"Don't you be mean to my car," Alexandria objected. "Sure, the engine sounds like it's going to explode and there's weird blue shit in the upholstery, but I like it. It's got character. I rescued a crazy girl in this car. She saved my life from a monster, definitely didn't get her ass kicked in the process, and then tried this whole 'I'm off-limits' routine on me. Turns out she goes to my high school. How's that for a CW plotline?"

"I don't know what that means," Neve deadpanned, mostly

to hide the enormous smile that spread over her face. The warm glow expanded until Neve felt like she'd swallowed the sun, like her skin should be suffused with light.

Alexandria grinned. "They're TV shows and they're *terrible*. You're going to love them."

She reached across the seat and took Neve's hand like it was nothing before launching into a breakneck explanation of *Supernatural*.

Neve had to bite her lip to keep from laughing, resolving then and there never to tell her that Neve had watched it before. Not only watched it, but sometimes on rainy days, she and Mercy marathoned the demon-centered episodes. Bay never joined them—she thought it was disrespectful or irreverent or something—but Neve and Mercy reveled in ripping the show apart for its blatant inaccuracy, munching on popcorn as they mocked the idea that humans could do what they did. Like demons could just appear *anywhere*.

Her amusement dimmed somewhat at that. Neve still didn't know why Mercy hadn't sensed the demon attack on the night she'd met Alexandria. At first it felt like a blessing, like Neve had gotten lucky, but the more she thought about it, the more it nagged at her. Whatever the reason for Mercy's blind spot, it wasn't a good thing.

It didn't help that Neve hadn't figured out what the talking demon had wanted, either. She'd turned it over in her mind a hundred times, but none of her explanations made any sense. She shouldn't have lied about it in the first place—it shouldn't have been her first impulse, to lie to her sisters, and her stomach twisted at how quickly she'd fallen into the habit—but the demon was dead now anyway. Neve tried to tell herself that it didn't matter what it wanted, but the worry remained.

Neve was distracted for the rest of the ride, preoccupied by the questions piling up, only returning to the present when the car stopped on a nondescript stretch of back road. The wind howled, and waves crashed close enough to make her skin crawl. Neve tapped her fingers against her leg and sucked a breath in through her nose. She couldn't be afraid of the ocean when half the town was coast, but she couldn't stop thinking about the way the water had greedily lapped up her blood while she struggled to stay conscious.

"Took you long enough," Tameka said, her eyes flicking between the two of them with a knowing smile.

"Not my fault that Puck drives like a maniac," Alexandria shouted back. "Also, can someone explain to the new kid where we are? Because I'm getting 'secluded place to dump a body' vibes."

Puck smirked and gestured the group forward, disappearing into the reeds with Ilma. Soon only their curly black hair was visible above the tall grass. Ilma's pink hijab was covered completely.

"If I die here, I'm going to haunt the *shit* out of this town," Tameka grumbled. Michael, Simon, and Alexandria laughed.

After another deep breath that tasted too much like salt water for her liking, Neve followed, one hand gripping the dagger hidden in her jacket. It wasn't long before the tall grass gave way to shale underfoot. The others were already settled when she arrived, perched on flat rocks arranged in a circle. Behind them was a shallow cave that extended into the cliff face. A fire pit and several logs had been set up inside it, placed far enough from the entrance that they were sheltered from the elements.

The ledge where they sat extended straight out from the cliffside, and beyond was nothing but empty sea and sky. It created the illusion that they were hanging in midair, suspended over everything. Neve's breath caught for a dizzy moment and she placed her hand on the rock wall behind her, anchoring herself.

"Don't tell me you're scared of heights," Michael said, scooting over to make room for her.

Neve's grip tightened on her dagger as she fought to keep her face neutral. *Keep it together, Morgan.*

"Forgive me for wanting to make sure that we don't fall into the sea." She didn't doubt her ability to survive the drop, but the others were human, so breakable that they may as well have been made of spun glass.

"We have to have a conversation about your trust issues," Ilma said, resecuring her hijab against the wind.

"What we need to talk about is that jujitsu shit you pulled back at school," Tameka interjected.

Neve stiffened as all their eyes landed on her, pinning her in place. Each excuse that ran through her head was less convincing than the last. "I just took him by surprise," she said, trying for a blasé shrug and failing.

"Mama-bear strength," Alexandria said in a stage whisper. It was enough to break the tension, and the others laughed. She shot Neve a wink.

Led by Alexandria, they quickly moved on to safer topics than Neve and her ability to pin linebackers without breaking a sweat. She was content to just listen as they quipped back and forth, laughing and telling stories. It was all silly, useless information, but Neve found herself paying attention anyway. It felt important, somehow. She'd protected these humans instinctively. They'd protected her too, in their own way. That meant something.

As it turned out, Ilma thought that the young new imam at her mosque a few towns over was cute. Puck made an adorably affronted face at this news, which everyone seemed to notice except Ilma.

Michael was falling in love with a boy he'd met online. They'd never hung out in person, but they texted and

FaceTimed every day. He hoped to visit him in Boston some-time over winter break.

Tameka was a brand-new big sister. She passed around her phone and everyone cooed over the tiny wrinkly baby and her chubby little fists. Neve couldn't help but notice how helpless the newborn looked. She couldn't imagine ever being so small and vulnerable. What did Tameka's little sister have except for a few equally breakable humans to shield her from all the darkness in the world?

Simon couldn't wait to get out of Newgrange Harbor. He'd applied to colleges all across the country to study archaeology. If he had his way, he was never coming back to New England.

"The Atlantic is overrated," he proclaimed before launching into an excited spiel about a promising archaeological dig in China. Neve should have been bored, but the light in Simon's eyes kept her engaged as he talked about the Qin Dynasty and terracotta warriors.

Alexandria talked about her time in Boston before coming to Newgrange Harbor, never mentioning her aunt and uncle or what had brought her here. If the others noticed, they were kind enough not to bring it up.

Only Neve and Puck didn't join in as the others told their stories, preferring to listen rather than share. It created a strange, quiet camaraderie between them. Neve's phone buzzed every once in a while, usually from Puck texting a GIF into the group chat or sometimes just to her. Mostly, Neve liked to watch the way Puck looked at Ilma when she wasn't paying attention—like she was hiding the sun somewhere on her person—and every time Ilma smiled, Puck blushed from their neck all the way to the roots of their curly hair.

It made her smile. Neve didn't even realize until her phone pinged.

Like The Library: Don't look now but there's something on your face. Your mouth is doing this weird thing where it's not frowning

Neve smoothed out her expression, mostly to make a point. Alexandria snickered when Neve gave her the finger. It was nice. This—cutting class, listening to their stories, all of it— was nice. Neve *liked* it. She'd never bothered with anything that wasn't to do with her sisters or her divinity or protecting the Gate, but strictly speaking, hanging around with this group of humans in particular wasn't the worst thing in the world.

Their cliffside visit lasted until storm clouds rolled in off the ocean and the sky opened, drenching them in seconds. They all shrieked, pulling jackets and hoods over their heads to shield them from the rain as they ran back toward the street.

Neve and Alexandria shouted their goodbyes over the wind as they dove into Alexandria's car to escape the rain.

Alexandria blasted the heat before turning to Neve and immediately dissolving into delighted laughter. "You look like a drowned cat."

Neve couldn't stop staring, entranced by the shape of Alexandria's lips when she laughed, the golden-rose blush on her cheeks, the way her long hair clung to her skin from the rain. Warmth pooled low in her belly when Alexandria's dark eyes met hers and darted down to Neve's mouth. Almost without meaning to, Neve leaned forward until there was less than a breath of space between them.

Then a shrill noise came from her pocket and they sprang apart, both sitting back firmly in their seats, cheeks flaming. Neve didn't dare look at Alexandria, her eyes cast downward as she fumbled for her phone.

"What?" Neve barked into the receiver, praying that her pounding heart didn't resonate in her voice.

"Where the hell are you?" Daughter Maeve demanded, sounding less like a High Priestess and more like a mom at the end of her rope. "I just got a call from the office that you were sent to the principal and then *skipped school.* You better have a good explanation, young lady, or Maiden help me, I will confiscate your weapons and smelt them into cutlery."

"I'm on my way," Neve snapped, and hung up before Maeve could shout at her again.

"That didn't sound good," Alexandria said.

"Apparently, someone told the Daughters that I made a scene today." Neve winced, already anticipating the lecture waiting for her at home.

Alexandria filled the car ride with idle chatter all the way back to the convent. Neve kept her eyes fixed on the road as Alexandria drove them back, twisting her fingers together in her lap. She felt . . . she didn't know what she felt. But for a second there it had felt like Alexandria was going to *kiss* her and—

"Should I still pick you up tomorrow?" Alexandria asked, catching Neve's wrist before she got out of the car. There was something hesitant in her voice, as if she expected Neve to refuse.

Neve was starting to realize that she couldn't refuse Alexandria anything.

"I'll see you in the morning."

She meant it, but all at once, Neve remembered her nightmare, hovering behind her eyelids with the lingering feeling that something was different this time. Like maybe living to see tomorrow wasn't guaranteed anymore.

CHAPTER TWELVE

Even days later, Neve's ego still smarted from the one-sided shouting match she'd endured from the Daughters, but it wasn't half as bad as it could have been. Neve didn't even want to think about what they would say if they knew about Alexandria. Daughter Maeve might bypass shouting altogether and just have an aneurysm. At this point, the magic it would take to erase Alexandria's memories would be more than Aoife spent in a year. Neve shuddered to think about it. That kind of intensive mind magic was dangerous, like trying to thread a needle in the middle of a hurricane. A million and one things could go wrong, and even the best-case scenario made Neve's heart pick up with panic.

She didn't want to go back to school without Alexandria waiting for her in the parking lot, or have to eat lunch without being able to listen to whatever Wikipedia rabbit hole she'd fallen down the night before. Neve didn't want to give that up. She didn't want to give Alexandria up.

In spite of Neve's feeling of foreboding, the rest of Spirit Week was uneventful. Alexandria picked her up every day for the rest of the week, prepared with a costume for each new theme. Neve was coerced into a hideous sweater and Puck sprayed gray dye into her hair for Geriatric Day. She thought she might have another respite on Thursday for Color Day, but as the others emphatically pointed out, "Black is not a color, *Neve*."

That argument led to Neve poaching Alexandria's purple hoodie and sneaking into the art room to splatter violet paint on her pants. The hoodie was so oversized that it actually fit Neve pretty well, and if Neve forgot to return it at the end of the day, she considered it a fair trade for a week's worth of being forced to play dress-up.

And finally, Friday. All Hallows' Eve. Halloween. Or as Neve knew it best: Samhain. All week the others had been planning a Halloween party, discussing the details at lunch and over text. Puck's parents were out of town, so Puck offered to host.

"I have plans," Neve said for what felt like the thousandth time when Michael brought up the subject of her attendance. Again.

"Is it a witch thing?" Michael asked. Of all of them, he'd internalized the Morgan rumors the most. Neve wondered if he was one of the kids who played chicken on the long road to the convent, each trying to get closer than the other before they inevitably lost their nerve and turned back.

"Yeah, I'm the fourth Sanderson sister, did I forget to mention?" Neve replied offhandedly, expecting the conversation to continue. "What?" she asked when the table fell silent instead.

"You've seen *Hocus Pocus?*" Michael demanded. *"You?* Neve *I-Don't-Understand-Pop-Culture* Morgan?"

"I have no idea what you're talking about," Neve replied, stone-faced. "I don't watch movies."

Michael's eyes looked like they were about to pop out of his skull. Neve gazed back, unperturbed. It didn't happen very often anymore, but when they were little, Neve and her sisters would watch a stack of Halloween DVDs as they counted down the days until Samhain.

Before any of them manifested, when all the magic of the reincarnation cycle was solely used to keep the Hellgate shut, Samhain was the scariest night of the year. No one in the convent slept, and Neve and Mercy spent the whole night in Bay's room, terrified that the worst would happen: the magic sealing the Gate shut would fail and they would have to fight without their full powers.

It never did, obviously, but watching silly human Halloween movies had been Bay's way of distracting Neve and Mercy. Neve had always liked *Hocus Pocus* best because there were three Sanderson sisters, just like there were three Morgans. And arguing about which sister was which was an excellent distraction. (Neve was *not* Winifred, no matter what Mercy said.)

"I knew it," Alexandria crowed. "You hipster asshole, you do get my references."

"I've never seen a movie in my life, let alone the 1993 classic *Hocus Pocus*. I have no idea what you're talking about," Neve said with a completely straight face.

The lunch table devolved into absolute anarchy after that as they all tried to get Neve to admit that she liked cheesy Halloween movies, but she wouldn't budge.

"Why are you like this?" Simon moaned, dragging his hands down the sides of his face.

Neve shrugged. If they thought she was bad, they'd never survive Mercy. Or Bay, even, when she was in a mood.

"Okay fine, fine, changing topics before my blood pressure goes through the roof," Simon said. "Who do you have these mysterious plans with? Last time I checked, we're your only friends."

"Harsh," Tameka said, as Alexandria snapped, "Watch it."

Neve made an appreciative noise before leveling with Simon. "You heard Michael, it's a witch thing. It's been in the calendar for months and if I skip out, they'll confiscate my broom."

If she skipped out, demons would rain hellfire and death on

Newgrange Harbor and everyone at this table—everyone in this building—would probably die.

"You know, I really wish I could tell if you're kidding," Michael said, breaking the silence with an uneasy smile.

Neve's phone buzzed.

Simon: Sorry. That was out of line.

Neve: Next time I'll curse your ass.

Simon snorted and caught her eye across the table. Neve met his gaze and smiled, a little surprised at both of them. They dropped the subject of Neve's attendance at the party after that.

"Is the reason you can't come one of the things you can't tell me about?" Alexandria asked at the end of the day, once they were alone in her car.

"Yes," Neve said softly.

"Is it dangerous?"

"I have my sisters." It wasn't an answer.

"And they're strong like you?"

She was fishing, Neve knew that, but she couldn't lie to Alexandria when she looked so worried. Her eyebrows furrowed, carving anxious grooves into her forehead. "Stronger. They'll keep me safe, don't worry."

"I know you mean that to be comforting, but it is *so* not comforting," Alexandria complained. "I don't—I don't like thinking of you getting hurt."

"You've seen me bleeding with two broken ribs. You saw my demon-bite scar."

That was the wrong thing to say. The furrow between Alexandria's eyebrows grew deeper. "I know, and I have nightmares about it twice a week."

"I'll be fine," Neve promised, purposely not thinking about the fact that she featured in Alexandria's dreams, nightmares or no. "I'll call you in the morning, okay? Just try to have fun tonight with the others. Do . . . what people do at parties."

Alexandria tried for a smile. "Okay."

Neither of them said goodbye when Neve finally got out of the car.

Neve tried to put Alexandria out of her head as she and her sisters prepared for Samhain. It was the most important day on their calendar, the day that began the darkest—and most dangerous—part of the year. As soon as the sun went down, the magic that separated their world from Hell was nearly nonexistent until dawn.

The Daughters had spent the better part of the last three months preparing everything they would need to shore up the Gate's defenses. Along with their roles as guardians and secret-keepers, their Order was tasked with protecting the spells and magical artifacts that acted as fail-safes in case the worst happened. In case Neve and her sisters died without starting a new cycle and the Hellgate was left without its defenders. It had never happened—it *would* never happen—but the Daughters had to be prepared, just in case.

Even with magic and steel on their side, Samhain never went smoothly. Once, a demon made it all the way to Main Street before Mercy killed it. It was a miracle no one had seen anything—if they had, they probably would have assumed that the demon was someone in a mask and wouldn't give it another thought. Thank the Maiden, Mother, and Crone for humans and their willingness to overlook anything strange.

"You ready, Nee-nee?" Mercy asked, strapping a long knife to her leg. Her broadsword was already in its sheath across her back. The glint in her eyes was familiar. Neve used to share it, the rush of adrenaline that made her look forward to every fight. It all used to be so much fun.

Not so much anymore. Neve's rapid pulse was a constant reminder of her own stupid mortality. If she and her sisters failed to protect the Gate, the whole town was in danger. Alexandria was in danger.

Alexandria, who was at Puck's party, worrying that Neve might not come back.

"Ready to run circles around you," Neve replied, because that was the answer Mercy expected. They had protected the Hellgate for a thousand years. They would not fail.

"Both of you, please," Bay admonished. "This is important and it would serve *you two* to remember that."

"Thanks, Mom," Mercy grumbled affectionately, reaching out to ruffle Bay's curls.

As the sun began to set, the Daughters perched on top of the cliff and took up their chant. The barrier appeared in the fading orange sunlight, invisible to everyone but those who knew what to look for.

Neve felt the moment that the magic failed. Something pulled in her gut, leaving a hollow place where the spellwork should be. Mercy and Bay fell into step on both sides of her.

"Stay safe," Bay signed, her voice gone with the sun. "I love you both."

"Love you too," Neve replied.

"Blah, blah, sentiment, sentiment, sentiment," Mercy said last. "Love you dummies."

No sooner were the words out of Mercy's mouth than her eyes blackened and the blood drained from her face. It was all the warning they needed. With the Daughters looking on, the three of them dove through the barrier.

The first two demons were easy enough to dispatch, but Neve knew better than to let herself relax. The attacks came in waves. If not for Mercy, they would be completely overwhelmed, unable to know when and how to brace themselves.

Even with the split-second advantage, they barely kept up with the onslaught.

It was the waiting that Neve couldn't stand. She hated not knowing when the next attack was coming, or how many were about to come through the Gate. Her pulse was so loud that it almost drowned out the sound of the ocean beating against the beach, and with every demon they killed, she couldn't help but wait for something bigger, stronger, worse. Something to justify the dread she'd felt for weeks.

Sometimes it felt like hours between attacks, but often they barely had time to flick the blood off their blades before the next. The demons came in pairs or groups of three, never one at a time, and they always went for Neve first. For once, she didn't take it personally, too preoccupied with staying alive. She lost track of time, of herself, as everything blurred into basic impulses. *Fight, dodge, stab, survive.*

Sunrise was just a few hours away when disaster struck. Neve was exhausted and bruised, blue-gold blood weeping from several wounds all over her body. Her arms and shoulders were especially battered, but the worst of it came from a deep cut on her forehead that kept dripping into her eyes.

"Incoming," Mercy warned as another demon ripped through the Gate. It looked like a shadow had come to life, eating up the light around it. Stark white eyes pierced the darkness, gleaming with hate as it tore through the barrier like it was made of gossamer, knocking Neve into the cliff in the process.

"*Shit*," Mercy swore. "Go after it! I'll hold things down here."

They didn't have time to argue. Bay and Neve jumped into the car they had waiting and took off. Neither of them needed to be able to see the demon to race after it, blowing every red light on their way into town.

"You go that way, I'll go this way," Neve ordered when the tugging *wrongness* inside both of them led them into a labyrinthine neighborhood and they were forced to abandon the car. Bay nodded, shoving her scythe into a sheath across her back before vanishing into the darkness.

Neve took off running, ducking around streetlights to keep out of sight. Of the two of them, she was much more likely to be seen and stopped. When Bay was like this, no one noticed her until she wanted them to, and by then it was usually too late.

It was luck more than anything that Neve spotted the demon outside a house on a darkened street, so camouflaged with shadow that it was almost invisible. Its head was tipped up toward an upstairs window, white eyes narrowed like it was looking for something.

Before she could reach it, the demon leaped onto the second-story sill.

"Bay!" Neve hissed into the night. Her sister would hear her. In the meantime, Neve pulled herself up by a bit of lattice on the side of the house and followed the demon inside. The window frame was cracked, the lock on the inside broken from being forced open.

Neve's heart hammered against her ribs so hard that she thought they would break—again—when she saw the demon crouched over a bed. A bed that was occupied by a small, sleeping figure.

She snarled, lunging at the demon with her weapons drawn. She didn't have time to worry about being seen—Aoife could take the human's memories later.

The shadowy creature batted her away without so much as looking up. Neve hit the wall hard. Her vision swam but she didn't let herself slow. Breathing heavily, she leaped back to her feet and attacked the demon again.

Wake up, she willed the person in the bed. *Why won't you wake up?*

This time she managed to wound the creature, drawing blood that burned through her armor. The demon hissed at her and Neve choked as an inky hand wrapped around her throat.

The person in the bed finally stirred. A mess of black hair emerged from under the covers, blinking blearily at the scene in front of her.

"*Shit*," Neve gasped, immediately recognizing Alexandria.

The demon increased its grip on Neve's throat, choking off any sound before it could escape.

"*Run!*" she tried to scream. "*Alexandria,* run*!*"

Maiden, Mother, and Crone, of all the houses in this gods-forsaken town. Alexandria was supposed to be at Puck's . . . why was she alone, why was she *here*? Neve fought even harder, feeling the demon's claws dig into her neck as she kicked and struggled. With a snarl, the creature tossed her aside, hard enough that she cracked her head on the dresser and fell to the floor in a boneless heap.

Alexandria remained frozen, her eyes massive as the demon loomed over her. Its free hand hovered above her chest, claws primed above her heart.

Neve hauled herself to her feet, using the demon's distraction to reach for the extra dagger hidden in her boot.

"*Get the fuck away from her!*" Neve shouted hoarsely, throwing the blade with all her strength.

The demon roared as blood spurted from the place where blessed steel pierced its flesh. It staggered back and shadows gathered behind it, sucking all the light out of the room.

"Neve?" Alexandria's voice was so woozy and small that Neve's heart gave a panicked squeeze in her chest.

Instinct prickled on the back of her neck. Neve whirled, her sword crossed over her chest, but she was already injured and exhausted and she couldn't defend herself from something she couldn't see. Something tensed deep within her, some untapped place beneath the hollow of her throat, and when the darkness grew even blacker, Neve didn't try to fight. Instead, she just opened her mouth and screamed.

Neve had screamed before—with anger, frustration, pain—but this was nothing like that. It was her rage and fear distilled into something new, something powerful like she'd never felt before. After a few moments, the darkness receded and the demon stood, trembling and frozen still.

The sound began to fade, and Neve didn't give the demon a chance to recover before she plunged her sword through its chest, using both hands to put her full weight behind the blow. The demon made a sound like the air escaping from a sealed vacuum, its eyes glowing doubly bright before it exploded in a whirlwind of brimstone and burning ash.

"Are you okay?" Neve asked as soon as she was sure that it was gone. Alexandria just stared, her eyes enormous, pupils blown. Some of the demon's blood had burned through her bedcovers, but she didn't seem to notice. Neve gripped her shoulders gently. "Look at me. Alexandria, I need you to look at me."

Alexandria's dark eyes found Neve for a second before they slid out of focus again.

"Gods *damn* it," Neve swore. She had to get back to the

Gate, back to Mercy. But she couldn't leave Alexandria alone when she was like this, and bringing her to the convent was a nonstarter.

"Alexandria," Neve said. Her voice was still raw from screaming, but she smoothed it out as best she could. "I have to go." Alexandria's pupils dilated even more and her hand came up to grasp at Neve's shirt. "I'll come right back, I promise."

Neve whipped around at a soft sound that came from the broken window, reaching for her dagger. Poe perched on the sill, head cocked, black eyes surveying them both. He cawed once. *I'll watch out for her.*

"Hey," Neve said, turning back. "That's Poe, remember? He's going to stay with you until I get back."

Alexandria still didn't answer, her eyes finding Poe for a split second before going hazy again.

"I'll be back soon," Neve promised. She squeezed Alexandria's hand before fleeing through the open window. Something in her chest burned and Neve patted herself down, checking for injuries, but there was nothing. Only the terrible, hollow ache of leaving Alexandria behind when she was terrified, like Neve had left her heart behind too.

CHAPTER THIRTEEN

M ercy!" Neve warned, already halfway out of the car before it came to a stop. It was almost sunrise by the time they made it back to the convent. Bay hadn't questioned it when Neve said that the demon was dead. There wasn't time, and the blood on Neve's blade was all the proof Bay needed.

Mercy spun, slashing at the demon poised to take a bite out of her.

The base of Neve's throat was hot like she'd swallowed a coal, and this time when she opened her mouth, the sound was beyond words.

Her scream shattered across the battlefield, and for a single moment there was perfect stillness. Neve exploded into violence, using the demons' hesitation to hack through as many of them as she could. It only took Bay and Mercy a moment to leap in after her, filling the air with ash.

She was lost amid a whirlwind of claws and teeth, each swing of her blade more frantic than the last as she fought to keep her head above the tide. And all the while, she just. Kept. Screaming.

Neve was barely aware that the sun had risen until she felt a hand on her shoulder. She whirled, sword and dagger raised, but it was only Mercy.

"It's morning," Mercy said softly. Blood streamed from her nose. It was lopsided and already bruising. Broken. "Nee, it's morning."

Bay hovered slightly behind, her face pinched with concern.

"What the hell happened?" Mercy asked. "Where did you guys go? What happened with that demon?"

Neve felt as if a bucket of ice water had been upturned over her head. Alexandria was still at her house, still waiting for Neve to come back.

"I killed it," she said finally.

"On your own?"

Neve's ego smarted at the surprise in Mercy's tone, but she couldn't exactly admit that this wasn't her first solo kill.

"Yeah," she said, already walking toward the car. "On my own."

The Daughters were waiting for them when they returned to the convent bleeding and exhausted, though as usual, most of the blood was Neve's. It took forever to scrub the blue out of her hair, and even after almost half an hour, her skin was still stained in a half-dozen places. Daughter Clara bandaged the worst of it—a nasty slash across her ribs and a puncture on her shoulder so deep it had almost gone all the way through—but she'd be sore for a few days. Neve almost didn't notice the sting of healing salve, preoccupied with the fact that Alexandria was still at her house, *alone*, after nearly being killed by a demon.

"You should eat something," Daughter Clara insisted when Neve tried to beg off breakfast.

Neve wiggled her bandaged shoulder. "I can barely hold a spoon right now. I just want to sleep." The Daughters exchanged looks, but they didn't object.

Neve locked her bedroom door behind her and waited fifteen minutes before throwing her window open and slipping out. She should've stayed longer to make sure that her sisters wouldn't come to check on her, but waiting this long had used up all her self-control.

Neve didn't know if it was grand theft auto to steal her own car, but it certainly wasn't subtle. She just hoped that everyone was too exhausted from their bloody all-nighter to notice her disappearance. It usually took most of the next day to recover from Samhain. Neve expected to be back well before anyone noticed she was gone.

The sun had only been up for a few hours and there wasn't a car in the driveway, but Neve still parked a few streets away from Alexandria's house, just in case. She didn't bother with the front door.

"Alexandria?" she called through the bedroom window,

voice pitched low. Neve knocked on the splintered wood and peered inside.

Alexandria was curled up in the farthest corner of the room, with clear eyelines to the window and the door. Her hood covered her hair, and her chest was rising and falling too fast to be healthy. Poe danced around her, hopping anxiously from foot to foot. At Neve's knock, he twisted his head around and cawed as if to say, *Get in here, you idiot.*

"Alexandria?" Neve said again, dropping onto the carpet with a soft thud. Alexandria's eyes found hers and her breathing hitched, as if she'd been holding back panic and seeing Neve set it loose.

"I was right," Alexandria whispered raggedly as Neve approached. "I was right. They told me that I was seeing things, but I was *right.*" Her breathing picked up again, until no words could escape between bouts of hyperventilation.

"Breathe with me," Neve said, scooting closer without touching her. This, she could do. For all Mercy's bravado, when she first turned eighteen, her connection to the Gate made her so anxious that she had panic attacks for months. Neve and Bay had become experts at helping her through them.

"We're going to do it together, okay?" Neve inhaled loudly for six seconds, held her breath for three, and then exhaled for seven, repeating the pattern until Alexandria's breaths began to match her own.

At last, Alexandria's heartbeat began to calm and some of the color returned to her skin. She exhaled once more, opening her eyes and reaching for Neve.

Alexandria's mouth twitched, halfway between a smile and a huff when Neve didn't move. "Come *here*, you ridiculous half giant."

"I'm not a giant," Neve grumbled, so relieved that she could have cried. She rearranged them so that she was the one pressed against the wall, tucking Alexandria into her lap. "Is this okay?"

"S'okay," she mumbled, leaning her head against Neve's chest. Alexandria was freezing, and the open window was not helping. Neve rubbed her arms to get the blood flowing again. "I *knew* that the monsters were real. I *knew* it."

"You've known for weeks," Neve said softly.

"Not just *your* monsters. *My* monsters. Everyone said that I was seeing things, but I was right. He's real. They all are."

Who? Neve wanted to ask. *Who taught you that monsters are real?* But Alexandria didn't need Neve's questions on top of everything else, not today.

"You were right," she agreed instead, resting her chin on top of Alexandria's head. "You were right about everything."

"I thought I was going to die. I thought he was going to kill me like—" Her voice broke off.

Poe cried, flapping his wings in response to her agitation.

He hopped into Alexandria's lap and made a soft, almost affectionate noise. Neve could feel Alexandria's ribs expand as she inhaled deeply through her nose.

"Sometimes I still think that the doctors were right," Alexandria said softly, half-asleep. "They told me I was seeing things. Maybe none of this is real and the monsters are all in my head. And if I made them up, that means I made you up, too."

Neve didn't know what to say to that. Her thoughts were slow, overwhelmed by exhaustion. The implications of Alexandria's quiet declaration were too big for her to wrap her mind around.

"I hope I didn't make you up," Alexandria said around a yawn. She mumbled something else, her eyes sliding shut, and before Neve knew it, Alexandria's breathing had evened out completely. She was asleep.

Neve didn't realize she'd drifted off too until she woke to Alexandria's head shifting on her chest.

"You look like shit," Alexandria said blearily, squinting. She frowned, and Neve realized that the cut on her forehead was visible. At least it had stopped bleeding.

Neve slowly reached her arms over her head, listening for the satisfying pop as her joints cracked. Thank the gods she hadn't broken any bones this time. Regrowing bone matrix was so *itchy*. "Good morning to you, too."

Alexandria made a face and poked a bruise on Neve's cheek. "Your bruises are black."

"Blue blood. Why do you think I'm so pale?"

"Irish genes and vampirism?" Alexandria asked with a wobbly, split-second smile. She stood and stretched, running her hands through her sleep-tousled hair.

"Are you okay?" Neve asked softly "Do you—I mean, what you told me . . . do you want to talk about it?"

Alexandria stilled, paling a little. Dark circles had bloomed under her eyes. "No. Literally not at all."

"What—" Neve hesitated, unsure of how to deal with an Alexandria who didn't want to talk. "What can I do?"

"I just—I just need time. To deal with all this."

Neve started to object, but Poe's sharp caw interrupted her. A quick glance at the sky revealed that she'd been gone for too long. Her family would notice her absence soon, if they hadn't already.

"He's playing your song," Alexandria said, nodding to Poe. "Go home, Neve. I'll, uh, I'll call you. Okay? Soon."

Neve swallowed hard and nodded, standing reluctantly. She squeezed Alexandria's hand once more before ducking out the way she came, tapping a new message to Tameka with one hand.

Neve: Check on Alexandria this weekend. Bring the others. Think she might need you guys.

Neve didn't know if she was doing the right thing, but she didn't want Alexandria to be alone.

Tameka: You joining us?

Neve: No. I'm not involved. Don't tell her I said anything. This was your idea.

Tameka: You want to talk about it?

Neve: No

Tameka emphasized "No."

No one was waiting for her when Neve returned. The Daughters hadn't sent out a search party. Her escape act, it seemed, had gone unnoticed.

Neve had been back for almost two hours, exhausted but unable to sleep, when there was a knock on her door.

"Can we talk?" Bay asked from the hall.

"I'm really tired," Neve tried. "Can it wait?" *Until tomorrow. Until never.*

"You know it can't." Bay's eyes were enormous, blue and cloudy with concern when Neve finally let her in. Bay paused before cocking her head to the side and sighing. "Just come in, Mercy!"

Mercy burst into Neve's bedroom so violently that the doorframe rattled. It was a good thing that everything in the convent was reinforced, or they would have destroyed it lifetimes ago.

"How the hell did you *do* that?" Mercy looked like she'd spent the last several hours in a windstorm, her eyes bright and her hair in furious disarray. "You are *way* too young to be warscreaming, little sister."

This was not the conversation Neve thought they would be having.

"Warscreaming?" Neve replied, latching onto the unfamiliar word.

Bay and Mercy made conspicuous eye contact that only served to fray Neve's ragged nerves.

"That's your gift," Mercy said finally. Bay made a distressed noise. "Come on, Bee, the cat's kind of out of the bag at this point. Besides, I'm pretty sure there's a loophole in the rules for when she starts *warscreaming* at *seventeen*." Bay gnawed on her lip but didn't protest when Mercy turned back to Neve. "When we come of age, our gifts are always the same. I sense the Gate, Bay goes all *Silence of the Lambs*, and you warscream. You can literally stop armies in their tracks. Paralyze them with fear. It's *awesome*."

Neve blinked, struggling to absorb that.

"How is this—I mean, is that possible?" Their abilities were fully locked away until they were eighteen. That was the way it had always been.

"I don't know," Bay said, picking at the cuticle on her thumb. "You . . . your voice—gods, it feels so *weird* talking about this with you so soon—your voice started developing a few months ago. That's never happened before, let alone full-blown warscreaming before you manifest."

"Is it a bad thing?" Neve asked after a long pause, thinking back to every strange thing that had happened over the last few months. Her nagging, persistent nightmares, a demon appearing without alerting Mercy; and now this. "Did I do something wrong?"

The question was out of her mouth before Neve could stop it, and she dropped her gaze to the floor. She sounded so young and stupid when all she wanted—all she'd wanted since the start—was to prove that she was strong. She just wanted to be like them.

Mercy grabbed Neve's shoulder, grinning. "Neve, you stopped an entire Hellgate full of demons. On *Samhain*. That's amazing!"

"We obviously need to do some research," Bay said, more slowly. "Any deviation from the cycle is something to look into. The Daughters are a little worried—" She noticed the look on Neve's face and immediately began to backtrack. "Not because of you, Nee. This isn't anything you did. You kept us safe when we were almost overrun. You killed a demon *on your own*. No one's angry with you."

"They're too busy being impressed," Mercy said, elbowing Neve in the ribs and looking like Christmas had come early.

"This is the best day. I've been waiting *forever* to spar against your scream."

"She's tired," Bay said when Mercy gestured meaningfully at the door.

"No, I'm not." Between Alexandria, warscreaming, and Bay and the Daughters *researching her deviation from the cycle*, Neve didn't think being alone with her thoughts was a good idea. "Let's do it."

CHAPTER FOURTEEN

The rest of the weekend was spent with Mercy, practicing Neve's scream over and over until her voice was so ragged, it sounded like she'd been gargling with barbed wire.

When she wasn't training, Neve checked her phone obsessively, but Alexandria's texts in the group chat gave nothing away. Not that Neve would know one way or another. As it had been pointed out to her more than once, she wouldn't know a social cue if it hit her in the face.

She very nearly texted Tameka or Simon—they were good at this kind of thing, they might be able to help—before deciding against it. That felt too much like conceding defeat, as if admitting that there might be a problem would speak it into existence.

Alexandria's spot was empty and she still hadn't reached out when Neve screeched into the parking lot on Monday morning. It was the longest time they'd gone without speaking since Alexandria put herself in Neve's contacts. Neve was trying not to take it personally.

She was absolutely taking it personally, beginning to wish

for the days when humans were the least of her worries.

She didn't care, she told herself. She could *choose* not to care. The fluttery, miserable feeling in her stomach disagreed.

The first few classes flew by, traitorously fast when they usually dragged. At lunch, Neve scanned the cafeteria for another place to sit and made her way to an empty table in the corner. She purposely avoided looking in the direction of where the rest of the group was beginning to congregate, trying not to imagine what excuse Alexandria would come up with to explain Neve's absence. She couldn't help the feeling of disappointment—of *loss*, like their weird little group had filled a hole she didn't know was there before—that ate at her, even as she pushed it away.

Neve picked at her food, her headphones planted firmly over her ears. She spun the pen in her hand like it was a dagger, finding a rhythm between her movements and the music.

"Simon!" someone bellowed over the noise of the cafeteria, so loud that Neve looked up. Michael waved to Simon as he approached the table. Puck and Ilma trailed behind, sitting down beside Neve. "We're over here today!"

"Why *are* we here today?" Ilma asked. Neve didn't answer. Samhain had left her twitchy and irritable, and not even training with Mercy had been able to rid her of the anxious energy that hummed beneath her skin. She'd expected it to be gone by now, but it was still there, that same lurking dread.

"Morgan needed a change of scenery," Tameka replied when Neve didn't answer. "And has apparently decided to take a vow of silence."

"Right, because she's always so chatty," Simon added.

Alexandria didn't show up, and Neve wasn't brave enough to ask the others if they'd gone to see her over the weekend. It felt like she would give herself away by asking. Like the moment she opened her mouth, the neutral veneer would crack, and they'd see what an absolute wreck she was underneath.

If they noticed her tension, none of them commented, and the conversation pivoted toward Puck's Halloween party. They talked about it like it had been fun, but for the life of her Neve couldn't understand the appeal of sitting in a basement and drinking poison. She and her sisters couldn't get drunk—thank you, divine metabolism—but even so, the allure of alcohol was lost on her. It didn't help that Alexandria was supposed to be with them, having fun or whatever, instead of leaving early and going home to be attacked by a demon.

Neve bolted the instant the bell rang, leaving them behind as she all but sprinted into her next class.

Her phone buzzed in her pocket, once, twice, five times.

Tameka: You good? This have to do with whatever happened over the weekend?

Michael: Everything okay?

Simon: Anything I can do to help? (Unless it's a girl thing or a witch thing because idk shit about witches or women)

Neve almost smiled at that one.

Ilma: Here if you need anything

Puck's message was a bunch of emojis and a sad clown meme.

They made her feel a little better, but Neve couldn't stop wishing that it was Alexandria texting her instead.

It only took fifteen minutes of Mr. Robinson's droning before Neve gave up on the day. She couldn't sit still, not with the desk to her left still conspicuously empty, or the rapidly expanding bubble of anxiety in her chest making it harder and harder to breathe.

I thought he was going to kill me like—

Like who? Who had been killed? Alexandria had *recognized* the demon in her bedroom, Neve was sure of it, but that was impossible. The Gate had never been breached, not in this lifetime.

Not just your monsters. My monsters. Her mysterious *him.*

And then Neve was moving toward the door, her backpack slung over her shoulder, despite Mr. Robinson's protestations. His voice was an insignificant buzz, easy to ignore compared to the echo of Alexandria's voice in her head and the roar of her pulse in her ears.

The Daughters would be furious if they found out that she was skipping again—and distantly, Neve recognized that the office would almost certainly call home—but in the moment she didn't care. She needed to get out of this school with its little people and their little problems, all blissfully unaware of the danger that lurked just down the beach.

What would you do if we were gone? Neve wanted to shout, to scream, to make them understand. *What would you do if we weren't here?*

Die. They'd all just . . . die.

Something in her, a tiny voice that wasn't her own, sneered at the thought. She could hear the boy's laughter from her dream, high and cruel, and Neve shook away the mental image of blood and chaos that accompanied it. She needed to get out of here.

Bay was working at the Three Crows when Neve arrived. The convent was a nonstarter, and her stomach turned at the idea of going to the outlook Puck and Ilma had shown them. It was too bound up with Alexandria and their friends. It was too *human.*

"Neve, you should be—Neve?" Bay's admonishment morphed into concern, and Neve wished she was a better liar so she could hide the way she was completely, utterly unraveling.

Bay came around the corner, reaching for her as if to pull

her into a hug. Neve backed away. Coming here was a mistake. Neve had always thought of the Three Crows as neutral ground in town, but right now it was too much of a reminder of all the secrets she was keeping, everything she was doing wrong.

It was all too much. Samhain, warscreaming, the shadow demon that had gone out of its way to target Alexandria. Gods, it had only been a couple of days.

"Neve, wha-what's wrong?" Neve felt more than heard the tremor of fear in Bay's voice. Shame pulled at her, dragging her further into the murk. She shouldn't have come here. She was making everything worse. *She was always making everything worse.*

"I need space," Neve said. *She* was what was wrong, and right now, everyone needed to get out of the blast radius before she detonated. "This"—she made an all-encompassing gesture—"is too much. It's all too much."

Wrong again. The hurt look in Bay's eyes deepened.

"What can I do?" she asked softly.

"Just leave me alone!" The words were out of her mouth before Neve could stop them, her temper snapping as anger filled the hole carved into her chest. The truth—not all of it, but the truth that started all this—poured out before she could stop it. "I need *space*, Bay. I can't go home because the Daughters treat me like I'm made of glass, and so do you! I'm not a kid anymore. I can fight and I can scream and I can take care of myself. I'm a part of this family! So start treating me like one and *back off.*"

Neve didn't know that it was possible to feel any worse until she saw the emotion drop off Bay's face, the emptiness from when she first manifested appearing behind her eyes. Bay inhaled once, the color in her cheeks the only indication that she felt anything at all, before speaking again.

"If that's what you want."

Then she shrugged on her jacket and left without another word, careful not to touch Neve as she went. Neve wanted to run after her, before realizing that Bay was just doing what she'd asked. Giving her space. Giving her a place to go that wasn't the convent.

Neve wanted to cry. She wanted to break something. She wanted to run after Bay and apologize, to admit everything. But she was too angry, too mixed-up, and too selfish, and by the time she looked again, Bay was already gone.

Gods, what was wrong with her?

Neve sat down behind the counter, laying her head on the old, scarred wood and praying that no one would come into the shop. Whatever gods she prayed to—Brigid, the Dagda, the rest of the pantheon who'd disappeared without a trace— they clearly weren't listening, because the bell over the door chimed less than five minutes later.

A glance up revealed Alexandria in the doorway, pale and bright-eyed.

"My parents died when I was nine," she declared without so much as a hello. "They were killed by demons."

CHAPTER FIFTEEN

Neve's first instinct was to disagree, but Alexandria barreled on without giving her the chance.

"My last name isn't Abbott," Alexandria continued in a rush. "Abbott is my mom's maiden name and I didn't want to chance it that anyone would recognize my last name. The mur—the Kuro case was kind of a big deal."

Neve's mouth opened and then closed as she tried to process what Alexandria was saying.

"I left after. My family's massive, but . . . bad stuff happened the farther away I went from home. So, I came back. Back-ish. Close enough."

And you chose Newgrange Harbor? Neve hadn't moved from behind the counter, she and Alexandria still standing at opposite sides of the shop, eyeing each other like wary animals forced into the same enclosure.

Alexandria shrugged like she'd heard Neve's question. "I don't know why. I've got family here—um, my aunt and uncle are pastors—so it made sense."

All the towns in all the states in this massive country, and she had to go and pick the one with the entrance to Hell.

Alexandria cleared her throat, visibly paling. "At the time—I mean, the night it—well, I, um, I didn't really know what had happened. But I woke up in the middle of the night feeling like something was wrong, and when I went into my parents' bedroom, they—"

She made a small, hurt sound and Neve wanted to go to her. But she stayed where she was, afraid that if she moved, Alexandria would stop talking. Or worse, leave altogether.

"They were gone. They weren't my parents anymore. They were just . . . ashes. And when I screamed, that was when I saw it, this thing like something out of a nightmare. He was shaped like a man, but it looked like he'd been cut out of the night sky or something. And his eyes were—"

"Glowing."

"Glowing," Alexandria confirmed. She took another deep breath and marched toward the counter, fishing her sketch-book out of her bag.

It was full of demons. And there, on the very first page, was the demon from Samhain. There was a date scribbled on the corner of the page from years ago.

Impossible, Neve thought again, even though the evidence was staring at her, rendered in pencil and charcoal.

"I tried to tell the police and the doctors and everyone, but nobody believed me. They said that I was just seeing things, and eventually I sort of accepted that I'd made it all up. I mean, I was a kid, it was nighttime, I was in shock. I still have PTSD about the whole thing. It was easier to think that I'd imagined it." She swallowed hard. "Bad enough losing my parents without having to deal with monsters too, you know?"

Neve didn't know. She didn't have parents. She and her sisters had been born of blood and war and magic. They'd grown up with all this.

"If anything happened to Mercy or Bay, I don't know what I'd do," she admitted softly, because it was true and Alexandria deserved the truth.

Neve knew that she might die before her sisters, or that they might die before her. It was always a danger. Technically, only one of them had to survive in order to renew the magic and create another link in the chain. They could survive for years, decades, without each other. The thought made Neve feel ill. She didn't want to live in a world without her sisters. She didn't know if she could.

"Yeah, you three are kind of dangerously codependent," Alexandria said with a watery smile. She sucked in a breath, steeling herself. "I was with my Aunt Bea for almost a year when there was a fire. The police said it was a freak accident, something to do with the wiring, but I felt *something* in the house right before it happened. I was home alone, and I only made it two steps into the kitchen before the whole place went up, but I swear I saw something in the fire. Something looking back at me."

Alexandria sighed and flipped to another page. Inky eyes glowered at Neve from charcoal flames. "It all went to shit after that. No one wanted anything to do with me. Relatives would let me stay for a little while because we're family and they had to, but they never lasted long. They'd get spooked and make up some reason for me to leave or—"

"They *what*?" Neve demanded, her voice too loud all of a sudden. Behind Alexandria, the glass panes in the door rattled, and Neve snapped her mouth shut, wary of shattering them by accident.

"I wouldn't have," she said after she'd reined in her temper enough to speak.

"Wouldn't what?"

"I wouldn't have left you."

Alexandria's eyebrows furrowed in a way Neve didn't know how to decipher. "I know." She held out her hand and Neve took it without hesitation. "I know. Some of them tried to keep me, but anytime I was in a place longer than a few months there were accidents. More fires, bad storms, floods. One night it rained so hard that a telephone pole came down. It shorted the entire neighborhood and Mrs. Green from next door died. Cardiac arrest. I looked it up and the internet says that it doesn't hurt, but sometimes I think about what it must have felt like for her heart to stop like that. What if she was still alive for a few minutes? What if she was in pain and all of it was my fault because I'm the one attracting the monsters wherever I go and—"

"It wasn't your fault," Neve interrupted, her voice so low and fierce that it actually stopped Alexandria mid-spiral. Alexandria blinked, her eyes inky-dark in the shop's hazy lighting.

"I know. I *know* that, but they're—the demons . . . I mean, they have to be looking for me, right? It's the only thing that makes sense."

"I don't know," Neve said at last, her mind reeling. "I didn't think that was possible, but I don't know everything."

"You don't?"

She shook her head. "I'm too young."

Something occurred to her and her stomach swooped. Neve gripped the countertop with her free hand to steady herself, digging grooves into the wood.

She hadn't considered it before, but Mercy's abilities were tied to the *Gate*. She was their alarm system, but what if nothing had tripped the alarm because the demons hadn't come through the Hellgate at all? What if there was another way for demons to break through? One without protection?

Alexandria went on, oblivious to the way Neve's thoughts

spun. "The last time I moved, I got to choose where to go. And then, I mean, you know what happened."

"You found the Hellgate."

"That is a super dramatic name." Neve would argue that the place where demons could escape from Hell was plenty dramatic. And she didn't know *what* to think about the idea that Alexandria might have some kind of connection to it. "I don't know why I had to go down there, but I did. I couldn't sleep for days and it felt like there were ants crawling all over my skin. And then I met you."

"And almost died," Neve said.

Alexandria clicked her tongue. "*You* almost died. I was fine, thanks to you and your Kryptonian genes."

"I don't know what that means," Neve said distractedly. She'd assumed the lapse in Mercy's sight was a one-off. A fluke. Not good by any stretch of the imagination, but what Alexandria was implying was catastrophic. Demons beyond the Hellgate, going out of their way to target a human. A human who had been drawn to it, somehow.

None of this made any sense, and she couldn't ask Bay or Mercy about any of it without having to tell them the whole story. It was too late to come clean now—too much had happened. There were too many lies between them and the truth.

"So that's me," Alexandria said after a moment of tense

silence, gnawing on her lip. "Cursed or demon bait or some-thing. And then there's you. Six feet of ridiculous ginger, demon-killing god of whatever."

"God of war," Neve said without thinking. Everything was backward and wrong and she shouldn't say anything more—she shouldn't have said anything in the first place—but she was so tired of lying.

"Excuse me?"

"You guessed right." Neve tapped an anxious, staccato rhythm on the counter. She paused, waiting for Alexandria to pull away before continuing. "I'm . . . my sisters and I, we're—war. I'm the god of war. Technically, we all are. Kind of." Neve scrubbed her fingers through her hair. It sounded so stupid when she said it out loud.

"Um," Alexandria hedged, looking about five seconds from bolting. Neve let go of her hand. "Okay."

"Look," Neve said carefully, terrified of puncturing what-ever strange bubble they'd made inside the shop, positive that it couldn't be recreated. This was her only shot.

After a moment of scanning the shelves for something she could use, Neve pulled a book off the wall. *The Bloody Isle: War Goddesses of Ancient Ireland.* There were at least a dozen books about them—the Morrigan, that is—scattered around the Three Crows. Neve's personal collection focused on the pantheon as a whole, but Mercy thought it was funny to see how wrong human historians were about them.

"The Morrigan," she explained, holding the book out. It was riddled with inaccuracies, but it would do for the moment. "That's us."

Alexandria's eyes darted between Neve and the book. "Okay, your turn. Explain. Right now."

Neve did her best, piecing it together as well as she could. It was harder than she'd expected. She'd been born and reborn into this life, but she'd never had to explain it before. And despite how many times she'd fantasized about telling the locals the truth about her family, just to see the looks on their faces, Neve felt herself stammering, struggling to find the right words. Maybe it was her audience.

"How old are you?" Alexandria demanded when Neve finally finished and her voice tapered off.

"Seventeen. In this lifetime."

Alexandria ran her fingers through her hair, looking moments from a full-blown mental breakdown. "This lifetime. Jesus Christ." She inhaled deeply through her nose. "How do you—how do you come back every time? Reincarnation? How does that even *work*?"

"I don't know," Neve admitted. "I told you, I'm too young."

"That is just . . . *so* stupid," Alexandria said. "I guess I get the whole memory-block thing, but the *rip-cord rein-carnation button* feels like pretty pertinent knowledge in *this* lifetime."

Neve didn't know what to say. Alexandria wasn't even really talking to her anymore, pacing and repeating parts of what Neve had said back to herself, sometimes multiple times over.

"I know that I was the one who wanted answers," Alexandria said at last, coming to rest again, "but I never expected—I mean, *gods*, Neve. I don't even think I believe in capital-*G* God."

Neve had messed up. Again. Hot shame burned through her—it felt like no matter how hard she tried, every choice she made was wrong. She should have just made something up. She lied to everyone else; why was this any different?

Because it was Alexandria. Because she was betraying her entire family and putting them all at risk. Because she didn't care about that anymore and really, really should.

"You know what?" Alexandria said after a few minutes that felt like they lasted hours. "Fine. Gods and demons in Newgrange Harbor." Her lips twitched. "But I'm telling you right now, if a gay angel shows up, I'm out."

Neve's mouth opened and closed in an excellent pantomime of a fish at how quickly Alexandria seemed to have absorbed and accepted . . . everything. All of it.

"What do we do now?" Alexandria asked, as if she actually expected Neve to have an answer.

"I don't know." She didn't. Neve didn't have her memories, she didn't have her sisters to confide in, and the rules she'd followed her whole life had gone up in flames. For the first time, she realized with a start, she was flying blind.

"But what if something happens? What if there's another accident and it's my fault? What if someone from school gets hurt this time? Puck or Simon or Tameka or any of them?"

"There won't be," Neve said. "We'll keep you all safe."

"But what about you?"

Neve shrugged. "I fight."

"That is *so stupid*," Alexandria said again. Her hands shook as she pinched the bridge of her nose.

"It's the whole point of me," Neve said. It was what she'd always done, even if these days the thought of picking up her sword and putting her body in harm's way made her nauseous.

"I hate it," Alexandria grumbled.

Neve hated that Alexandria had been chased from home after home until *something* drew her to Newgrange Harbor. She hated that demons had chosen Alexandria at all. She hated that there was a possibility of an unprotected Gate. She hated the feeling that, beyond all this, something worse loomed on the horizon. She hated it all, but she couldn't change any of it.

What she could do was fight.

"Thank you," Alexandria said softly, after a few moments. "For listening. And for telling me the truth."

She reached out her hand and Neve met her halfway, threading their fingers together again.

"It's not . . ." Alexandria started, gnawing on her lip. "I don't want you to think that you have to put yourself on the line for this mess. I don't—I couldn't handle it if you got hurt because of me."

"Don't worry about it," Neve said. She didn't understand where this was coming from. War was her purpose, her birthright. Neve meant to be comforting, but Alexandria's lips turned down, and her grip on Neve's hand tightened.

"Okay, but the thing is that I do worry," Alexandria continued, her words picking up speed. Her voice hitched. "I can't stop worrying because I keep thinking about you and monsters and you *fighting* monsters instead of just running away like a rational person because you think it's your job to save people. Every time I think about you in that big scary convent on top of that big scary cliff I feel like I can't breathe because what if you *die?* What am I going to do if you just don't show up one day and I hear that you died under mysterious circumstances and *it's my fault*—"

"Alexandria," Neve started, but Alexandria was spiraling.

Neve moved before her mind could catch up, skirting around the counter. "Hey," she said, taking Alexandria's face in her hands. They were so close that Neve could see the flecks of amber in her dark eyes. "I'll be okay. I'm going to be okay. I'll always come back."

Alexandria sucked in a breath, her cheeks warming under Neve's palms. Her eyes darted downward, landing on Neve's lips, and Neve didn't think. She just pulled Alexandria even closer, her thumb skating over Alexandria's cheek as she brought their mouths together. There was a single moment of awkward stillness, and Neve almost pulled away before Alexandria began to kiss her back.

Neve was lost, overwhelmed by the softness of her lips and the smell of her pomegranate shampoo. Her head spun, and her hands moved to the back of Alexandria's neck and curled around her waist to pull her closer. Alexandria's fingers wound through her hair and Neve shivered, sparks crackling up and down her spine.

They were both flushed and out of breath when they finally broke apart. One of Alexandria's hands was still cupped around Neve's jaw, her thumb against Neve's cheek.

"Wow," Alexandria murmured. Her eyes were even darker than usual. Neve was sure she must look the same, wild and incredulous. "I didn't think you'd make the first move."

Neve smiled, bending her neck to bring their foreheads together. "I like you."

"You like me?" Alexandria repeated. Her mouth wobbled like she was trying not to laugh. "Took you long enough. I've been flirting with you since we met."

Gods, it had only been a few weeks. Neve almost couldn't remember her life before Alexandria had turned it upside down. The memories seemed gray now.

"I'm always going to come back." *To you.*

"Because you like me?"

"Because I like you," Neve agreed.

"Has anyone told you that you're a little emotionally stunted?"

"You have." Neve smiled. "More than once."

Some of the amusement drained from Alexandria's face. "Promise me you'll be safe? I know you're super strong and you have your sisters, but my imagination kind of gets away from me and—"

Neve stopped her with another kiss. This time Alexandria surprised her by nibbling on Neve's bottom lip.

"You know you're just giving me more incentive to talk if *that's* how you stop me," Alexandria said. Neve's cheeks burned even redder.

They both hesitated, neither wanting to break the moment.

"Please be careful," Alexandria said finally. "I know you're going to look into all this and it's going to be stupid and brave and—just *please* be safe."

"I will," Neve swore, with a slight twinge in her chest. Even as she made the promise, something deep inside knew that it was one she was destined to break.

CHAPTER SIXTEEN

The shop was closed, but Alexandria stayed until the shift would've normally ended, asking so many questions that Neve's head spun with them all.

Also, kissing.

Bay was notably absent as Neve walked through the front door and into an ambush by the Daughters. The buzz in Neve's veins fizzled somewhat at their expressions.

"Keep that up and your faces are going to get stuck that way," Neve said. She tried to breeze past them, but the Daughters weren't having it.

"Explain yourself, young lady," Daughter Clara demanded.

Not that young, Neve thought automatically. "I'm going to need you to be more specific." Her voice was sharp, but the squirmy feeling returned to her stomach. She'd broken so many rules lately—told so many lies and too few truths—that she really did need the specificity.

"I don't know what's gotten into you," Maeve said, planting her hands on her hips. "Phone calls home, getting called into the office, cutting class? Help me understand what is going on and why you *insist* upon causing trouble."

Neve knew that she should just let it go, take her punishment, and go to her room without calling any more attention to herself, but after Alexandria's revelation, Samhain, the dreams and laughter that now filtered into her waking hours, it was too much.

For the second time that day, Neve's temper snapped.

"Trouble?" Her voice pitched high, the harmonics shifting as if she was building to a scream. "Cutting class isn't trouble. Almost dying is *trouble*. Spending my lifetimes fighting a war I don't remember starting is *trouble*. Getting slaughtered once every hundred years only to be reincarnated to do it all over again is *trouble*. Not to mention that the rest of our family just up and disappeared and no one seems to care where they went or if they're even still alive, or worry that all this has been for nothing if we vanish too."

Neve took a deep breath through her nose, squaring her shoulders and leveling her gaze at each of her stunned guardians in turn. "You guys are the ones who always insist that I embrace humanity or whatever, so congratulations, you got what you wanted. I've decided that I actually want to live this time around before I'm ripped to pieces, so forgive me if I've got better things to do than waste my time at Newgrange Harbor *fucking* High School!"

There was a collective inhale and Neve used the split-second pause to break past the Daughters.

The convent felt crushingly claustrophobic, the high walls and vaulted ceilings pressing in on her and making it impossible to breathe. Instead of going to her bedroom, Neve slipped out the back door and into the wildest part of the garden. She inhaled deeply, the sea air immediately tempering her anger. She was hollow without it, and the wind whistled as it blew through the hole in her chest.

Above her, Poe cawed from his roost in the enormous oak tree before screeching into the sky.

Neve watched the sun begin to descend below the horizon, leaching the world of color and replacing it with the same darkness that had taken root inside her. She wasn't alone for nearly long enough when Mercy found her.

"Poe's a snitch," Neve complained when she saw her sister's head poking out of the shrubbery.

"Poe is worried about you," Mercy said, uncharacteristically serious. "That was some speech. And your second of the day, that's got to be a record."

Neve winced. Bay must have told Mercy about Neve's tantrum at the Three Crows. Gods, it felt like this afternoon had lasted lifetimes.

"I didn't mean it."

"Didn't you?" In the fading daylight, Mercy's eyes were black and unreadable.

"I don't want to mean it." That wasn't good enough, not

even close, but Neve didn't know what else to say.

"I didn't realize how hard this has been for you," Mercy said when the silence became uncomfortable. "Being the youngest. I thought . . ." Mercy sighed. "We're overprotective because we love you. And we're scared. There's no more cycle if you die before turning eighteen, Nee. Bay and I—we know how good you are. We *know*. But you're our baby sister We're not meant to live without each other."

You three are kind of dangerously codependent, Alexandria had said earlier.

"Living without you sucks shit, Neve," Mercy said. Neve inhaled sharply, barely moving in case Mercy suddenly remembered how explicitly forbidden it was to tell Neve anything about their past lives. They were all breaking the rules this cycle, it seemed. Another disruption in the pattern.

"It's bad," Mercy continued. "It's so, so bad. I never want to go through that again, okay? The only thing that got us through was knowing we'd see you in our next life."

Mercy ran both hands through her hair, fluffing her bangs. "I wouldn't make it. If the cycle was broken and you were already gone and there was no way to ever see you again, I'd go bugfuck crazy. I know we're being suffocating and it's the absolute worst, but it's just a few more months, okay? Then you'll know everything, and Bay and I will unclench, I promise."

Neve nodded, any fight left in her thoroughly washed away

by Mercy's confession. Mercy didn't do sentiment. She and Neve were too much alike that way, way more comfortable facing a problem with steel than their feelings.

They watched the sun finish its descent below the horizon in silence. Neve laid her head on Mercy's shoulder. Just a few more months and she'd know everything. She'd remember it all and step fully into the light with her sisters where she belonged.

Neve sighed. Gods, that's all she'd wanted since Bay turned eighteen. To be strong. To remember.

In the back of her mind, the persistent sense of wrongness keened. If they remembered everything at eighteen, how was it possible for another Hellgate to exist? Why didn't Bay and Mercy know that there was some other way for demons to break through to this world? What was the point of them, if their divine mandate was bullshit? Why were they still here? Why hadn't they disappeared like the rest of their family?

And why didn't Bay or Mercy know where they'd gone, or why? What had *happened* to the pantheon? With every new question, it felt more and more like the foundation of Neve's existence was crumbling beneath her.

Gods, how would her sisters even react to the news of another Hellgate? It would be devastating. It could destroy them. The Daughters, too. They'd devoted everything to this cause—they'd given up families and safety and their mortality—to ensure that Neve and her sisters fulfilled their sacred duty.

There were too many unanswered questions, too many loose ends. She couldn't fathom the scale of it, but she couldn't risk telling anyone until she had a better idea of what they were dealing with. She could protect them for once, for at least a little while.

"How much trouble am I in?" Neve asked eventually, putting her questions aside and focusing on the most immediate problem.

Mercy kicked a rock. "Grounded for two weeks, minimal weapons."

It could have been worse. In fact, it should have been worse.

Neve sighed, straightening up. "I have to go talk to her, don't I?"

"I mean, you could always talk to me about your problems," Mercy said. She stretched her arms out over her head. "But I won't lie, I've pretty much hit my mushy bullshit quota for this lifetime. Next time you come home reeking of hormones and angst, I'm going to put you in a headlock until you get over yourself."

That sounded about right. Mercy laughed as Neve flipped her off on her way out of the garden.

Any leftover good humor from Mercy was gone by the time Neve ascended to the second floor. Bay's door was closed, which was a bad sign.

"Bee?" Neve called softly, rapping her knuckles on the wood. "Can I come in?"

There was no answer, but the door wasn't locked, so Neve let herself in. Bay was lying on her bed with her back to the door.

"Bay?"

"What do you want?" Bay's voice was muffled by her nest of pillows.

"To say that I'm sorry," Neve said. Bay didn't respond, so Neve flopped onto the bed, nearly launching Bay into the air.

"Cut it out," Bay snapped, turning to reveal red-rimmed eyes. "Go away."

"No," Neve said, folding her legs beneath her. "I was awful and I'm sorry."

Some part of her wondered if she was always like this, if she unraveled every lifetime or if her behavior was another deviation. Even if she was different in her past lives—a better sister, probably—who she was in *this* life was more important, no matter what the memories dredged up. Bay had explained it a little when Mercy manifested.

"We get to choose," Bay had said. "Who I was in those lifetimes is still me, even the things I don't like, even the things that scare me. Who I was is a part of who I am, and it's hard to differentiate at first, but it gets easier. I can choose to . . . to be gentle with the difficult stuff, acknowledge its presence, and then try to let it go."

It didn't matter who Neve was in the past; what mattered

was who she was now. And who she was now was someone who'd hurt her sister's feelings.

Bay sniffed. "It's *fine*, Neve."

"No, it's not."

Bay pushed herself into a seated position, her hands in her lap. "I know it's frustrating not having your memories, but you know how much we love you and how proud we are of you, and you don't get to take it out on me."

"I'm sorry," Neve said. "I just—I'm sorry."

Bay didn't say anything for a long time, just stared at her hands. She started to pick at her cuticles, worrying the thin skin until it was blotchy and irritated.

"Can you please say something?" Neve said when she couldn't take the quiet any longer. She couldn't stand the sight of Bay crying, and the fact that she'd caused it made Neve feel small and horrible. "Just tell me what to say to make this better. I'll do it."

"I want you to stop *lying*," Bay said finally. The words sounded as if they'd been wrenched from her throat. "I know you've been keeping things from us. I don't even know what to say to you anymore because I don't trust that you'll be honest with me."

Another demon bite would've hurt less. Neve's mouth opened and closed as she tried to come up with words, excuses, *something*, but there was nothing she could say that would come even close to the truth. Not after everything Alexandria had told her. Not after everything she'd told Alexandria.

Bay turned her face away, eyes fixed on her bedspread. "Just go, Neve. I don't—please just go."

Neve left without another word, closing the door behind her with a quiet *click*. She felt sick, like there was a piece of herself that had been yanked from its alignment and the sharp, dislodged edges were digging into her skin.

She ignored the Daughters' calls for dinner, locking herself in her room and throwing the window open.

"I think I really messed up," Neve whispered to Poe. For once, the raven held still and let Neve bury her face in his feathers. Bay had never been so angry with her before—gods, Neve couldn't remember the last time Bay *was* angry.

You don't get to take it out on me. Bay was right. Of course she was.

"I'm sorry," Neve said again, as if it did any good. As if *I'm sorry* could make up for the hateful things she'd said. Neve and Mercy both cycled through emotions so quickly that Bay's quiet serenity sometimes felt alien to them, but they relied on it. *Neve* relied on it, and she'd taken for granted that Bay would always be there, no matter Neve's moods.

But now Bay was hurt, one-third of the triad was splintered and bleeding, and Neve didn't know if she could fix it. She didn't know if she could fix any of it.

CHAPTER SEVENTEEN

A lexandria was perched on the hood of her car as usual when Neve pulled into the parking lot the next morning. Her headphones hung around her neck as she sketched in her demon notebook.

"Hi," Neve said, suddenly nervous. With all the drama from the night before, she'd somehow pushed Alexandria—her revelation and everything that had come after—to the very back of her mind.

This time Neve anticipated the flush that colored her cheeks and the back of her neck when she thought about kissing Alexandria. Her first kiss, in this lifetime at least. *Kiss*es, *actually*, Neve thought, blushing even more furiously. She'd momentarily entertained the idea of asking Mercy if she'd ever dated in their other lifetimes and quickly decided she'd rather die.

"Tell me you dropped your phone into the ocean," Alexandria demanded as she hopped off the hood of her car. She held her notebook close to her chest, her eyebrows furrowed, and Neve panicked immediately. What if Alexandria thought the whole thing was a mistake? What if it was just something that happened in the heat of the moment, after an emotional afternoon? What if—

"Um, no?" Neve withdrew her phone from her pocket as evidence. "It's dead? I forgot to charge it."

"You forgot to charge it."

". . . Yes?"

"You give me heart palpitations," Alexandria announced, throwing her hands in the air. "Neve, you idiot, I thought—I thought you were upset about, you know. Yesterday. Everything. And I might have been freaking out about it. A little."

Neve immediately felt guilty. "I'm sorry, there was . . . stuff I had to deal with at home. I didn't mean to make you worry." Gods, she was terrible at this. "But, um, yesterday was good. It was—it was good."

"You still like me?" Alexandria asked with a grin, the tension vanishing.

"Despite my better instincts," Neve grumbled, but she couldn't hide her smile and didn't really want to try.

"Shut up, you said you like me. No take backs."

Alexandria tucked herself close to Neve as they made their way into the building, summarily invading her personal space. Neve didn't mind, leaning into the closeness.

Halfway through first period, Neve's phone powered back on, thanks to the charger that Alexandria had all but thrown at her. It buzzed a moment later with a text from Simon, a blurry photo of Alexandria smiling down at her notebook.

Simon: She sure looks happy. Something to do with you?

Neve bit her lip, glad that none of her friends were in her first-period class.

Neve: No idea what you're talking about

Simon: ;)

Simon: Also get Instagram you Luddite

Neve: I don't know what that is

"Bullshit," Simon said without preamble the moment he sat down at lunch.

"Well, that's one way to start a conversation," Alexandria said, raising an eyebrow.

Simon ignored her, pointing his fork at Neve. "You know what Instagram is, admit it."

"I've never heard of it," Neve said without breaking eye contact, her expression utterly earnest. Compared to lying to her sisters, who could sense her emotions, bluffing her friends was too easy. "Is it a website?"

Simon stared at her for nearly a minute, his eyes darting back and forth as if the truth was written in her freckles, before giving up. "You are the *worst*. If I ever decide to learn how to play poker, you're not allowed to come."

"Don't be a sore loser," Ilma said, sitting down opposite Neve.

"He called me a Luddite, too," Neve added in a conspiratorial stage whisper.

"Well, that's just rude," Alexandria said. "Those are fighting words."

Simon scowled, muttering to himself. *"Oh, look at me, I'm Neve Morgan. I live in a convent and I think I'm too cool for Instagram."*

"I *am* too cool for Instagram," Neve said without looking up. "And the filters are ugly."

That, of course, led to Simon losing his entire shit, and the table devolved into chaos. Neve barely noticed, suddenly and irrevocably distracted by Alexandria's mouth when she laughed.

"You're staring," Alexandria whispered.

Neve blinked. "You're cute when you're indignant," she said, her brain stalling out. Not great, but better than admitting that she'd gotten distracted by Alexandria's mouth.

Alexandria pouted, which did not help the whole not-staring-at-her-lips thing. "I am not cute. I am tough as nails. I'll kick his ass. I'll kick your ass. I'll kick my own ass."

"Huh," Michael said, and Neve realized that the table had gone quiet again. Everyone was looking at them.

Neve fought the urge to hide from the weight of their collective gaze, blushing again. Alexandria just grinned, slowly and purposefully reaching for Neve's hand.

"Finally," Tameka said, shaking her head. "I thought you two would never get your heads out of your asses."

Michael and Simon high-fived, whooping loudly and smiling like idiots.

"About time," Ilma said.

"Pot, meet kettle," Alexandria replied, looking significantly between Ilma and Puck, who determinedly did not make eye contact, flushing nearly as red as Neve.

"Welcome to our club," Simon sang as they walked out of the cafeteria. Neve slouched, but Alexandria joined in immediately, jumping up and down with the boys.

"I knew," Michael said sagely. "We always know."

Alexandria punched him on the arm. "You did *not.*"

"Please," Simon said, adopting Michael's beatific tone. "As if I wouldn't recognize gay yearning when I saw it. And the boots, Neve?"

"Queercoded," Michael chimed.

"Obviously queercoded," Simon agreed.

"Oh my God," Alexandria laughed. "People aren't queercoded, stupid, that's not a *thing.*"

"Whatever you say, Miss Cuffs-Her-Jeans—gah!" Simon yelped as Alexandria leaped at him, jumping onto his back in an impromptu piggyback ride that nearly toppled them both.

"I hate you all," Neve grumbled.

"Sure you do."

She didn't. Not even a little bit. They were *important*, these humans she'd collected and who had collected her. She wasn't supposed to have this—any of it. Even Bay and Mercy's friends were kept at arm's length. They had to be. Neve had never understood why they bothered at all before she'd made friends of her own, but now she didn't know how her sisters hadn't caved and let them in entirely. It was like she'd been missing them her whole life—maybe for lifetimes—and she'd only just realized.

Though, by the end of the day, Neve was about ready to throw her phone into the ocean after the way the group chat had exploded. She opted to put it on silent instead of taking more drastic measures.

"You okay?" Alexandria asked as they walked out of the building at the final bell. "I know this is a lot for you."

"It is," Neve agreed. "But it's good."

Neve wasn't ready for any of this—she wasn't ready for what was coming, whatever it was—but she had her friends and she had Alexandria. She just hoped that she could protect them.

It was strange to be happier at school than she was at home. It was happiness built on lies and at the expense of her family and her duties, and yet Neve couldn't find it within herself to regret it. The resulting guilt was familiar at this point, which dulled its sting.

"On a scale of one to ten, how uncomfortable is it going to be when we get home?" Neve asked as she and Mercy locked up the Three Crows after their shift. Mercy wasn't even supposed to be working, but Bay had changed the schedule.

"Eleven. Maybe twelve," Mercy said. Neve glared at her. "What? You asked."

"You're supposed to lie and say that it's going to be fine."

"Am I? Huh."

Mercy was right. Dinner was strained, the silence punctuated only by the clatter of cutlery. Between the Daughters and Bay, Neve didn't know where to look.

Bay was the first to excuse herself, citing homework. Neve tried to help with the washing up, but Daughter Clara waved her away.

"I'm sure you have something to do for school, Neve," she said coolly.

"Not really," Neve replied.

Mercy's hand landed on her shoulder. "That's so weird, because I remember you telling me about that big project."

Neve rolled her eyes but took the out. Mercy had given her an idea, anyway, and Neve didn't know why it had taken her this long to think of it. Her sisters' memories weren't the only repositories of knowledge in the convent. They weren't even the most accessible. The mythology books in the Three Crows and in Neve's bedroom might be bullshit, but the Daughters' collection in the library was legit. If there was anything, any whisper about another Hellgate, it might be in one of those books.

Figuring out where to start took longer than she would've liked, and it wasn't as if Neve could ask Daughter Maeve for the "other ways out of Hell" section, but eventually she settled on one of the squashy armchairs with a stack of books by her side and a notebook in her lap. She fiddled with the pen between her fingers, taking notes on anything promising.

Most of the text was so dense that it was almost indecipherable, but Neve plowed through, losing track of time as she searched for any mention of another Hellgate. There was nothing, nothing she could find, nothing to explain what had happened to Alexandria's family or why Mercy hadn't sensed the demon on the beach the night Neve and Alexandria had met.

The more she thought about it, the more her stomach turned. If her sisters had no memories of another way through, and the Daughters, in their thousand years of recordkeeping, didn't even mention the *possibility* that there was another Gate, it meant they'd missed something huge. It meant they were wrong. Wrong about demons. Wrong about Hell.

Wrong about themselves.

CHAPTER EIGHTEEN

N eve didn't know how long she'd been asleep when she startled awake to find books strewn haphazardly around her. One still rested on her lap, jostling as she slowly sat up from her slumped position.

It took her a few moments to realize that she'd been awoken by her phone ringing.

"Alexandria?" Neve answered. The back of her neck prickled.

"Something's happening." Alexandria's voice was warped and high.

"Where are you?" Neve demanded, but she already knew the answer.

"The Gate."

"I'm coming. Stay on the line."

Neve flung herself out of the chair, sending the book flying as she beelined for the armory. She was still in her clothes from yesterday and the Daughters had taken her weapons from her room.

Poe was waiting for her when she slipped out the back door, flying in tight, agitated circles over the training yard. He was almost invisible against the darkness of the storm clouds that gathered in the sky, his cries drowned out by the rain pelting the convent. Neve was drenched in seconds.

"Mab's tits." Neve stabbed her sword into the ground and hastily tied back her hair before flipping her hood up, for all the good it did her.

Keeping up a steady stream of curses, Neve picked her way to the beach, nearly slipping on the slick grass. Below her, the ocean pounded against the sand, frothy waves whipped up by the storm. Neve felt the cold spray on her neck and smelled brine as seawater lurched up her nose. She felt her skull cracking against a rock, her blood leaking into the water until there was nothing left of her, and—

No. Neve shook her head, burying those thoughts as deep as she could. Now wasn't the time to lose it. Alexandria needed her.

"What the hell are you *doing* here?" Neve shouted over the storm as soon as she was in earshot of Alexandria. There was only a tiny spit of beach left by the rising ocean, forcing them way too close to the Gate for comfort.

"Couldn't sleep." Alexandria looked a little dazed, her eyes wide and slightly unfocused. "I don't—I didn't mean to come." Her eyes flicked to the cliffside as if it was about to transform into a monster, something with a wide, gaping mouth that would swallow them whole. "It's that same feeling, like something horrible is about to happen. Like something is call-ing me here."

Neve knew she should take a second, think about the impli-cations of what Alexandria was saying, but—

"Then let's answer."

—it wasn't in her nature.

Alexandria's eyes snapped to Neve, her mouth dropping open, but Neve was already striding toward the Hellgate. If it was calling Alexandria, there had to be a reason. Demons couldn't have targeted her out of nowhere, and maybe, if she'd been drawn to it, there was someone on the other side. Someone with *answers.*

"I want to try something," Neve said, gesturing Alexandria forward. It was an exceptionally stupid idea, but she hadn't found anything on her own, and the attacks would only get worse as the season grew darker. If this was how she got answers, so be it.

But what if, whispered a voice in her head, *they're waiting for you, too? What if it comes to a fight?*

Neve adjusted her grip on her sword. Then she would fight. Better now, here, where she could face the enemy head-on. Neve was tired of trying to fight something she couldn't see.

Alexandria shuffled from foot to foot. "This is the moment in the horror movie where someone in the audience shouts, 'Don't do it!' at the screen."

"If you've got a better idea, I'm all ears."

Alexandria swallowed hard. "This is going to end so badly."

Nothing happened at first. Neve thought that Alexandria's closeness to the Gate might trigger something, but there was no sound except for the rain against the cliff and the furious tide behind them.

Then Alexandria made a sharp noise and stumbled forward like she was being dragged by some unseen force. Neve's hand shot out, grabbing for Alexandria's jacket to pull her back, but not before Alexandria pressed her hand against the cliff.

The moment she made contact, everything happened at once. Neve's ears popped from a sudden shift in barometric pressure and the Gate began to warp, shifting and changing beneath Alexandria's fingertips. It began to peel away, revealing dark glimpses of what lay beneath. Neve gripped her sword, trying to peer closer, but the images slipped away like ripples across a disturbed pond. Muted colors swam across the surface, with flashes of brightness that disappeared just as fast. It smelled acrid, like burnt tires and rot.

"I can't—" Alexandria grunted, tugging on her arm. Her hand was still splayed against the cliff. "I can't move."

Well, shit.

Inside the Gate, something moved toward them. It lumbered close, drawn to Alexandria just like she'd been drawn to the beach.

"You have to let go," Neve said, pressing against Alexandria's shoulder. Something inside her, a pull in her blood, warned that whatever was coming for them, it was very old and very, very angry. She stepped closer to the Gate, crossing her blade over her chest as her heart pounded against her ribcage. "Alexandria, you need to let go *right now.*"

"I'm trying," Alexandria said, her voice tight with strain. The demon loomed, its shadow falling on them.

Neve gripped the hilt of her sword so tightly that her knuckles went white. "Stay still," she ordered.

"You just told me to let go!"

"Stay still!" Neve said again as a massive shape began to emerge, just inches from where Alexandria's hand was still stuck.

"Neve . . ." Alexandria shouted. An enormous, tusked head broke free of the barrier, roaring so loud that chips of shale and stone shook free and skittered down the rock face onto them. *"Neve!"*

Neve didn't let it get any farther before she stabbed her blade at the demon's forehead. Her sword glanced off, but not without leaving a bloody slash that carved down the side of its face. The demon howled and Neve used its distraction to yank Alexandria away as hard as she dared. Her palm came away with an awful ripping sound and the moment she was no longer touching it, the Gate solidified again.

"Son of a bitch," Alexandria swore. The palm of her hand was red, the skin patchy and raw as if she'd been burned. She tucked herself against Neve's side, staring at the trapped demon with enormous eyes. "How is . . . how did—did I—?" Her voice petered out as the demon roared again, a terrible dying sound. Black blood scorched down the stone.

The demon thrashed its head, trying to catch Neve with its tusks as she took a step closer, sword still at the ready. The Gate had cut it in half, but she wasn't going to risk getting speared while it died.

"You won't stop us."

Neve's blood cooled in her veins at the sound of the demon's voice, craggy and rough like it was being scraped over gravel.

"Holy shit," Alexandria whispered. The demon locked its eyes on her, bright with pain and hellish rage.

"We will have you, girl. It's only a matter of time."

"What do you want with her?" Neve demanded, forcing her voice even. "Tell me, or—"

Out of the corner of her eye, Neve saw the convent lights flick on. Mercy must have sensed the demon come through.

Shit, shit, shit.

The demon laughed. Blood dribbled out of its mouth. "You can't stop us, little queen. The sea will run with your blood. And once you're dead, we'll take her and burn this whole world to ash."

Alexandria made a small noise and Neve moved without thinking. She lunged, driving the tip of her sword so deeply through the demon's throat that it struck the stone behind it.

"Burn this," she snarled, leaning over the pommel. Her vision was limned with red and blood pounded in her ears.

She didn't wait for the demon to explode before turning away to face Alexandria. "Where's your car?" she asked in a voice that wasn't entirely her own.

Alexandria blinked twice. "What?"

"You have to go, right now."

"I'm not leaving."

"My sisters are coming," Neve said urgently, coming back to herself. "And if they find you here, they're going to take your memories. They'll—" *They'll take you away from me.* The thought was a stone in her gut. "Unless that's what you want."

Alexandria stared, her eyes suspiciously bright as they reflected the rain.

Neve swallowed hard. "Daughter Aoife can take your memories away. You won't remember any of this. You can forget."

All this time, she'd never thought that maybe Alexandria might *want* to forget. Aoife's ability to take away her memories was never far from Neve's mind, but it had always been a danger, a threat. She'd never even considered that after everything Alexandria had been through, she might want the memories gone.

"We can still keep you safe." Maybe Alexandria would be happier that way, without the burden of knowing what was after her, but Neve had been too wrapped up in her own desires to consider it.

"But I won't remember." Something blazed in Alexandria's expression, lighting her up from the inside as if she'd swallowed a star. "I won't remember *you*."

Neve didn't trust herself to answer. She sucked in a breath, preparing for a goodbye, when a hand snaked around the back of her neck and pulled her head down.

"No," Alexandria said fiercely. "I'm a target either way and I'm—I'm not giving you up too." She tugged Neve down farther until their foreheads were touching. "I choose you."

Neve swallowed thickly. "Okay, um. Right. That's good. Then you have to go. Now."

"You really, really suck at this."

"I know." Neve pressed a small kiss against Alexandria's valiantly smiling mouth. "I'll call you as soon as I can."

"I won't be sleeping. Probably ever."

Alexandria was long gone by the time Bay and Mercy reached the beach, both bristling with weapons.

"What the *hell*, Neve?" Mercy demanded. The rain plastered her hair against her forehead. Bay stalked forward, eyes black and enormous as she took in the demon trapped in the rock. "What happened?"

"I was patrolling," Neve lied. It was almost true. She'd been patrolling when all this started, trying to prove herself. Gods, that felt like a lifetime ago.

"Alone?" Mercy's voice spiked toward a screech, and Neve knew she was thinking about the conversation they'd just had in the garden. "Are you *shitting me?*"

"It's not like I expected this to happen!" Neve shouted back.

Bay's scythe thwacked against the cliffside, drawing their attention back to where the demon remained lodged in the rock like massive, hideous taxidermy. It should have exploded by now. "We have bigger problems," she fingerspelled with one hand.

"I don't know what happened," Neve said. That, at least, was the whole truth. She *didn't* know how the demon had been drawn here, or how Alexandria had been able to call it, or why it was still intact. None of this was meant to be possible. "It started coming through and I stabbed it and the Gate closed again."

"How is its body still here?" Mercy asked, edging closer. She held her sword ready, as if the demon was only playing dead and would lunge at any second.

"How the hell should I know?" Neve demanded, her ragged nerves making it hard to remain calm. She was just glad the demon had stopped talking.

You can't stop us, little queen.

Fury was easier than fear, and Neve held it tight to her chest, letting her anger propel her forward. Ignoring Mercy's panicked squawk, she sidestepped her sisters and ripped her sword out of the demon's throat. The creature sagged without the blade holding its weight and after a few tense seconds, exploded into ash. The embers scorched Neve's skin where they landed, sizzling in the downpour.

"Well that answers that question," Neve said under her breath. Mercy and Bay gaped. "Unless you two want to stand out here in the rain," she said before marching to the car.

The silence was so tense that Neve almost choked on it on the way back to the convent.

"What is going on?" Daughter Maeve demanded, awake and alert despite the early hour. The other Daughters assembled behind her, all dressed in nightgowns. It shouldn't have been as intimidating as it was, three old women in their pajamas, all looking at her expectantly.

"I couldn't sleep," Neve lied. "So I went to patrol."

The Daughters sucked in sharp breaths in unison.

"If that's it—"

"No. No it is absolutely *not* it," Mercy shrilled, running her hand down her face. "We *literally* just talked about this. You could've gotten hurt, or killed, or—"

"I know!" Neve interrupted, unable to bear the way Mercy's voice shook. "But I couldn't sleep, and I've been so worried about—" She snapped her mouth shut, suddenly way too close to the truth for comfort. Bay tipped her head to one side, blinking owlishly. Gods damn it. "I was worried about . . . my friend."

"What are you talking about?" Mercy started up again before Bay put a hand on her shoulder.

Neve gnawed on her lip, shifting her weight from foot to foot. She shouldn't have said anything. She shouldn't have let Alexandria touch that stupid wall. She should lock herself in the armory until she turned eighteen and hope that her memories washed all the stupid away before she could make another bad decision she'd have to lie her way out of.

Before Mercy could gain steam, Bay interrupted, very deliberately fingerspelling a word. A name.

"Alexandria?" Mercy repeated out loud, her eyebrows climbing. "What, library girl?" Her eyes widened with sudden understanding. "Wait, holy shit, are you two dating? Is that why you've been acting so weird?"

"Um," Neve started, but Mercy's face split into a grin and Neve was pulled into a fierce hug before she could come up with an excuse.

"I don't understand," Neve said when Mercy finally released her. "You aren't mad that I went out alone?"

"Furious," Daughter Maeve interjected, a small smile creasing her mouth.

"In fact, we're extending your punishment indefinitely,"

Daughter Aoife added, clasping Clara's hand tight. Clara didn't bother to hide her fond look as she dropped her head onto Aoife's shoulder.

"Thing is," Mercy said delightedly, "you've always been a solitary pain in the ass, little sister. In every lifetime. And if you've finally found someone—"

"I didn't mean to," Neve said, the truth spilling out of her mouth before she could stop it. She'd expected them to be angry that she'd gotten so attached, not *giddy*. "I didn't even want to, but—"

"It just happened," Bay signed.

Neve nodded, every bit of swallowed emotion rising to the surface at once. The corners of her eyes pricked with unshed tears and she bit her lip hard. "I don't want anything to happen to her because of me—because of what we are." Neve stepped away from all of them and wrapped her arms around herself, tasting bile. "I'm so scared."

"I know," Bay said, her voice tiny as it slowly returned.

"I'm sorry," Neve said, unable to look her sisters in the face. "I'm so sorry." For lying. For not telling them about Alexandria. For lashing out and hurting Bay. For *breaking them*.

She was sorry for all of it. For everything. "I'll do better," Neve swore. "I know . . . I've been awful. Just so awful and I'm sorry and I promise I'll do better."

Neve finally looked up, still sniffling and swiping at her nose. Bay was crying too but reached out to wipe the tears from beneath Neve's eyes.

"I don't want space," Neve said softly, catching Bay's hand. "I don't want space, Bee. I want us to be us again and I know I'm the one who broke it and I'm so sorry I—"

Bay cut her off with a hug, pulling Neve into her chest and holding her so close that it should've been hard to breathe. It wasn't. In fact, it felt like the first time Neve had exhaled in months.

Mercy made a strangled sound and threw her arms around them both. "Gods damn it, you two."

Neve didn't know how long they stood like that, crying and clinging to each other, but for the first time since the night she snuck out of the convent to the Hellgate, Neve felt whole. She had her sisters. She had Mercy and Bay, the missing pieces of her soul. There were still secrets—gods, too many secrets—but in this moment, they were together again.

"Well, it's about time." Daughter Maeve's voice floated into their weepy little huddle.

"How do they get so stubborn?" Clara asked.

"Centuries of practice," came Aoife's reply.

"We are trying to work through some stuff over here," Mercy grumbled, blinking balefully at them. She turned her gaze on Neve and grinned, her eyes sparkling. Neve's little-sister instincts tingled. "You know this means she has to come over for dinner."

The apprehension at the prospect paled in comparison to the slightly hysterical giggles that bubbled out of her, and Neve started crying all over again, feeling for the first time in a long time that maybe things were going to be okay.

CHAPTER NINETEEN

The days turned into weeks as the temperature continued to drop and the sun set earlier and earlier. Neve scoured her family's spellbooks and historic texts for any mention of another Hellgate, anything to give her an insight into why Alexandria was being targeted.

Nothing. No mention of any of it. She even tried looking online, though that was an exercise in futility. Gods, she didn't understand why anyone bothered with the internet.

Thanksgiving came and went without making much of an impression. The Daughters didn't care for "American holidays," and despite Michael's insistence that the post-turkey nap was the best he slept all year, Neve didn't think there was enough tryptophan in the world to override her supercharged metabolism.

Like many of her habits, this baffled the rest of the group.

"Wait, okay, explain this to me one more time," Simon said the day before their break. He goggled at her like she'd sprouted another head. "You've never had pumpkin pie? Never? Not ever?"

"That's what *never* means," Neve said without looking up

from her phone. Alexandria was tucked against Neve's side. Her dark hair tickled where it touched Neve's neck.

"Apple pie?" Michael asked.

"No."

"Blueberry pie."

"No."

"Pecan pie?" Tameka added, her eyebrows climbing toward her hairline.

"I don't think she's ever had pie, period," Alexandria said like it was a secret. She snickered at the collective gasp around the table. Neve looked at Ilma, who was usually her ally in these kinds of arguments, which were becoming a weekly occurrence.

"Sorry, this time I'm with them," Ilma said, raising her hands. "My parents love Thanksgiving. Puck's actually joining us this year."

For a moment Neve's dessert faux pas was forgotten as everyone at the table swung around to stare at Puck. They hid their face behind their hands, mumbling something about finding halal marshmallows for the sweet potatoes.

Neve's phone buzzed in her pocket.

Like The Library: If Ilma doesn't put them out of their misery, Puck is going to explode into confetti and candy hearts

Neve smirked.

"But seriously," Michael said, turning back to her. "No pie?

Ever? Is it, like, against the rules of your . . . religion?" He trailed off, looking uncomfortable.

"Yeah, the denomination draws the line at pastry," Neve deadpanned. She let Michael squirm for a few seconds, his forehead creasing as he tried to tell if she was kidding. "Not really. We're just not dessert people, I guess."

The Monday after Thanksgiving brought what looked like an entire bakery's worth of pies to their lunch table and the unified insistence of the group that Neve taste-test each and every one. Pumpkin had an unpleasant texture that she could do without, and the blueberry was gooey and weird, but she could—and did—eat the entire tin of Tameka's pecan pie. Tameka was smug about it for days.

"Why did they bother?" Neve asked Alexandria afterward as they walked to their next class. "Did you ask them to do that?" It seemed like something she would do.

Alexandria smacked her, which Neve didn't think was fair. "It's because they love you, you big dummy."

Neve's chest lit from the inside, but the warmth was accompanied by a weird feeling of déjà vu. Like she hadn't realized there was this cavernous hole inside her until someone lit a match.

November trickled into December. The Thanksgiving Pie Incident, as it came to be known, gave way to an epic debate—spearheaded by Puck and Simon—over whether sour cream or applesauce was best on latkes, which, naturally, led to another taste test.

Neve liked them best with sour cream, which made Puck pout for the rest of the day, though they quickly forgave her when Neve offered to teach them ASL as a Hanukkah present.

Neve: So we don't have to text when we want to talk shit

Puck grinned and gave her a high five over the lunchroom table. Neve kept on glowing.

Even with the lessening daylight, there were no more demon outbreaks than usual for this time of year. None of them went for Alexandria, but Neve still panicked every time.

And Alexandria . . .

Alexandria was everything. She had thousands of questions, usually in the middle of the night. Neve kept trying to nail down her sleeping patterns, but they were utterly random, and no matter how many questions Neve answered, Alexandria's curiosity was endless.

"So you're saying you *don't* know if Egyptian gods are real?" Alexandria insisted early in the morning one random Monday. No, it was Tuesday now. It didn't matter.

"Why would I know that?" Neve asked around a yawn. She didn't bother taking her phone off the nightstand, just put one earbud in her ear with slow, sleepy movements. She'd gotten used to falling asleep to the sound of Alexandria's voice. "We're Irish, not Egyptian. My knowledge of other pantheons begins and ends with my family."

"Okay, what about all the other Irish myths? Faeries and elves and stuff?"

Neve snickered, images of tiny, Tinker-Bell-like figures dancing behind her eyes. "Faeries definitely aren't real. But if I ever see one, you're my first call."

"Wasted," Alexandria grumbled. "Reincarnation and weird magic are wasted on you."

"How about you tell me how to not waste my reincarnation and weird magic?"

"I have some ideas."

"Naturally."

December also brought nightmares, along with the anniversary of the Kuro murders. Alexandria never talked about what happened, not after her declaration in the Three Crows, but Neve couldn't help but notice when Alexandria started to come to school with darker and darker circles under her eyes, like she was getting even less sleep than usual.

"Do you want to talk about it?" Neve asked every morning. "No."

And then the subject was dropped, though Neve made it a point to bring disgustingly sweet coffee whenever she picked Alexandria up for school. It didn't help much. Nothing did.

. . .

Neve knew something was different even before her phone rang. Poe had been finicky and loud all night, flying in and out of the open window and cawing at nothing.

"What's wrong?" Neve asked, answering the phone on the first ring. There was only high-pitched breathing on the other end. Neve sat up straight, wide awake in an instant. "Alexandria? I need you to talk to me."

"Bad dream." Alexandria's voice was reedy and tight. "Really, *really* bad dream. Can you—can you come here? I need—" She drew in a deep, shuddering breath.

"I'll be there in ten. Do you want me to stay on the line?"

"Yes, please."

Neve pulled on a ratty pair of sweats and Alexandria's purple hoodie, plugging in her headphones as she rifled for her keys.

"Neve?" Alexandria sounded so small and scared that Neve's chest hurt.

"On my way."

She made it to Alexandria's house in seven minutes flat, which had to be a record, breaking every local traffic law in her hurry.

"I'm here," Neve said when she arrived. "Open the window, okay? I don't think your aunt and uncle would appreciate me breaking in through the front door."

There was a click over her head and Neve disconnected the call. Getting to the windowsill was no challenge, but Neve still winced at the creak of old wood beneath her weight.

"Hi," Neve said softly, stepping through the recently repaired window. Alexandria stood on the opposite side of the room. She'd pressed herself into the corner with the best eyeline to the door and the window, the same corner where Neve had found her after Samhain. In the dusky light coming in from the lamp outside, her eyes were inky black and enormous.

"My war god girlfriend is sneaking in through the window," Alexandria said with a hysterical giggle. "This is some teen drama bullshit."

Neve's heart clenched in her chest. "Can I come over there?"

"Yeah," Alexandria said. She was perfectly still, holding herself as if she was going to fly apart any second. "I'm kind of—I'm kind of freaking out so if you could please get your ridiculous self over here—"

Neve crossed the room in two steps, too fast, but she didn't care. She wrapped her arms around Alexandria and pulled her close, feeling a frantic heartbeat pound between them.

They stood like that for a long time, until Alexandria's breathing evened out and she began to relax.

"Do you want to sit down on the bed?" Neve offered. She rubbed Alexandria's arms, feeling the topography of goose bumps on her skin.

"Don't," Alexandria said when Neve let go of her hand to close the window. "Don't."

"Okay." Instead, Neve climbed into the gap in the covers and opened her arms, making room for Alexandria to snuggle against her side. She didn't ask about the nightmare, but she could sense where fear had taken root, concentrating someplace behind Alexandria's eyes.

You can literally stop armies in their tracks, Mercy had said. *Paralyze them with fear.*

Causing fear. That was her gift, like Bay's shark-like silence and Mercy's connection to the Gate. And if she could cause it, maybe she could take it away. Maybe. Magic always had a flip side, a way to be reversed or undone.

"I was there," Alexandria said, drawing Neve's attention to her again. "I saw it happening and I saw the monster that did it and I couldn't stop it. I couldn't stop any of it and then he—it—*looked* at me." She took a shallow, shuddering breath.

Neve felt as if she'd been punched, hollowed out by the horror in Alexandria's voice. Gods, to have seen something like that.

Poor, scared little Neve, hissed the laughing voice from her nightmares. She shoved it away. This wasn't about her. She was raised into this life; she knew the dangers. She was prepared and protected. Alexandria had none of that. Her family had been ripped away from her by creatures that shouldn't have been able to get to her in the first place.

"It was just a dream," Neve said, trying to smooth out the edges in her voice. She winced at how stupid that sounded with the literal entrance to Hell only a few miles away, but she didn't know what else to do. There was nothing to fight, no place to direct her scream.

"They died because of me. They died because demons want *me.*"

"Hey." Neve pulled back so that she could see Alexandria's face. "Hey. Stop. It's not your fault."

"It was there for me. I'm the reason they died." Tears collected on her bottom lashes and threatened to spill over. "And I'm so—I'm so fucking scared."

Neve kissed both her cheeks, thumbing the tears away. "Nothing is going to happen to you," she said gently, running her hands through Alexandria's hair.

"Not for *me,*" Alexandria said, suddenly agitated. "For you. You're the one throwing yourself in front of them and looking for answers and—" Her voice broke and took Neve's heart along with it. "What if you die too? I can't lose anyone else."

"I'm not going anywhere," Neve promised. "I'm a thousand years old and I've got my sisters watching my back. Sorry to break it to you, but you're stuck with me."

It was a long time before either of them spoke again. If not for the steady thrum of fear under her skin, Neve might have thought that Alexandria had fallen back asleep.

"I see them whenever I close my eyes. I can't sleep. I can never sleep when I'm like this. I'm too—I'm scared. All the time. It's making me crazy."

"I think I might be able to help with that."

Alexandria blinked up at her, eyes luminous with what looked like hope.

"I'm not sure if anything will happen. I don't know if my ability works in reverse, but I want to try. Is that okay?"

Neve prayed it would work, but more than that she hoped that Alexandria would at least let her try to help. The thought of doing nothing felt like she had swallowed an entire nest of snakes, writhing and useless and terrible.

"Yes."

Armed with permission, it dawned on Neve that she really had no idea how to go about this. Warscreaming brought fear, and it wasn't as if she really knew what she was doing there either. It just happened. Now Neve wanted to do the opposite, take away fear instead of causing it. So, she reasoned, what was the opposite of screaming?

Feeling thoroughly ridiculous, Neve reached for a low note deep in her throat. At first nothing happened, and she almost started to apologize before the harmonics of her voice shifted. The note shivered in the air and Neve could *feel* the fear draining out of Alexandria, like brackish sludge washed away by cool, clean water.

Alexandria shifted, leaning up to catch Neve's lips with her own. Neve kissed her back, still humming a little, and the note lingered for a few seconds longer.

"Feel better?" she asked when they broke apart.

Alexandria nodded, her eyes already drooping. "You're better than Xanax."

Neve listened to Alexandria's breathing even out. She stayed awake for a little while longer, just in case the dream came back, but she couldn't ignore the weight dragging on her bones. Eventually, she let herself settle in the nest of pillows that made up half the bed, resting her cheek against the top of Alexandria's head. They were close enough that Neve would know if the nightmare returned.

Her own dreams were peaceful and amorphous, warmed by the girl in her arms, suffused with light. It was the best night's sleep Neve had had in a long time.

As it turned out, the Abbotts were morning people. The sun had just begun to peek through the window when Neve heard footsteps from down the hall. Neve snapped awake and was out of bed like a shot. She pressed a quick kiss to Alexandria's forehead before scuttling out the window. No doubt there would be a snarky comment lobbed her way for sneaking out before sunrise, but she'd rather that than risk two pastors finding her in bed with their niece.

Neve drove around the block a few times before returning, unwilling to stray too far while the Samhain attack and Alexandria's nightmare lingered in the forefront of her mind. That impulse made sense at least, unlike whatever temporary insanity prompted her to announce herself by knocking on the front door.

"Hello?" A tall woman with her hair pulled into a bun at the nape of her neck answered. She didn't look much like Alexandria.

"Hi, um, Pastor Abbott?" Neve said, trying to make herself look smaller and less imposing, which was wildly out of character in a way she didn't have time to examine. "I'm Neve?" It came out sounding like a question. This was a bad idea.

"Oh, you're the mysterious Neve," Pastor Abbott said warmly. "I've heard a lot about you."

"Um." Neve twisted a strand of hair around her finger. "I'm actually here to pick up Alexandria?" She cast about for a halfway-convincing lie to explain her presence so early in the morning. "We have a Shakespeare presentation today and I was supposed to pick her up early so we could practice. Did she tell you?"

"She didn't, in fact," Pastor Abbott said with a look that Neve couldn't decipher. "Would you like to come in?"

Neve's brain stalled. "Um."

"Please, I insist," Pastor Abbott said, stepping aside to let Neve in.

Without much of a choice, Neve plodded into the house, following Alexandria's aunt into the kitchen.

"Greg, this is Neve," Pastor Abbott said, introducing Neve to the short, balding man who stood at the stove. He looked like a bacon-making garden gnome.

"Alexandria's Neve?" Alexandria's uncle—Greg—asked cheerfully. Neve ducked her head to hide the pleased blush at being known as Alexandria's anything. "Welcome. Please take a seat."

Which was how Neve ended up sitting at the breakfast table with a steaming plate of bacon and eggs in front of her.

"Eat," Pastor Abbott—she insisted on being called Carol—said. "Greg is an excellent cook."

The bacon *was* excellent. Maybe even better than Daughter Clara's, though Neve would never admit it for fear of invoking Aoife's wrath.

"Isn't that Alexandria's sweatshirt?" Carol asked as Neve was mid-bite.

"I think it is," Greg said. Neve struggled not to swallow her own tongue.

"Explains why Xandria has been so cheerful lately."

Neve's cheeks burned. Maybe if she wished hard enough, the floor would open up and swallow her.

Neve was saved from coming up with a coherent response by footsteps on the stairs. "Hi, Neve," Alexandria said, coming to an abrupt stop when she saw Neve at the kitchen table. "What's up?"

"Shakespeare presentation, remember?" The look on Alexandria's face was almost worth the awkward introduction to the Abbotts.

"Oh yeah, sorry. Didn't sleep a whole lot last night."

"Bad dreams?"

A smile. "Could've been worse."

Carol clapped her hands. "Well, you two should get going then. Can't leave the Bard waiting."

Neve stood, and Alexandria swiped a piece of bacon off her plate. "Thanks," she said, yanking her backpack off the back of a chair.

"Nice to meet you both," Neve said after an awkward moment. Maeve would be pleased that she remembered her manners.

Neve was two steps away from her car when hands gripped the back of her hoodie. She allowed herself to be spun around to face a very smiling Alexandria. Before Neve could get a word out, a hand curled around the back of her neck, pulling her into a kiss. Alexandria tasted like mint toothpaste.

"Good morning to you too," Neve said warmly. "How'd you sleep?"

"Better than I have in forever." She looked it too. Alexandria was buzzing, some of her missing energy returned.

"Apparently, I am better than Xanax," Neve said.

"I did not say that."

"You snore, too, in case no one ever told you."

"I do *not*."

Neve grinned, letting her mouth drop open and making soft snoring noises. Alexandria smacked her.

"Sorry I left without waking you this morning," Neve said once they were in the car and on the road. "I didn't want to get you in trouble."

"Sorry I didn't warn you about my aunt and uncle. They're enthusiastic." Neve thought they were nice. A little over the top, but nice. Mercy would love them.

"Can you—um, will you do that thing again?" Alexandria asked suddenly. "If it gets bad?"

Neve reached out and squeezed her hand. "Of course I will."

CHAPTER TWENTY

As if in defiance of Neve's ability to soothe Alexandria's nightmares, Neve's own dreams were getting worse. Sometimes she ran around a hazy, warped Newgrange Harbor that she barely recognized, searching for someone she'd lost. Neve couldn't remember who was missing, but they were important. They were important and she'd forgotten them. How had she forgotten?

In others, the Hellgate was open and the onslaught of demons was too much. Neve screamed herself hoarse, but she couldn't do anything against the advancing horde. Hundreds, thousands of demons tore through the boundary, shrieking, as the same laughter echoed above the din.

Sometimes Bay and Mercy were lost, killed in front of her, and Neve woke up in a cold sweat, still reaching for them. Sometimes they survived, but Neve was so entrenched in the battle that she couldn't distinguish her sisters from the demons they were fighting.

In every dream, Neve couldn't find Alexandria. She wasn't where she was supposed to be; she wasn't anywhere. Neve would end up back at the Hellgate, injured, broken, but still fighting, and Alexandria was nowhere to be found. It made her want to scream. She *did* scream, but that wasn't what woke her up. Not this time. Instead, Neve was jolted into consciousness by the sharp knock on her door and the imposing-dread feeling she'd recognized even in her nightmare: Mercy had sensed something.

Neve shot to her feet, her body moving automatically. She stripped off her pajama shirt, throwing open her closet to retrieve her armor before flying downstairs to the armory.

"How many?" Neve demanded as they sprinted outside and piled into the car. The doors weren't even shut before Mercy hit the gas and they screeched down the hill.

"Six," Mercy breathed.

Neve swore, and she was sure Bay would have too if her voice wasn't already gone. Six. Gods damn it all. It wasn't even the Solstice. There shouldn't be six, not tonight.

A high note keened in the back of Neve's mind, a warning. Some kind of intuition that this wasn't random. It couldn't be random, not so close to the anniversary of the Kuro murders. Was this it? The disaster she'd been waiting for?

Focus, Neve. Neve had prepared for this, had sent the sos text to Alexandria's phone, certain that she would be awake to receive it. She would be okay. She had to be okay.

"Well, let's not leave them waiting," Mercy snarled, already out of the car and stalking toward the Gate. Bay was the first one through the barrier and Neve wasn't far behind. The place below her throat grew hot, building to a scream even before she broke through the gossamer curtain that separated the Gate from the rest of Newgrange Harbor.

Immediately, Neve knew that something was wrong. The demons were *waiting* for them, not scrambling to break free of the Gate. Neve hesitated for a split second, reeling at the strangeness. Had she fallen back asleep? Had she never woken up in the first place? She whipped her head to the side, searching frantically for Mercy and Bay among the chaos, half-sure she wouldn't find them. But there they were, their weapons flashing as they charged through the fray. Neve didn't have time for relief before three of the demons rushed her.

She screamed two of them into the sand before one caught her by the back of the neck and hurled her into the cliffside. Neve's vision swam, her breath exploding from her lungs in a painful rush. She rolled the instant she could force her body into motion, sliding out of the way as an enormous, muscled tail crashed into the rock face where she'd been just seconds before. Blood trickled down her cheek, and she didn't have time to recover before the demon struck again.

"I thought this would be harder," it said in a crackling voice, pinning her to the rock with hands like pincers. Pain rocked up and down Neve's torso where the demon's talons bit through her skin.

You thought right, asshole. Neve sucked in as much air as she could, feeling her ribs groan in protest, before screaming in the creature's face.

The change was instantaneous. The demon howled, dropping her into the sand. Neve rolled onto her side and struck, slashing its heel with her dagger. She wrenched herself to her feet as the demon staggered, lifting her sword to hack at the demon's neck. It took three swings to part its head from its shoulders, and by the time Neve was done, her armor was so covered in black blood that it began to eat through to the clothes beneath. Her breath came in harsh gasps and her muscles ached, shaking from the effort.

There wasn't time to celebrate the victory. Her sisters were still grappling with their own demons while two more stalked toward Neve, as if they'd expected the first one to take her out. As if they were backup.

As if Neve and her sisters had walked into a trap.

Neve's gaze slid away from them, landing on a third creature as it rushed Mercy's exposed side.

"Mercy!" Neve shouted over the chaos, rolling out of the way of the two advancing on her. Neve leaped, landing on the demon's back before it reached Mercy. She latched on tight, winching one arm around its neck. Neve stabbed her knife through the base of its skull and cursed as the demon exploded in a maelstrom of burning ash, dumping her back onto the ground.

Neve had time for a single breath before a massive weight landed on her chest. It pinned her to the sand and her ribs creaked, straining against the pressure. It felt like her breastbone was being pulverized, jagged chips of bone spearing her organs as she struggled. *Not again*, she thought desperately. *Not again.*

Neve tried to suck in enough oxygen to breathe, to scream, to do *something*, but the demon pressed hard on her throat. It watched her with glowing, dispassionate eyes as she struggled for air, the points of its claws heating up until each one was like a white-hot poker stabbing through her skin.

"You will not interfere any longer."

The voice was clear, unmarred by fangs or a forked tongue. White stars danced in her vision, and Neve could feel blood gush out of the punctures on her neck. It sizzled against the demon's claws, filling the air with a horrible, acrid stench and clotting in the sand like spilled ink.

"Get away from her!" Mercy's voice was accompanied by the swish of steel slicing through the air. The demon ducked, only narrowly avoiding the blow. Mercy rolled with the force of her swing and Bay appeared in the space she vacated. Bay swung her scythe in a deadly arc, slicing the creature from shoulder to navel, practically cutting it in half. The demon screeched and its blood poured onto Neve's chest, eating the rest of the way through her already damaged armor. Neve screamed in pain, and for a moment their howls of agony were perfectly in sync before the demon exploded in a plume of ash.

Two pale faces swam above hers when Neve's vision finally began to clear. Mercy's mouth moved, but Neve couldn't quite make out the words.

You will not interfere any longer.

She'd been right and wrong. It had been a trap, but not for all of them. Just for her. She was the target.

Which meant—

"Alexandria." Neve's voice was a croak and she could barely speak through the pain in her throat. Her sisters eased her into a seated position and Neve had to grit her teeth to keep from crying out, her cracked ribs and scorched chest screaming in protest at the movement.

"It's okay, Nee," Mercy said, one shade shy of desperate. Neve spat into the sand, adding to the blue-gold carnage around her. That was so much blood.

"I have to—" Neve tried to stand. Her vision whited out and only Mercy and Bay's reflexes kept her from hitting the ground again. "I have to go. I have to find Alexandria."

"She's fine, little sister. We need to get you home."

"She's not!" Neve's voice was too loud and it hurt her ears, but the sudden flash of anger helped dull the pain somewhat. "They're after her. They have been since—since the fall. I have to find her."

Mercy and Bay exchanged looks that Neve doubted she would be able to translate even if she wasn't precariously close to passing out.

"You've lost a lot of blood. We need to get you to Aoife and Clara."

"I'm fine." She wasn't.

Neve wasn't sure how she got to the car, but the next thing she knew, the passenger door closed beside her. She blinked and catapulted over the divider to dive behind the wheel.

"Neve!" Mercy shouted.

"I have to make sure she's safe," Neve coughed. Blood splattered onto the window. She threw the car into drive and sped off before Mercy could rip the door off its hinges.

The fact that she made it to Littletree Lane without wrapping the car around a telephone pole was nothing short of a miracle. It was early, too early for most humans to be awake, which was good because they'd certainly call the cops at the sight of her. Neve had enough presence of mind to park on the other side of the street before staggering up to the Abbotts' little white house, trailing blue boot prints.

With none of her usual grace, Neve clambered up the trellis, thanking each of the gods that the window was open despite the cold, because she didn't think she had the strength to break in.

Neve ducked inside, her head swimming, and badly

overbalanced. She crashed onto the carpet with a dull thud. Neve pushed herself onto her hands and knees, eyes glazed as she scanned the room.

"Neve?" Alexandria's voice was small and incredulous, but she was there, she was okay, she was alive.

"You're okay," Neve breathed.

"Jesus Christ, what happened to you?"

Neve's chest hurt. Her neck hurt. Her everything hurt. "I had to make sure you were okay."

This wasn't the plan they had agreed on. She was being rude. Social cues again.

Neve was bleeding onto Alexandria's carpet. That was rude too. Neve opened her mouth to apologize when the adrenaline keeping her conscious finally faded.

"Sorry," Neve wheezed. She wondered who had replaced her blood with fire. She wished they would put it back to normal. "I'll go now."

Then she passed out.

CHAPTER TWENTY-ONE

S natches of conversation sounded above her. She knew the voices, but she couldn't remember how. Gentle hands gripped her, and Neve vaguely recognized the sensation of being lifted. Some part of her mind whispered that they were safe—they were family—and they would never hurt her, but Neve's body was broken glass and she thrashed against them.

After that it was just a lot of screaming.

Neve's first conscious thought was of feathers. More specifically, Poe's feathers as he sat on her head like a broody hen on a nest. Neve coughed and he hopped away with a squawk.

"Don't yell at me," Neve said fuzzily. Poe cawed again, the picture of avian anger.

"He was worried." Bay's voice came from the doorway, and the rest of the room filtered into her vision. Familiar blue, sloping walls greeted her. An empty cage hung from the ceiling, and mismatched trinkets lined the shelves. Her walls, her birdcage, her trinkets. She was back home.

Neve didn't remember getting here, or much of anything after falling into Alexandria's bedroom. Just the bright glow of relief and a lot of pain.

"We were all worried. That was a stupid thing you did."

Neve coughed and tried to sit up. Bay kept her down with one hand on her shoulder.

"Good thing I'm not the smart one."

"You could've died."

"Hazards of divinity?" It came out as a question. Neve didn't want to fight with her sister right now. In fact, all she wanted to do was close her eyes and sleep until she could breathe without her ribcage feeling like it was going to collapse into powder. "Wait . . . how did you—?"

"Your girlfriend is kind of pushy, did you know that?" Mercy appeared in the doorway, her arms crossed over her chest. "She called us. Something about you bleeding out on her rug, although she didn't look super concerned that your blood is the wrong color. Anything you want to share with the class?"

"Um," Neve said slowly, trying to come up with a halfway-convincing lie. Her brain wasn't working. Her thoughts were hazy and slow.

Mercy didn't budge, though her mouth did tick up into a tiny smile before smoothing out again. "I thought she was going to start throwing things when Daughter Maeve tried to get her to leave. You're dating the world's most indignant hobbit."

"She's here?" Neve's mouth opened and closed. "In the convent?"

"I'm pretty sure she'd chain herself to the doors if we tried to make her leave."

Neve's blood chilled despite Mercy's nonchalance. "Is she okay?" she demanded, trying to rise. Bay stopped her again. If Alexandria was in the convent, then Aoife might have already taken her memories. "Did Aoife—"

"No," Bay cut in firmly. "Alexandria's fine. She was worried about you."

"She—" Neve started, but her lungs chose that exact moment to seize up, and she coughed so hard and for so long that blood speckled her sheets by the time she finished. "Oh."

That wasn't good. She'd known that her injuries were bad, but not like this.

"Next time," Mercy said, rubbing her temples in a way that Neve knew meant she was channeling her concern into exasperation, "maybe don't drive away like a maniac after having six different kinds of shit kicked out of you. You're giving Bay worry lines. Look at her. She could've been so beautiful."

Neve tried to laugh, but it only led to more coughing. More blood.

"I'll take it under advisement," she wheezed. The smiles were gone now, and both of her sisters looked pale and drawn. "I'm sorry." Exhaustion weighed her down, pulling her back into the warmth of unconsciousness. "I'm sorry I made you worry. They're . . . they're after her. I don't know why, but I had . . . I had to make sure she was safe."

Neve's vision fogged, but she remained present enough to feel familiar fingers carding through her hair. "It's okay. We're not mad. Just rest. We'll keep her safe while you sleep."

They would keep Alexandria safe. That was good.

Gods, she was so tired.

This time when she woke up, another familiar figure sat in the chair by her bed.

"Alexandria?" Neve mumbled, half-convinced that it was a dream, a figment conjured by her mind as her body healed. Even imaginary, Alexandria made Neve's heart do somersaults.

"Hey, I'm here," she said gently.

"Are you real?" It was a stupid question, but Neve couldn't seem to get her brain to work, too busy trying to memorize the starburst of freckles across Alexandria's nose and the way her eyes looked almost black until they hit the light and transformed into a kaleidoscope of copper and gold and amber.

Alexandria's lips twitched. Neve wished she would smile. "I'm real. I'm here, I'm not leaving you, okay?"

The drag on her bones started up again, too strong for her to fight, but Neve nodded.

"You're here. Good. Here is safe."

She thought Alexandria might have said something, but it was muffled by a blanket of darkness and Neve couldn't make it out.

There was a weight on her stomach.

Neve woke slowly, a stark departure from her usual head-first leap into consciousness, and she focused on the weight as the rest of her senses filtered back one by one.

Maiden, Mother, and Crone, she hurt. It felt as if her body had been replaced with one enormous, pulsing bruise. Her chest twinged with every inhale, her healing ribs and sternum creaking their displeasure. Breathing was only made more difficult by the burning sensation that scalded from her chin to her belly button. Neve shuddered at the memory of the demon's clawed fingertips buried in her throat and how its blood had burned her skin. That had . . . not been fun.

It only took a second to do an internal diagnostic. Things were better. Painful as hell, but healing.

Neve opened her eyes last, sucking in a breath at the sight of a head of pitch-black hair lying on her stomach. Not Bay or Mercy, then. Her gasp and subsequent cursing were enough to wake Alexandria, who looked up at her blearily. Half her hair was plastered flat to her head, and the tiniest ribbon of drool was hanging out one side of her mouth. Even so, Neve couldn't help the warm feeling that ignited in her extremely injured chest.

"You look like shit," Neve said, because she knew it would

make Alexandria laugh. She was rewarded by a snicker and the briefest hint of a smile. Victory.

"Says the girl who looks like she got hit by an eighteen-wheeler and went back for seconds." This time Alexandria smiled fully, her dimple flashing against the constellation of freckles on her cheeks.

"What day is it?" Neve asked.

"Monday."

Monday. Gods, the attack had happened Friday. She'd been in and out of consciousness for three whole days.

"You should be in school." The look Alexandria shot her was so incredulous that Neve felt stupid for saying anything. "Education is important, Alexandria-like-the-library."

"You're more important," Alexandria said, her dark eyes blazing. All of her was blazing, imbued with fierce, determined light that shone through her skin. She was so beautiful that for a moment, Neve had a hard time believing that she was real.

I love you. Neve almost said it out loud as the thought occurred to her. She loved Alexandria. Of course she did. How could she not? The ease with which her mind formed the words took her breath away.

"Don't you look at me like that, I'm mad at you," Alexandria said.

"Is it about the window?" Neve asked, searching through her fuzzy memory of the attack.

Alexandria's eyebrows rose. "No, you idiot, it's not about the window. It's about you almost *dying on my carpet.*"

"I'll ask Aoife to mix up something. She's good at getting out bloodstains," Neve offered.

"It's not—" Alexandria spluttered. "Who *cares* about the stains?"

Neve blinked, wondering if she had a concussion. "I thought you said—"

"You almost died!" Alexandria shouted, throwing her hands into the air. "*Died*, Neve. Right in front of me."

Oh. "I had to make sure you were safe," Neve said softly. "I was worried."

Alexandria dragged her hand down her face, muttering something about *no self-preservation instincts or a single working brain cell* before making a shooing motion. "You're giving me gray hair, I swear to God. Now move the hell over so I can make sure you don't stop breathing in your sleep."

Neve would give her the moon on a necklace if Alexandria asked.

Alexandria folded herself against Neve's side and tucked the covers around them. The bed was plenty big enough for both of them to have space, but Neve pulled Alexandria even closer.

"Am I allowed to talk?" Neve asked after a few minutes filled only by the sound of their breathing.

"Were you not allowed to talk before?"

"Well, you were on a roll before and I didn't want to interrupt. Also, you said that you're mad at me, which seems unfair but—"

"You are an ass, Neve Morgan," Alexandria said, cutting her off with a laugh. Neve hummed happily.

"I love you," she said with only a moment of hesitation. She'd barely thought the words to herself, but this wasn't a secret she wanted to keep. She didn't think it was a secret at all. "I think I've loved you for a while, but I'm . . . new at this. I've never . . ." She trailed off, suddenly unsure.

"In this lifetime?" Alexandria asked.

Neve shook her head.

"In any of the others?"

"You're the first," Neve whispered. "In any of my lifetimes."

"Wow." They sat in heavy silence for exactly four seconds before Alexandria punched a fist into the air. "Hell yeah. Suck it, historical hotties, she likes me best."

Neve groaned and squeezed her eyes closed, her cheeks flaming. "You're the worst."

"I love you too, you know," Alexandria said after a moment, snuggling closer. "I mean. Duh."

Neve wanted to tell Alexandria about the attack, about how the demons had gone after Neve to get her out of the way, but she still didn't know *why* they were after Alexandria in the first place. Why her? Why the Kuros? What was so special about one human family that it warranted this much concerted effort from demons—demons, who were meant to be chaotic and disorganized by nature. None of it made sense.

But Alexandria loved her. Alexandria loved her and she was safe and Neve had almost died, so it could wait a few hours. The world would keep spinning until then.

"Your family might know that I know," Alexandria said through an enormous yawn. Her eyes were half-lidded, on their way to fully closed, and Neve realized that she couldn't have slept more than a few hours in the past few days. What had she told the Abbotts to explain her whereabouts? *Sorry, I have to go sit by the bedside of my severely injured supernatural girlfriend.*

Somehow, Neve doubted it. Gods, what had she told their friends? In the few hours she'd been conscious, Neve hadn't so much as thought about her phone, but she could guess that there would be dozens of texts waiting for her, wondering where she and Alexandria had disappeared to over the weekend. Her first instinct was to just make something up and be done with it, but the idea made her sick to her stomach. Neve was so tired of lying.

"I might have yelled at them," Alexandria continued, oblivious to the direction Neve's thoughts had spun. "A little. Poe backed me up. He's a good bird. Kind of gave up the game, though."

"You think?" Neve snorted. Pain ricocheted through her chest, into her throat. "Ow."

"We'll deal with it in the morning. Afternoon? Whatever."

The *we* made Neve glow from the inside. "Can I kiss you?" she asked.

Alexandria cracked an eye open. "I'm in your bed. I love you. You can kiss me whenever." Another yawn, this one interrupted as Neve pressed her lips to the corner of Alexandria's mouth. Alexandria turned her head, catching Neve's mouth, and kissed her back.

"I love you," Neve whispered into Alexandria's hair. She pressed their foreheads together. "I love you so much."

"You're sappy," Alexandria said sleepily.

"Go to sleep," Neve urged, pressing a kiss to Alexandria's temple.

"*You* go to sleep," she mumbled, eyes already half-closed. "Guess what?" Alexandria asked after she'd been quiet for so long that Neve was certain she'd fallen asleep.

"What?"

"I love you."

CHAPTER TWENTY-TWO

A booted foot kicking open the door served as their wake-up call. Neve almost jumped out of bed, but Alexandria's weight on her chest and the encyclopedia of injuries kept her still.

"Good morning, lovebirds," Mercy called, far too loud and cheerful for the unholy hour. The sun wasn't even up yet. Neve groaned, trying to close her eyes and snuggle back under the covers. Somehow, Alexandria hadn't moved.

"Come on, up and at 'em, you have one hell of an explanation to give and I, for one, am excited to hear it."

"Why are you like this?"

"Lifetimes of practice," Mercy trilled. "Now how about you wake Sleeping Beauty and officially introduce her to the family."

"Five more minutes," Alexandria mumbled against Neve's shirt.

Mercy chose that moment to make an unnecessarily graphic gagging noise. "You two are gross. Out of bed. Chop chop!" She paused on her way out the door. "Also, you should probably shower, because you smell like blood and bad decisions. Bye!"

Neve groaned, laying her head back against the pillows.

"Your sister is . . . the most," Alexandria mumbled, still half-asleep.

"It runs in the family."

Watching Alexandria wake up was an exercise in patience. Unlike Neve, she woke up degree by minuscule degree, dragging her head up as if it weighed a thousand pounds. Her hair was tangled from sleeping against Neve's chest. There was an imprint where Neve's shirt had bunched up in the night and pressed against her cheek.

"What?" Alexandria's eyes were still cloudy, her voice sleep-rough and adorable.

"I love you," Neve said, because it was true.

Alexandria's eyes closed halfway, and she hummed like a pleased cat. "What are we going to tell your family?"

"The truth." It was the only thing Neve could think of. "As much of it as you want to tell them."

"But what about—?"

"I'm not going to tell your secrets. They know that you know about us, but that can be the end of it. We don't have to tell them anything else if you don't want to."

"Is that what you want?"

After a moment, Neve shook her head, gnawing on her lip. "I don't want to lie to my family anymore."

Alexandria straightened and she inhaled deeply through her nose. "Then we tell them everything."

"You don't—"

"Yeah, but you do. And I'm not getting between you and your sisters any more than I already have." Neve opened her mouth to protest, but Alexandria kept talking. "And that's not just because Mercy scares me. We're telling them. End of story." Her nose wrinkled a little. "Now point me to the bathroom. I need to make a good second—third?—impression."

Showering took a lot longer and was significantly more painful than Neve expected, the warm water collecting in wounds that were so deep that they hadn't even scabbed over yet. By the time she was done, the tub was stained blue and she ached all over.

"Heads up," Alexandria said when Neve emerged almost forty minutes later. A piece of fabric hit her in the face. The purple hoodie. "I was wondering where that went."

"You can have it back if you want," Neve said, making no move to hand it back over.

Alexandria snickered at Neve's obvious unwillingness. "You keep it. You need more color in your wardrobe anyway."

Neve grinned, reeling Alexandria in for a kiss. Alexandria made a soft, pleased noise and kissed her back. It occurred to Neve that there was a girl in her room. A girl she was kissing while mostly naked.

The thought made Neve blush and she pulled Alexandria closer. So human.

"Okay." Alexandria squared her shoulders once they were both dressed, which had taken longer than strictly necessary. They'd gotten distracted. "Let's do this thing."

What awaited them downstairs was a breakfast table laden with so much food that Neve almost asked if they were expecting guests. Mercy was already seated and way too excited, considering the circumstances.

"You look better," Bay said, pulling Neve into a gentle hug. Something in her settled at the tone of Bay's voice and the comfort that swept through the bond between them. She wasn't angry. Neve didn't think she would be able to handle that again on top of everything else.

"Liar," Neve replied. She still looked terrible and she damn well felt it. Whatever pit those demons had crawled out of, they weren't messing around.

"How about all of you come sit down?" Daughter Maeve said in a voice that brooked no argument. All at once, Neve's courage fled and she seriously considered grabbing Alexandria and making a break for it. Unfortunately, in her condition, she wouldn't make it two steps before falling flat on her face.

Alexandria's hand slipped into hers, squeezing tight. *I'm here.*

"Alexandria, we've been facilitating phone calls to your school, and they are under the impression that you are severely under the weather. Your aunt and uncle believe that you have been house-sitting for a friend in need since Friday," Daughter Clara said, not unkindly.

Alexandria opened her mouth and then closed it again. "Um, thank you?"

"We take our charges very seriously," Daughter Aoife went on, her eyes glimmering with magic. Showing off. "We take our secrets even more seriously, which means that we make sure that certain questions aren't asked."

"Enough," Neve snapped. "She gets it."

Aoife's eyes dulled, but Neve knew that there must have been an argument about wiping Alexandria's memory. Her grip tightened at the thought.

"Wanna ease up, Ginger Spice?" Alexandria asked with forced lightness. "You're crushing my hand."

Neve loosened her grip but didn't let go, glaring at each of the Daughters in turn. Bay stood off to the side, looking supremely uncomfortable. Mercy rested her chin on her folded hands without bothering to hide her smile. Neve wished she could laugh the whole thing off as well, but she could feel the sword hanging over her neck, threatening Alexandria as it swung back and forth.

"Please." Daughter Clara cut through the tension, setting her hand on the small of Aoife's back and leading her to the table. "Everyone sit down and eat something. We have a lot to talk about and these conversations are best had over a meal."

With the threat of Aoife's magic momentarily set to rest, Neve allowed herself to exhale, and she and Alexandria sat down. Mercy was to their left and Bay to their right, while the Daughters sat opposite. Neve breathed a little easier knowing that her sisters were with her on this.

"This," Mercy prompted after a few tense moments when no one had touched their food, "would be a good time to start talking, little sister."

"Demons killed my parents," Alexandria blurted. She was practically vibrating, her leg bouncing under the table. Neve's mouth dropped open. She'd thought they might work their way up to that and had anticipated doing most of the talking. If the looks on her family's faces were any indication, they hadn't expected it either.

Alexandria took a deep, steadying breath, still fidgeting. "Demons killed my parents and they've been after me ever since."

It was Bay who broke the silence. "That's impossible." Her voice held no accusation, but Neve couldn't help the way her hackles rose. "There hasn't been a breach like that in this lifetime."

Neve sucked in a steadying breath. "Not out of the Gate, no."

They told the story in turns after that, filling in the gaps when the other faltered. The night they met and how Mercy hadn't sensed the Gate opening, the attack on Samhain,

Alexandria's run-ins with demons in the past, the one that had come through the Gate when Alexandria touched it. Nothing was left out.

To their credit, no one said another word until they finished. Neve knew that they weren't telling the story well, but she just wanted it all out in the open. She wanted it done.

"They were after me on Friday," Neve said as she and Alexandria wound toward the end of the story. Everyone swiveled to stare at her, Alexandria included.

"What?" Alexandria demanded, eyes wide and very, very dark.

"It was a coordinated attack. I think they were trying to get rid of me so that they could get to you. They know I'm protecting you."

Alexandria made a sharp noise. "And you didn't think, 'Hm, I was almost murdered with extreme demonic prejudice, maybe I'll tell someone about it?'"

"It wasn't relevant until I knew you were safe." Neve raised one shoulder and dropped it. "After that, everything got a little fuzzy."

"What if you'd died?" Alexandria was almost shouting. Her voice echoed off the vaulted ceilings and made Neve wince. "You promised me you would be careful."

"But I didn't die," Neve pointed out, which didn't help the situation at all.

"I'm with library girl," Mercy piped up. "You should have mentioned it."

"See!"

"She's right," Bay added.

Neve raised her hands in surrender, thoroughly outnumbered. "I'm saying it now."

Three voices broke out, all speaking over one another.

Daughter Maeve stood. "Macha. Badb. Nemain."

Neve's breath hissed through her teeth. Bay and Mercy went still, silenced by their true names.

Maeve's gaze fell on Neve, and suddenly she looked exactly her age. "You know the implications of all this."

"Yes."

If demons could get into the world another way—if there was another Gate—that meant their divine purpose, their literal reason for being, was pretty much moot.

"What?" Alexandria broke through the heavy silence that had descended over the table, weighted down with a particular kind of existential dread. "What does it mean?"

"It means that everything we've been doing for millennia hasn't amounted to anything," Neve replied with no small amount of bitterness in her voice. "Demons aren't supposed to be able to get into the world except through the Hellgate."

"But they got to me. They came after my family."

"Meaning the whole point of us is bullshit," Neve finished.

There was supposed to be one Gate, three Morrigan to guard it. If there were other ways that demons could cross through, then what was the point?

"No."

For once, the hands slapping against the table did not belong to Neve or Mercy. Bay's skin was so pale that it was almost translucent, turning her into a specter of herself. "No," she said again, so quiet that Neve almost didn't hear it.

"Holy shit," Mercy breathed at the same moment that Neve pushed up from the table. Her body protested, but a spike of adrenaline numbed the pain.

"What the—" Alexandria asked, because she was Alexandria and she couldn't not ask.

"Stay sitting," Neve ordered, one hand on Alexandria's shoulder. Neve never took her eyes off Bay, stark and silent and terrifying despite the conspicuous lack of demons to fight.

Mercy gripped Bay's shoulders. "Bee, I need you to calm down, okay? We're fine, we're safe. No one is under attack and we have a guest, so I need you to please not go into the scary quiet place, okay?"

"It's not pointless." The words were barely louder than a breath, though Bay was clearly fighting to be heard. In the depths of her eyes, now enormous and alien, was heartbreak. "It can't be."

Of course it couldn't, not for her. Neve and Mercy loved

what they did, what they were, but of the three of them, Bay was the one who *believed* in it. With all her heart and soul, she believed that they were doing something good, something noble and worthy. She had to. She was too gentle to be able to take on a thousand years of blood and carnage without fully devoting herself to the cause. Bay was both worshipped and worshipper, a god who believed in her own divinity with everything she had.

"It's not." Alexandria sidestepped Neve to stand directly to Bay's left, undeterred by Neve's urgent look. "You know what Neve said to me when I told her about my family? She said that she would fight. Like that's some kind of normal response. Like fighting the demons up my ass is just another Tuesday."

Neve couldn't help the small growl that escaped at the harsh frankness of Alexandria's words.

"But that's what you guys do, right? You fight. That can't be for nothing. I don't know why they want me, but I think it would be a whole lot worse if you guys weren't around. Maybe it would be everyone, every family, not just mine. It means something. It has to." Alexandria's voice cracked and she faltered for a moment before managing a small, rueful smile. "Sorry, I'm not really sure where I was going with this. I'm great at starting speeches, not so great at ending them. It's the ADHD."

"I'm sorry," Bay whispered after a few minutes of tense silence. "I'm—" Her eyes shone with tears, and Neve could feel the depth of her sorrow.

Mercy and Neve reached Bay at the same moment, and the three of them stood close in a tangle of limbs and hair. They pressed their foreheads together like they used to when they were little.

"Triad," Neve whispered, because Bay needed to hear it.

"Triad," Mercy agreed. Bay didn't respond, just sniffled and pulled them closer. They stayed that way, in their lop-sided, uncomfortable embrace, until a soft sound pulled them apart. Daughter Clara cleared her throat, though her eyes were damp too. All the Daughters' eyes were. This wasn't just traumatic news for Bay. The Daughters had devoted their lives and a thousand years to raising and protecting Neve and her sisters. They'd given up everything to do it.

"We, erm," Daughter Clara cleared her throat again, visibly trying to rein in her emotions in a way that made Neve's chest hurt. "We clearly have to look into all this."

"I can show you the books I've been reading," Neve offered, desperate to do anything to stanch the bleeding. She was the one who loved Alexandria; she was the one with secrets. She was the one who had brought all this crashing down on their doorstep. "There isn't much, but—" She winced as a spasm of pain scraped up and down her spine, reminding her that she had been standing for too long.

"You can show us from your bedroom," Maeve ordered, clapping her hands together. Neve nodded. "Alexandria, would you be a dear and help Neve, please?"

Alexandria said something, too fast for Neve to pick up as her hearing began to fade in and out. Her injuries were tired of being ignored. She felt like she was going to break in half as Alexandria took her arm and led her up the stairs.

It was only because she was moving so much slower than usual that Neve was still within earshot to hear Mercy sob softly.

"I failed," she said in a hollow, thunderstruck tone that Neve hadn't heard since Mercy had turned eighteen. "I . . . I failed. I didn't know. I'm—I'm so sorry. I—" Her words choked off as Neve crested the top of the ironwork staircase, leaving her family below to reckon with the shattered remains of their lives.

CHAPTER TWENTY-THREE

Alexandria broke the silence first. "Are you okay?"

"I was going to ask you the same thing," Neve deflected.

"We are not worrying about me right this second," Alexandria said, shaking her head.

"I'll be fine."

"You almost weren't." Alexandria took a deep, shuddering breath. "I need you to be okay. I can't lose you. I thought I was an expert at losing people, but I can't lose anyone else, all right? So you're going to let someone take care of you for once."

"I'm sorry," Neve said softly as Alexandria guided her back into bed. "You shouldn't have to worry about any of this. Nothing is going to happen to me. I have my sisters." It was her go-to promise to Alexandria that she wouldn't get hurt, that she had protection, but Neve remembered the ache in Mercy's voice when she recalled the lifetimes where Neve had died first. They'd been at the height of their power then and it still hadn't been enough.

"Am I allowed to ask what happened to Bay back there?"

"It's her ability," Neve answered, because why not? Everything was already out in the open. "She gets . . . quiet." It was hard to explain. "'Death on silent wings,'" she said, quoting from one of Mercy's Irish mythology books.

Alexandria stared at her for a moment before she burst into laughter. "I'm sorry," she said, waving her hands over her mouth. "I'm sorry, that's literally so inappropriate, but why is everything about you guys so dramatic?"

"It's not."

"It so is."

Neve made a wounded noise, placing a pillow over her face. "You're supposed to be nice to me. I'm injured."

"Don't start pulling that card now." Alexandria let out another peal of laughter as Neve's fingers snaked around her wrist and pulled her down onto the bed. Alexandria burrowed under the comforter and pulled it over their heads, making a warm cocoon. "Hi."

"Hi," Neve said, trying for a smile that wouldn't come. "How are you handling all this?"

"I'm fine."

"Liar." That was met with a pout, and Neve crossed the tiny bit of distance between them to kiss it away. "Tell me the truth."

"You're rude," Alexandria huffed. Her cheeks were pink.

Neve just looked at her, expectant.

"It's a lot," Alexandria said at last. "All of this. You and your sisters, and the Hellgate—which is totally not dramatic *at all*. It's just a lot."

"You know that you can—" Neve started, but Alexandria kept talking.

"But I'm not alone anymore." The quiet sincerity took Neve's breath away, without the help of her injured ribs this time. "I'm not wondering if I'm crazy or seeing things. I know that what happened to my family is real, and I know that you three are out there, putting your lives on the line to keep it from happening to anyone else."

Guilt twisted in Neve's stomach. "I'm sorry we didn't save them. I'm sorry we didn't know."

"You're here now and we'll figure it out together." Alexandria sighed. "I thought it was going to get easier, but I think it's always going to suck. I don't think the Gate was the only thing that drew me here. I think it was you, too. And everything is terrifying and shitty, but I'm not alone."

"No," Neve promised, low and fierce. "You're not."

She wished that was enough, that her promises meant anything at all, but it wasn't that simple. There were still demons out there somewhere, plotting something hideous. This wouldn't be their last attempt. There was still so much they didn't understand.

In the meantime, they had to go back to school. Neve

was no stranger to skipping weeks at a time, but Alexandria needed to graduate. She was still human, and things like getting good grades and college applications were still important to her. Or so it was explained to Neve.

She wasn't fully healed by Wednesday, but it was the earliest that the Daughters would let her return and if Alexandria was going back, so was Neve. She wasn't going to leave her unprotected, not after such a brazen assault.

"I'm not going to get attacked in the hallway," Alexandria grumbled, watching Neve pack up her stuff. She'd more or less moved into the convent since the weekend. Whatever lies Daughter Clara had spun, neither the Abbotts nor the office staff at Newgrange Harbor High had made so much as a peep about their absence.

"That you know of," Neve replied, but she was distracted. And if she was being fully honest with herself, she didn't know if she wanted to go back. The convent was safer, and it didn't help that her phone had been buzzing nonstop since she'd plugged it in. She'd been a little busy fighting for her life, but clearly their friends had noticed Neve and Alexandria's vanishing act.

By the time they made it to school, Neve's parking space was already occupied. Five unsmiling figures waited for them, all looking at Neve's car expectantly as she pulled into the lot. Alexandria waved her phone in response to Neve's questioning glance, looking far too pleased with herself.

"Rip off the Band-Aid."

"So you two want to explain where the *hell* you've been?" To everyone's surprise, it was Puck who spoke, their usual mild-mannered softness nowhere to be found.

"And why do you look like you got hit by a truck?" Ilma added.

"I did," Neve said, her eyes never leaving them as they absorbed the lie. Her stomach twisted, but she and Alexandria had discussed it and for now, their friends were safest if they didn't know the truth. "I've been in the hospital since Friday. Alexandria stayed with me."

There was a pause before several voices spoke at once.

"A truck, Morgan? You couldn't just get hit by a car like a normal person—?"

"What the hell? Did you file a police report—?"

"Are you okay? Should you even be walking right now—?"

"I'm fine," Neve insisted, stonewalling. "I don't really want to talk about it."

No one was satisfied with that answer, but the bell rang before someone—probably Michael—could decide to be nosy. Ilma held Neve's gaze for a few seconds longer than the rest, looking as if she was doing some kind of mental calculation before she shrugged and started toward the building like everyone else. It set Neve's teeth on edge, but she had bigger things to worry about at the moment.

With Tameka on her left, Puck on her right, and Simon and Ilma ahead and behind, Neve felt like she was being guarded. Like *they* were protecting *her*. Michael went so far as to hold the door for her. Simon insisted on carrying her backpack.

"You got hit by a truck," Michael reminded her when Neve tried to protest. "How about we shove the Morgan pride for a second, yeah?"

Neve really couldn't argue with that.

She stuck close to Alexandria for the rest of the day, mostly to reassure herself that she was still there, but also because Neve was seconds away from making a mad dash out of the school. Alexandria kept her present.

Neve didn't even bother pretending to pay attention in Mr. Robinson's class. She just sat back in her chair, blatantly not taking notes and daring him to comment. He didn't, though there was a fair amount of glaring in her general direction. Eventually, Neve's eyes fell on the calendar on the wall, where the Winter Solstice was printed in tiny script. December twenty-first.

It didn't take long for her thoughts to spin away from *King Lear* and Newgrange Harbor High, trying to put together the implications of the Kuros being killed on the darkest day of the year. It couldn't be a coincidence; there was no such thing.

At least she wasn't searching alone anymore. The Daughters had spent the last few days locked in the library,

and her sisters were trying to find any sort of similar cir-
cumstance in their past lifetimes. Both would take time. Time
they might not have, considering that the Solstice was this
Saturday.

Alexandria tugged on her sleeve. "Where'd you go?"

"Just thinking."

"Well, stop," Alexandria said. "You're making your doom-
and-gloom face and it's going to give you worry lines. I like
your face the way it is."

Neve blinked at her. "I do not have a doom-and-gloom face."

"Your nose gets all scrunchy."

Neve rubbed her finger down the bridge of her nose like she
could smooth out the alleged scrunches. It made Alexandria
laugh.

They fell into a routine after that. Neve insisted, and, to her
surprise, her sisters agreed, that Alexandria should stay at the
convent until after the Solstice.

"What is up with this day?" Alexandria asked when Neve
laid out her plan. "Besides, you know, it being the anniversary
of the day I became demon-bait?"

Neve winced. Alexandria was matter-of-fact about it, but
Neve knew her well enough to recognize when she was trying
to grin and bear it.

"I mean, I know the science of it. Darkest day of the year
and all that, but what's got you freaked?"

"It's the darkest day of the year," Neve repeated slowly, wishing she were better at this. "There's magic in that. Old magic. The Gate is practically all the way open and the attack is usually . . . bad."

Neve knew that she was being overprotective and suffocating, but she wasn't willing to leave anything to chance. Not with this. The Daughters made them breakfast in the morning and dinner at night. Alexandria offered to help cook and always joined the clearing up after dinner and they actually seemed to warm up to her, which was nothing short of miraculous.

Neve drove them to and from school and they roamed the convent grounds in the afternoons, exploring the gardens or library, or the hundreds of nooks and crannies that Neve and her sisters had discovered as children in this lifetime and all their lives before. Alexandria even made a point of watching their training sessions, though she was more of a distraction than anything else. She delighted in heckling Neve from a safe distance and laughing when she got knocked down.

"Your girlfriend is mean," Mercy said, hauling Neve to her feet. "I like her."

"Me too." Neve said, breathing hard. She shouldn't be training, but she wasn't willing to fall out of practice. She could take the pain. "Again."

"You're done for today, little sister." The air blurred and

Neve's weapons were removed from her possession. "If you break anything else, Bay and Maeve are going to kill me, and I'm on thin ice for sparring with you in the first place."

They had a routine. They had half a plan. They had each other. It would be enough to keep Alexandria safe.

It had to be.

CHAPTER TWENTY-FOUR

The Solstice started with a phone call.

"No," Neve protested as Alexandria rolled away from her, reaching toward the nightstand. "Too cold. Too early. Let it go to voicemail."

"It's my aunt," Alexandria said through a yawn. Neve tried to pull her back and plug the spot against her side where the cold seeped in. Convents were great for housing young gods, but they weren't insulated for shit. "Hi, Aunt Carol."

Neve groaned, pulling the covers over her head as Alexandria tried to force herself to sound alert and awake and not like she'd been spending her nights in her supernatural girlfriend's bed. With her supernatural girlfriend's equally supernatural family. While supernatural monsters plotted against her from an entrance to Hell literally right beneath them.

All together like that, it really did sound dramatic.

"Good morning to you too," Alexandria said after she hung up, burrowing back under the covers.

"It's Saturday," Neve complained.

"Do gods care about sleeping in on the weekends?"

"They do when they're stuck in seventeen-year-old bodies." Neve yawned, stretching her arms and feeling her joints crack. Alexandria made a face. "Something-something circadian rhythms something-something. You're the one who pays attention in bio."

"I didn't know that kind of thing affected you." Neve cracked one eye open at Alexandria's tone. She was frowning, a tiny mark appearing beneath her bottom lip.

Neve ran her thumb over the place where Alexandria's skin creased, smoothing it back out again. "What's the look for?"

"I feel like . . . like I'm never going to know everything about you. I mean, you've lived *forever*, basically."

Neve considered this before sticking her hand under Alexandria's chin in a cramped handshake. "Hi. I'm Neve," she said briskly. Alexandria snorted. "I'm seventeen in this lifetime, but in total I'm closer to a thousand even though I don't know the actual number. I'm not human, but I'm close enough to want to sleep in on Saturday mornings. I'm part of an ancient trio of war gods. I live in a convent with a bunch of nuns and my sisters, who are both faster and stronger than me. I love a girl named Alexandria, who I met when I was sneaking out and she tried to drive me to the hospital after I got my ass kicked by a demon."

"She sounds like a cool girl. You should probably listen to her more."

"I should."

Alexandria's smile didn't last.

Neve bit her lip. "What did the Abbotts want?"

"Just to check in on me. Today. You know."

Neve nodded, feeling a strange swell of affection for Alexandria's aunt and uncle. They were in an impossible position, one they couldn't begin to understand, but they cared. They were good people.

"I was thinking," Neve said, finally sitting up and drawing Alexandria into her lap. "We should go to the cemetery today. If you want to."

Alexandria looked at her for so long that Neve began to squirm. "My parents aren't buried here."

"I know, but I just thought . . . cemeteries are supposed to be places of mourning, whether or not your parents are there. It could be . . . cathartic."

"Did you Google that?"

Caught. "I don't know a lot about human grief."

Neve understood the emotion by itself, but humans put a lot of ritual significance into the act of mourning. She didn't get it, but if it would help Alexandria get through today, she was willing to sit in the cold and pretend to be moved by a bunch of tombstones.

"If you don't want to, we can always steal a bunch of liquor."

"You can't get drunk."

"But you can. Google says that alcohol helps sometimes."

"I'm taking away your Google privileges." Alexandria sighed, releasing some of her chipper exterior and letting the tiniest bit of grief show. She laid her head on Neve's chest. "I think the cemetery would be nice. You sure you want to come?"

Neve did not dignify that with a response.

"Where are you off to?" Daughter Maeve asked when they made their way downstairs almost an hour later. Solstice or not, Neve was still reluctant to be up and moving before nine in the morning on the weekend. Mercy was probably still fast asleep, though Bay was already eating at the kitchen island.

"Cemetery," Neve answered before casting a glance at Alexandria. "Should I have lied?"

Alexandria heaved an enormous, put-upon sigh. "No, you goober. It's not a secret."

Neve nodded, pleased that she'd gotten it right. She didn't want to make any mistakes today.

"Good timing," Daughter Clara said, flipping a pancake in the air. It landed on an electric griddle that Neve had never seen before and would be willing to bet hadn't existed before this morning. "Breakfast is almost ready." She scraped the pancakes onto a serving dish and retrieved a pan of sizzling bacon from the oven. "Coffee?"

Alexandria nodded, nonplussed, as a plate was set in front of her and Clara slid a steaming mug across the marble counter. "Thank you," she said. "How did you—?"

"Today's about you," Neve said. "And you like a ridiculous amount of sugar in the morning. I guessed the rest."

Alexandria stared at her plate for so long that Neve thought she'd done something wrong. "My mom used to make us chocolate chip pancakes on Saturdays." She cleared her throat. "She always took the whole day off so we could spend it together. Before she, uh . . . yeah. Before."

Neve was frozen, paralyzed by Alexandria's grief and helpless to do anything to stop it except squeeze her hand. *I'm so sorry*, she wanted to say but didn't. *I'm so sorry that happened to you. I'm sorry my sisters and I couldn't protect you. I'm sorry you lost them.*

"Sorry," Alexandria said with forced brightness, shaking her head. "Got a little weepy there for a second. I'm back."

"There's nothing wrong with mourning the ones we've lost," Daughter Maeve said. "The ache stays with you forever, but so do they. As long as you're around to remember how much they loved you, they're not really gone." Maeve's eyes were clouded, and suddenly Neve remembered that the Daughters had to watch her and her sisters die, over and over again. "It sounds to me like you love your parents very much."

"Yeah," Alexandria's voice was small. "Yeah, I do." She

didn't eat much of her breakfast but made a point to compliment Clara on the coffee, which meant that it must have been mostly sugar.

"Do you still want to go?" Neve whispered as they loaded their plates into the dishwasher.

"I want to remember them." Alexandria exhaled, leaning against Neve for a moment. "It's a good idea."

"One last thing," Aoife said, producing a bouquet of white flowers that glittered with magic. "For you."

"These . . ." Alexandria said, staring at the flowers as she took them with both hands. "We had these at the funeral. How did you know?"

Aoife shrugged primly. "I'm a witch, dear. Now shoo, both of you."

There was only one cemetery in Newgrange Harbor. It was small, attached to the only church in town, but expertly maintained. The grass looked very green against the backdrop of steel-gray sky. The tombstones waited like warriors in formation, standing fast against grief.

Neve didn't know how, but the air was stiller here. Still and heavy, as if the memories of passed loved ones added physical weight. It felt like she was trespassing. This place wasn't meant for her. She wasn't ever going to be buried in one of these plots. She wasn't ever going to have a funeral. To the people in this town, she would simply disappear one day until the reincarnation spell made them forget that she even existed.

"This is weird," Alexandria sighed a moment after she finished explaining that technically this was a graveyard, not a cemetery, because of its connection with the church. The delighted buzz that usually accompanied her ever-expanding list of fun facts was conspicuously absent.

Alexandria clutched the flowers in white-knuckled fingers. "I feel like I'm being disrespectful. My parents aren't even here."

"These places are exactly what humans need them to be," Neve said gently. Besides, it wasn't as if there was anyone around to care what they were doing. The darkest day of the year was also the coldest they'd had all season. It was enough to keep everyone away.

"You do that a lot more now," Alexandria commented.

"What?"

"Talk about what you are. You never used to before."

"I can stop if it bothers you," Neve offered. Alexandria wasn't wrong; Neve had stopped pretending this past week. The convent was the one place where she and her sisters didn't bother with the façade of humanity. They got to let go, be exactly as strong and fast as they wanted to be. Neve had tried not to make a big deal of it, but she still felt as if she were on display, waiting for judgment.

"No," Alexandria said, winding her arm tighter through

Neve's. "No, I like it. Just an observation." They walked in silence for a few minutes more. "I need you to talk to me. I'm getting a little lost in my head here."

"What do you want me to talk about?"

"Anything," Alexandria said in a rush. "I need a distraction."

"I'm never going to have one of these." Neve winced as her previous thoughts slipped out. She wasn't used to talking on command, and spending so much time around Alexandria had well and truly eroded her filter. "We—my sisters and I—don't die like people do. Our bodies only last a day or so before they just kind of disappear and we're reborn."

"Disappear," Alexandria repeated slowly, drawing out each syllable. "What kind of magical loophole bullshit is that?"

Neve shrugged. "I don't make the rules."

"And you don't know how the chain works," Alexandria mused. "But you're all different ages. How's that work?"

"More magical loophole bullshit," Neve admitted after a moment. "When the last one of us dies, there's a spell. The town forgets that we existed and then Bay comes back, and then Mercy two years later . . ."

"And then you."

Neve nodded. Even when she had her memories, she didn't think she'd ever fully understand how the reincarnation worked. According to Aoife, they had to come back staggered so that there was never too much magic diverted from sealing the Hellgate. The spell kept them safe until Bay turned eighteen, when it was weakened by manifesting her abilities. After that, it was up to Neve and her sisters to protect it.

Neve sighed. It was . . . complicated. Magical loophole bullshit all the way down.

She talked about nothing for a while as they walked, her eyes scanning the headstones. She didn't know exactly what she was looking for until she found it: a grave in the northernmost corner of the cemetery, so worn with age that the name carved into the stone was indecipherable.

"Here," Neve said, stopping in front of it.

"Ah yes, a very old grave," said Alexandria, fidgeting.

Neve generously ignored her. "You said it was weird because your parents aren't here. This could be them."

"Neve . . ."

"I would want to talk to Bay and Mercy," Neve said. Mercy hadn't said so, but there had to be lives where Neve had lived without one of them. Or, gods, *both*. The thought made her ill. "Even if they were gone and even if they couldn't hear me. I would want to talk to them. So, I'm going to go over there, and you can say—or not say—whatever you want."

Neve nodded, concluding her speech, and extricated Alexandria from her side. She stripped off her outermost layer and dumped it over Alexandria's head before ambling away. She didn't go very far, keeping one eye on the corner of the graveyard, but she didn't want to stare. This moment wasn't for her and she didn't want to intrude.

Neve wondered if the people laid to rest here had actually found peace. She wondered if there was any peace to be found. There certainly wasn't any in life, not for any of them. Mortal or divine, they were all fighting. Some fights were just more literal than others.

Neve kicked at a pebble. She would never go to heaven or find paradise or whatever humans believed in. She would be reborn into another cycle, and another, and another. The thought made her tired all of a sudden, when it had only ever been a comfort.

Gods, though, she hoped that something was out there for them. She hoped there was more, and that it—whatever it was—was quiet, and safe. Humanity deserved a gentle afterlife. Alexandria most of all.

Neve's eyes flicked to the old grave and her heart jumped into her mouth. Alexandria wasn't there anymore. Nerves jangled beneath her skin as Neve scanned the tombstones, searching, and the hair stood up on the back of her neck. Something was wrong.

The tiniest shift of air behind her was her only warning. Neve spun, a scream on her lips that died instantly.

A demon stood among the gravestones, and Neve had a moment of disbelief as she recognized the demon she'd killed on Samhain. It was back. But how? She'd killed it. It had *exploded.*

The demon held Alexandria against its side, one arm wrapped tight around her shoulders, its claws poised just above her collarbone.

"Get away from her," Neve shouted, the words coming out distorted. Heat built in her throat, but she couldn't scream without hurting Alexandria too.

"Neve—" Alexandria's voice cut off as the demon's claws pricked her skin. Blood beaded around its black talons and Neve's vision went red.

She was only a few steps away, but gods, she wasn't *fast enough.* She couldn't even go for her weapons without running the risk that the demon would part Alexandria's head from her shoulders. Neve wasn't willing to take that chance. She was frozen in place, useless.

The demon snarled at her, its teeth flashing yellow in a face mostly obscured by shadow. Black lines like spidery veins appeared where its claws bit into Alexandria's skin.

"I said," Neve said, squaring her shoulders, *"get away from her!"* She had to move, she had to do something, she couldn't just stand here and watch.

Something shivered against the back of her neck and Neve whirled. She yanked a dagger from its place at her waist, but the second demon was a blur of motion, and there was a sharp sting in her side before she could stab it. Neve's insides writhed and she choked on bile as something burned through her bloodstream. She inhaled around the pain, gritting her teeth as she waited for her body to metabolize the toxin.

It didn't. Instead, her throat closed, cutting off her voice, and Neve was only able to stay upright for a few seconds more before her body went slack. Her vision dimmed and the world tilted around her. She wasn't aware of falling, only of the sudden wet press of grass against her cheek.

A kick landed squarely in her midsection and there was a moment of perfect agony as something gave inside her. The air parted, whistling in her ears as her body flew backward. She was airborne for only a second before she slammed against something solid. The jagged edges of a broken tombstone dug into her back. Neve blinked as a dark shape loomed over her, but she couldn't make out the details, her vision too hazy to focus.

She was going to die. She was going to die here, in this cemetery, just four months shy of her birthday. She was going to break the cycle. She was going to lose Alexandria.

"No!"

The single word was all Neve could make out as her hearing went the way of her vision, fading so quickly that she wasn't quite sure what was real anymore. Voices sounded above her, but she couldn't make out the words.

Whatever poison was coursing through her veins, she wasn't strong enough to fight it, but gods damn it, she had to *try*. Alexandria needed her—her sisters needed her. Neve refused to let this be the end of them, not like this. She needed to *fight.*

But she was too weak, too young, and the crushing darkness dragged her under.

CHAPTER TWENTY-FIVE

N eve woke up, which was unexpected but not unwelcome. She should be well beyond dead. The thought made her shudder as if an icy hand had clutched her insides.

A quick glance at her phone revealed that she'd only been out for a few minutes. Whatever had been injected into her bloodstream, it was only meant to keep her down for a moment. There was still time.

Muttering curses, Neve gripped the broken edges of the tombstone and dragged herself upright. She staggered to her car, head throbbing. Her vision was still fuzzy, but she threw herself behind the wheel anyway.

"Neve?" Mercy's voice crackled through the receiver when Neve unlocked her phone and hit the first number on speed dial. This was her fault. She'd let Alexandria out into the open; she'd made her a target.

And, some sinister voice whispered in the back of her mind, she was selfish. Neve knew the risks, she knew the danger of getting involved with humans, and she'd done it anyway. *You thought you could be happy with her*, the voice cackled. *You thought you could have a* future, *you arrogant—*

"They took her," Neve shouted, too loud. Trying to drown out the voice. The despair. Both.

"Where?" Mercy replied immediately.

There was only one place they would take her. Her palms itched for her sword and black fear threatened to drown her. She could barely hear her own voice over her heart hammering in her ears. "The Gate."

"On our way."

Mercy and Bay were already on the beach by the time Neve arrived, skidding to a stop so violently that the car torqued. They weren't moving, just hovering by the KEEP OUT sign.

Why the hell weren't they moving?

"Neve!" Bay called. "Neve, stop—the poison!"

"Alexandria!" Neve cried out, all desperation. She blew past her sisters, her feet pounding against the rocky sand. Something was wrong with the Hellgate. It was rippling and black, the edges seething as if she was staring down into an active volcano. Even during the worst demon attacks, she'd never seen it look like that.

Alexandria was too close. The warped edges of the Gate seemed to reach for her in Neve's blurry vision. Another two steps and Alexandria would fall through. She was too close, *too close—*

"Stop!" The terror in Alexandria's voice was enough to

freeze Neve in her tracks. "Neve, please stop. Don't come any closer. It'll kill you."

Her hesitation didn't last, and the sliver of Neve still capable of rational thought prayed that her sisters would forgive her for this. The breathless panic that had dogged her thoughts for months now vanished into smoke, incinerated by her rage. Her side still throbbing, Neve screamed and the force of it parted the air, making it shift and shimmer like heat waves over a flame. The demon by the Gate lashed its scorpion-like tail and her voice choked off again before it could do any damage.

Neve's legs gave out, her knees bending as if she'd been forced to the ground by an enormous invisible hand. Panic thrilled in her blood and she thrashed against the pressure.

"Neve, stop!" It sounded like Mercy, but Mercy would never ask her to do this. Mercy would never ask her to stop fighting. That wasn't who they were. They were the Morrigan, and they fought. "It's going to kill you—*Neve!*"

"I don't care," Neve ground out, spitting blood. "I don't care."

She fought until the poison stole the breath from her lungs, and then it was all she could do to stay conscious.

Neve didn't know if she was hallucinating from the lack of oxygen, but a gentle hand on her cheek forced her to focus again. Alexandria's face swam in front of her own.

"I'm sorry," she whispered, tears shining in her dark eyes

and trailing down her cheeks. She looked so scared that it made Neve's chest hurt. "It'll kill you if I don't go. I . . . I can't let you die too."

"Not a *fucking* chance," Neve spat. Pressure built against her spine until she was almost bent in half. "You're staying here with me."

"You'll die."

"I've died before."

"*Neve.* Let me save you this time." Alexandria's face was pale and she'd stopped crying, but her lips still trembled as she spoke. "I—I love you so much. But not enough to let you die for me."

"No," Neve said again.

"I love you," Alexandria repeated. She tried for a smile, and this time the ache in Neve's chest had nothing to do with her broken rib or demon poison. "I'm so glad I met you."

Neve couldn't force her arms to move, couldn't will her body into motion. She could only remain perfectly still as Alexandria's lips brushed against her sweaty forehead.

Then she was gone, walking back to the seething Hellgate where the two demons waited. Neve wanted to close her eyes, wanted to scream, wanted to do *something*, but all she could do was watch as the shadowy demon closed one clawed fist around the arm of the girl she loved and pulled her into Hell.

CHAPTER TWENTY-SIX

Neve didn't know how long she remained there, half slumped over with the rocks cutting into her knees, unable to look away from the spot where Alexandria had vanished. With the demons gone, the Hellgate looked like it always did, an insignificant stretch of cliff directly beneath the convent.

"Neve."

The gentle touch on her shoulder was like an electric shock. She was wobbly and stiff, still metabolizing the poison, but Neve sprang to her feet and sprinted to the Gate as best she could. Some hazy, half-mad part of her was sure that it would give beneath her grief, but then what? Alexandria was still gone, still in Hell where Neve couldn't follow. That knowledge didn't stop her from pounding her fists against the stone until the cliff was splattered with her blood. It didn't stop her from screaming for so long and so loud that some of the loose stones shook free and tumbled into the ocean.

"Neve, stop!" Mercy's arms wrapped around her, unyielding as steel, and pulled her away.

"No!" Neve cried out, but she wasn't strong enough. She was never strong enough. Not when it mattered.

Mercy dragged her back to where she'd left the car, mumbling nonsense the entire way, but Neve was beyond hearing. All she could see was Alexandria walking away from her, Alexandria disappearing through the Gate, Alexandria gone.

"Stop. Stop! You have to stop!" Mercy shouted when Neve kept fighting.

"I have to—" Neve panted, her voice harsh and jagged. "I have to—"

"It would've killed you."

"You should've let it!" She whirled on Mercy and in that moment, Neve hated her. She hated both of them for standing by and doing nothing. Bay clapped her hands over her mouth, her blue eyes wet with tears. "You should have saved her. That's the whole point of us—*that's the whole point!*"

"There is no us without you!" Mercy shouted back, grabbing Neve by the shoulders and holding her so that they were eye-to-eye. "You haven't manifested yet. If you die now, it breaks the chain and I will not lose you, do you hear me?"

"You should've let me die," Neve growled. Mercy's eyes widened with shock, but Neve didn't care, not now. Not at this moment, when there was a great cavernous hole where her heart should be.

"Nee—"

"Get away from me," she snarled, shoving hard. "Just get *away!*"

Mercy released her as if she'd been burned and Neve spun away without another word. She didn't know where to go. She didn't have anywhere *to* go.

She wanted to hit something; she wanted to hurt something. She wanted to die. She wanted to scream and scream and scream until the entire world felt exactly what she was feeling.

She wanted Alexandria. Gods, how had this happened? They'd been so careful. Neve thought that she could keep her safe. But the truth was that she couldn't even protect herself.

"What happened?" Daughter Maeve's eyes were enormous when Neve finally arrived home. She had nowhere else to go.

"She's gone," Neve said through her teeth, all the anger flooding out of her in an instant. She had to throw out a hand to keep from collapsing, barely catching herself against a wall. "They got Alexandria. They took her."

"Oh, Neve."

This time Neve didn't fight the arms that embraced her. She just fell against her oldest guardian and sobbed. Deep, aching sobs that reached the very core of her.

The other Daughters came and went, shooed away by Mercy and Bay and no doubt told the whole, horrible story.

Neve barely noticed them, too busy trying to keep breathing as she cried like she hadn't since she was a little girl. Maeve held her all the while, until Neve had no more tears left. She felt numb, wrung out.

"I'm so sorry," Maeve whispered when Neve's hiccupping sobs finally subsided.

"What am I going to do?" Neve asked. Gods, it was going to be like Alexandria had just *disappeared*. Vanished without a trace. What was she going to tell the Abbotts? What was she going to tell her friends? How was she possibly going to find a lie big enough to cover up the truth?

How the hell was she going to survive this?

"We'll do everything we can," Maeve promised. "But right now, you need to rest. This has . . . You need to lie down, Neve, before you fall over."

Neve wanted to argue, but she knew Maeve was right. Daughter Aoife met her in the corridor, her eyes shining. She held a steaming mug in her hands and Neve took it without question. At Aoife's expectant look, she swallowed it in three burning gulps, tasting the sugary sweetness of the healing tincture that they'd used since they were children.

Neve wasn't entirely sure how she got to her bedroom, but the next thing she knew there were covers tucked up to her chin and the door clicked closed. After a week of sleeping with Alexandria curled into her side, her bed felt cold and empty.

Poe's cage swung from the ceiling and the old raven made what could only have been a noise of mourning. Neve let it lull her to sleep.

Even in her dreams, something was missing. Neve scrambled around, blind and deaf, nerveless in the dark, but wherever she went, she couldn't find her. Jagged stone penned her in from every angle. She was trapped, terrified, and *useless*.

Neve had to find her.

"Alexandria!" Neve's voice echoed back to her from every angle, the harmonics shredding into a scream. "Alexandria, where are you?"

Gone, whispered a little voice inside her. *Dead.*

No. No, that wasn't right. She wasn't dead. She hadn't died.

Gone, the voice insisted. *Dead.*

"Not dead," Neve said aloud, shivery and strange. "Taken."

Taken wasn't dead. What had been stolen could be retrieved.

And Hell was just a place.

Neve woke with a start, half out of her bed before the dream solidified into something more tangible. Alexandria was gone. Taken, not dead.

Hell was a *place*.

Neve didn't even make it out of her bedroom. She didn't

know why she was surprised to see Mercy and Bay there, sitting on either side of her door, but a small, furious part of her still hissed and spat at the sight of them.

"You shouldn't be up," Bay said gently, her eyes shining with concern. "It's only been a few hours."

That was already too long.

"Go away," Neve said. Her voice came out harsher than she meant it, and both Bay and Mercy flinched. Neve wasn't sorry. They'd let the demons take Alexandria through the Gate. They'd let her go, just like that, like it was nothing.

Neve shoved away the slightly more reasonable voice that reminded her that they were trying to save her life. After this afternoon, after losing Alexandria, she didn't have much use for reason. Blaming her sisters was easier than blaming herself.

"Neve—" Mercy started, but Neve didn't give either one of them a chance. They had their chance. They made their choice back on the beach, and now Neve had made hers. She pushed past her sisters without a word, hoping that they would get the hint and leave her alone.

No such luck.

Mercy and Bay trailed her to the library, their worry buzzing in Neve's ears. She ignored them.

"What are you looking for?" Bay asked as Neve marched into the demonology section. "Maybe I can help."

"Like you helped before?" Neve snapped, and Bay slunk

back a few steps, stung. Neither of her sisters tried to talk to her again as she tore through Maeve's meticulously organized collection. Before today, the Gate only opened when demons pushed their way through from Hell, but they'd opened it from this side to pull Alexandria through with them. If it was possible for them, it should be possible for her. Neve would smash through with her fists if she had to.

They had more books than she would ever read in this lifetime—maybe several lifetimes. Spellbooks and firsthand historical accounts and everything in between. Hundreds of books—*thousands*—and absolutely nothing about how to get into Hell. Neve didn't know why she was surprised, after there hadn't been a single mention of another Hellgate in their expansive collection, but it still made her want to scream the convent apart with frustration.

"Neve . . ." Bay tried again. Neve didn't know how much time had passed, but she whirled on her sister, another biting comment on her lips before Bay's expression stopped her short. Bay was holding one of the books Neve had abandoned, tossed behind her in her haste. Maeve was going to go apoplectic at the mess.

"Bee?" Mercy prodded when Bay didn't say anything.

Bay's eyes darted between the books Neve had discarded, her lips parting in horror. "Please tell me you're not serious."

Neve tilted her chin up in defiance.

"Serious about what?" Mercy demanded. She took a step closer, sensing Bay's agitation.

"You can't stop me," Neve said.

"Stop you from what?" Mercy insisted.

"She's going to try to get Alexandria back," Bay said softly, her voice strained like she was about to lose it. Her pupils were enormous. "Neve's trying to get into Hell."

CHAPTER TWENTY-SEVEN

Mercy's mouth dropped open, but she recovered quickly, her expression furious and incredulous by turns. "Quick question, are you fucking insane?"

"You can't stop me," Neve said again, hackles high.

"Like hell we can't!"

"I love her!" Neve cried, her voice ragged, scraped raw. "I love her and I'm not leaving her in there. I'm *going*. I'll find a way." She would find a way, the world be damned. The *chain* be damned. The chain, reincarnation . . . Neve would burn it all down to get Alexandria back.

Bay made a strangled noise and fled the library, her hair trailing like a red flag behind her.

"It's Hell!" Mercy said, lowering her voice. Neve shifted from foot to foot, fighting the urge to bend with the full force of Mercy's intensity bearing down on her. Mercy ran her hands through her hair, scraping it back like she did when she was trying to calm down. "It's Hell. Actual, literal Hell. How long do you think you'd last in there, even if there was a way in?"

"Long enough," Neve replied.

"You're grieving, it's—"

"I'm not *grieving.*" The word morphed in her mouth until it was just shy of a scream. "She's not dead, she was taken."

"Neve—"

"She's not dead!"

"Nemain, lower your voice."

Neve and Mercy spun toward Aoife's voice so fast and so completely in unison that it would've been funny under different circumstances. As it was, Neve didn't think she'd ever laugh again.

Daughter Aoife stood in the door of the library in her black nightgown, her severe mouth pinched so tight that her lips were white. Bay was behind her. Neve cast about for an excuse, a reason to be up against explicit orders for bed rest, but Daughter Aoife held up a hand.

"I think I know what you're looking for," she said. Her voice was measured, but Neve could see the wet shine of her eyes in the darkness. "Come with me."

Aoife didn't wait for any of them to respond before spinning on her slippered heel and leading the way out of the library. Bay was close behind, and after a moment of hesitation, Neve followed. Mercy brought up the rear, muttering under her breath the whole way.

Aoife walked past the doors to her and Clara's chambers and the infirmary to a third door at the end of the hall in the Daughters' wing. The room was small, crammed with books piled in every corner and overflowing from their shelves. Stray papers, maps, and bits of parchment sat on every available surface. They wouldn't have looked out of place in those weird, historically inaccurate period dramas Daughter Clara swore she didn't like.

It looked like the Three Crows, and the magic inside settled over Neve's skin like a blanket.

"Sit down," Aoife said, gesturing to one of the armchairs stuffed in a corner. Neve remained standing. "You're dead on your feet. Sit."

Neve slid into the chair, childhood instinct reacting to Aoife's tone of voice. Bay stayed by Aoife's side, her face still drained of color. Aoife watched Neve sit, her eyes narrowed and appraising. "You really love this girl?"

Neve blinked. That was not what she'd expected. "Yes."

A long, drawn-out sigh. "Fine."

"Aoife," Mercy said, hanging back by the door. She pulled her hands through her hair again. "I don't know what Bay told you—"

"She told me enough," Aoife said severely before turning and disappearing into the stacks of magical detritus that littered the room. She rifled through shelves and drawers, looking for gods only knew what.

"What are you doing?" Neve asked after a few moments. She fidgeted in the chair, loath to waste any more time.

"Trying to find a book," Aoife replied shortly. "And deciding whether or not to give it to you."

Gods damn it, this was not the time for some kind of contrived moral lesson.

"Badb tells me you're planning a jaunt into Hell," Aoife continued, her tone as casual as if they were going on a late-night snack run, despite her use of Bay's real name. Neve's blood chilled and she gripped the sides of the armchair so hard that the stuffing almost burst. She didn't think Bay would actually *tell* Aoife what she was planning. "I don't think I need to tell you what a *monumentally* stupid idea that is."

"I—"

"*You* can't open the Gate from this side, for one thing, and I doubt you have five humans who would be willing to put their lives on the line for you."

Five humans . . . Neve knew five humans. She hesitated, weighing the danger. She couldn't ask her friends to do this. She *wouldn't* ask them to do this.

But what if there was no other way?

"Say that I do," Neve said cautiously. Hope ignited in her chest, and she kept waiting for Aoife to crush it. "What's the problem then?"

Aoife sighed. "Despite your desperation to prove otherwise, you're mostly human, and you'll be hunted the moment you pass through."

Neve heard the tremor in Aoife's voice despite her usual steely demeanor, but she focused on the fact that it was possible. She could get in.

"I'll take my chances." Neve had already killed more demons than she thought was possible at her age, and she had her scream. She'd last long enough.

Aoife nodded, her mouth impossibly thin, and vanished among the bookshelves again, only the top of her head visible as she dug around for something. Behind her, Mercy grabbed Bay by the wrist and whispered furiously in her ear, too hushed for Neve to hear.

Mercy and Bay's whispering cut off sharply as Aoife finally returned with a book in her hands. The book didn't look like what Neve would have expected for what was essentially a road map to Hell. It was ordinary. Hardback and matte red, without a title or design on the cover.

"You're sure that's it?"

"What were you expecting?" Aoife asked sourly. "Something bound in human skin with a skull and crossbones on it?"

Neve stayed silent, because that was exactly what she'd expected. "And it'll work?"

"If humans cast it."

"Okay, *enough!*" Mercy stamped her foot, drawing everyone's attention to her. Her eyes were wild as she placed her hands on her hips, glaring at each of them.

"No," she said. "No. This is insane." She pointed at Neve. "You are not going to Hell. I know you love her, but Alexandria is *gone*, and there's nothing you can do about it."

Aoife shook her head. Neve didn't know what was worse, the sheen of tears in her eyes, or the tiny, miserable smile on her face. "You're wrong, dear. You've . . ." She swallowed hard. "Gods, you're running out of time. There's so much you don't know—any of you. There's so much we couldn't tell you. When you're inside, find the Three Crows. There's something there that might help you survive long enough to rescue Alexandria."

Aoife swallowed hard, pinching the bridge of her nose before she collected herself. "You'll find your answers there."

The Three Crows? How could they find the Three Crows where they were going?

"What is *wrong* with you people?" Mercy shouted. "'Find the Three Crows'? Aoife, that's *nothing*. Gods, when did I become the voice of reason in this family?"

"Mercy," Bay started.

Mercy held up her hands. They were shaking. "No. *No.* We're not doing this. We're not just *letting her walk into Hell.*"

"Of course not," Bay said, like it was obvious. "I'm going with her."

Neve's head snapped to Bay so hard that if she'd been human, she would've given herself whiplash. "What?"

"You're going and we can't stop you. But you're not going alone."

"*Bay!*" Mercy yelled.

Bay's gaze was unyielding as she looked back at Mercy, and for a second Neve thought they might start throwing punches—or worse, crying—when Mercy threw her arms up in the air.

"*Fine*, then. A little field trip to Hell, why not? Let's just go hang out in the place where literally everything wants us dead." She stormed toward the door. "I'm getting my weapons. Meet you at the armory."

Neve didn't know what to say, staring at the space Mercy had occupied a moment before. She hadn't asked them to come with her—she didn't *want* them to come with her—but she couldn't deny the rush of relief in her chest. She wouldn't be alone. She didn't have to do this alone.

The relief was quickly overwhelmed by gnawing guilt. They were leaving the Gate unprotected. She was putting everything on the line, and worst of all, Neve didn't care. She knew the risks, she knew the dangers, and she would make the same decision in a heartbeat.

"So dramatic," Aoife said, shaking her head. "Now take the book and get out before I change my mind."

"Why?" The question slipped out before Neve could stop it, but she had to know. Aoife shouldn't be helping her with this;

she should be magically locking Neve in her room for the rest of this lifetime.

Aoife took a deep breath, sadness flitting across her face for a moment before she hid it behind the stern mask. "Because it's what I would do if anything happened to Clara. Or you girls. Now go."

Neve was halfway out the door when she turned back. Her ribs twinged, and Aoife made a small *oof* as Neve pulled her into a crushing hug.

"Thank you," she whispered, her voice thick.

Aoife patted her on the head. "You're wasting time, Nemain. Go get your girl."

Neve nodded, swallowing hard around the lump in her throat, and fled Aoife's workshop without another word. She was halfway up the stairs when she pulled out her cracked phone and dialed.

"Morgan?" Tameka's voice was heavy with sleep, which Neve couldn't fault, considering it was almost midnight. "Why are you calling me?"

Neve sucked in a breath. She needed them, but she had to give them a choice. The truth, if they asked for it. "I need your help."

"You need my help in the middle of the night?"

"I need you to get the others and meet me past the warning signs on the beach. Right under the convent."

"Shit, Morgan, what the hell is going on? Are you okay?"

"No," Neve said in a rush. She clenched her fists to keep her hands from shaking. "No, I'm not, but I need you. All of you."

Tameka only hesitated for another second.

"We'll be there."

CHAPTER TWENTY-EIGHT

I s anyone going to tell me what the *hell* is going on?"
Simon demanded when Neve and her sisters arrived on
the beach.

Mercy had been uncharacteristically silent as they made
their way down to the water, hostile energy crackling around
her like Aoife's magic. Bay's quiet was less aggressive, and
Neve wanted to say how grateful she was that they were coming with her, but she kept her mouth shut, sure that as soon
as she said anything, Bay would come to her senses and drag
her home.

The whole group was there, huddled together in the dark,
illuminated by the beams of a car's headlights. Neve noticed
their unease at Bay and Mercy's presence. They'd gotten used
to one Morgan's worth of weirdness, but the full set was something else altogether, especially in the middle of the night.

"I need your help," Neve started. This was her idea, her
girlfriend, her friends. She had to lead. "I—I know it's late, but
I can't do this without you."

"Do what?" Michael asked, crossing his arms over his chest.
His gaze darted between Bay and Mercy and the convent

looming above them. He'd always bought into the spookiness of the Morgan mythos more than the others.

"Where's Alexandria?" Tameka added.

"Look," Neve said, trying to find a way to articulate herself without sending them running. Part of her hoped Bay would step in and explain—she was so much better at talking to people—but no such luck. "I can tell you everything right now, but you might not want to know. And you'll never be able to go back to the way things were."

Silence dragged on for a few seconds too long, and Neve was sure that they were going to turn around and leave.

"Just spit it out," Simon said at last. Mercy twitched, reacting to Simon's tone, but Bay placed a hand on her arm. "You're acting even weirder than usual. Where's Alexandria and *why* did we have to have this very creepy meet-up in the middle of the night?"

"And, um . . . no offense, but why did you bring your sisters?" Ilma asked. Mercy waved with a grim smile that set absolutely no one at ease.

"Hell," Neve said, her nerves making her even more blunt than usual. She pointed to the cliff behind her, watching each of their expressions. "Alexandria is in Hell and I need you five to open the Gate so I can go in and get her."

None of them ran away. Not yet, at least.

"And you're not a part of this, why?" Ilma asked, her reassuring tone coming out a little too forced.

It wasn't the first question she would've asked, but Neve took it as an encouraging sign. "Because it needs to be done by humans. And I'm . . . not one." The admission hung in the air for a few long, *long* moments.

"We're not either," Mercy said, pointing to her and Bay. "For the record. Oh, and we hunt demons who try to come through there." She jabbed a thumb over her shoulder at the Gate.

"Mercy," Bay warned.

"What?" Mercy asked. "Apparently we're being honest with the locals. I'm just trying to keep up now that *you two* have torn up the rule book."

"Okay, I'm out," Michael said, holding up his hands. "I'm sorry, this is too much for me. All this witchy stuff was funny when we were kids, but this is too weird."

"Gods damn it, I don't have time for this. Every minute we waste out here is another minute Alexandria is stuck—" Neve started, desperate.

"Stuck where?" Puck added their voice to the din. "Hell?"

"Yes, Hell," Neve spat. She swore again, kicking at a rock. Gods, she was terrible at this and she didn't have *time* to convince them.

"I've got an idea," Mercy chimed in again. The joking tone in her voice had an icy edge as she flipped a knife out of a sheath on her hip.

"Hey now," Tameka said, taking several steps back and raising her hands. "Let's not do anything stupid."

Behind her, Puck put their arm out in front of Ilma, as if prepared to shield her from whatever came next. Neve hated the fear on their faces.

"You wanted proof," Neve said, guessing Mercy's plan.

Bay shook her head at the theatrics as Mercy jammed the knife into her forearm, blue blood pearling where her blade stabbed into her flesh. It shone under the glare of the headlights, sparkling and distinctly not human.

"What the hell is *that*?"

"Blood," Neve said. "Mine looks like that too."

None of them said anything. They just kept staring as the shallow cut began to knit itself together before their eyes. That was one way to convince them that she was telling the truth.

"Happy now?" Neve asked as Mercy flicked blood into the sand and stowed the knife away again.

No one spoke. Maybe they were in shock or maybe they needed more proof. Neve didn't know, but she wasn't willing to wait around until they got used to the idea that a blue-blooded freak of nature had been hanging out with them for the past few months. She wanted to scream. This was a mistake. She didn't have time to tell them the whole story, and more important, *Alexandria* didn't have time.

"Demons." Ilma's voice cut through the thick silence. "Is that what worked you over last week? Because you didn't get hit by a car." Everyone turned to her and she shrugged. "My mom works at the hospital. She would've told me if Neve had been admitted."

"And you were just sitting on this information?" Michael demanded.

"I figured she had her reasons."

"Yes," Neve cut in, eager to speed this along. "Yes, I got the shit kicked out of me by demons and yes, demons took Alexandria, and the only way I can get to her is if you five help me."

"Because you need to get into Hell," Tameka said slowly.

"Yes."

"And rescue Alexandria. Who is also in Hell."

"Yes."

"And you can't do it because you aren't human. None of you are."

"*Yes.*"

Amazingly, Tameka shrugged. "I'm down." Michael and Simon gaped at her. "I mean, come on. It explains some things. No offense, Morgan, but you've never been normal. If you say demons, then sure, demons."

"I'm in too," Ilma added. Puck nodded their assent and Neve's heart swelled. Three out of five. She might be able to pull this off after all.

"Simon?" Tameka turned to the boys, both of whom stood pale and silent.

"You're not going to be in any danger," Neve promised. "It's just to get us inside. I'll protect you."

A laugh bubbled out of Michael, high-pitched and half-hysterical. "You're going to protect us? You're . . . you're in *high school.*"

"I'm a thousand years old," Neve said, the truth heavy on her tongue. Bay laid a hand on her shoulder and Mercy pressed in close, flanking her like Neve was leading them into battle. "My family has protected this world for lifetimes. I promise I'll keep you safe now."

"Okay," Simon said softly.

Michael's head whipped to the side, his mouth parting in disbelief. "You cannot be serious."

"I just saw someone bleed the wrong color. I'm willing to go with it."

"Jesus Christ, *fine.* If you guys want to go along with this insanity, then fine." Michael squared his shoulders and looked Neve dead in the eyes. "What do we have to do?"

It was a simple spell. As it turned out, all it took to open the literal entrance to Hell was a few candles, five humans, a pentagram drawn in the sand, and some chanting in a long-forgotten dialect.

Setting up the pentagram was just a matter of Neve dragging her foot along the sand until they had the approximate shape, and then they each took their places along the five points.

"This is way more cinematic in movies," Tameka grumbled when Neve handed her the red-bound spellbook. Nervous laughter tittered along the beach.

"Just read the words," Neve instructed, touching her weapons to calm her heart. "The pronunciation doesn't matter, it's about feeling. You need to *mean* it." Neve's eyes found Michael. "You need to believe that Alexandria is in there."

Tameka had been the first to agree, so she started, setting the candle at her feet as she read from the book. The flame flickered and danced as she butchered the words, but the buzz in Neve's blood told her that it was working. Ilma, Puck, and Simon all read their bits and with every verse, the hum of magic grew stronger, until Neve felt it vibrating in her bones. Wind whipped around their heads and the roar of the waves beating against the sand grew louder and more frantic, as if nature itself was objecting to what they were trying to do. In her ears, the hum grew so loud that it was nearly a shriek.

"Michael, I'm going to need you to finish up," Neve said, tense.

The book trembled in Michael's hands and he had to shout to be heard over the waves, but moments later the spell was completed. The final words had been spoken.

"Shouldn't something be—?"

The flames from the candles leaped until they were five feet tall, holding their height for a few seconds before guttering out.

"Did it work?" Ilma whispered, her dark eyes darting to Neve.

The Hellgate answered for her. The cliffside began to warp, churning and black, and from the inside, something roared so loud that the cliff shook.

"Don't move!" Neve shouted, knowing what was about to happen a split second before it did. "Whatever happens, don't move!"

Neve prayed that they would listen as she turned her back to her friends to face whatever monster was bearing down on them. It was massive and furry, almost bear-like, with claws like corkscrews and too many eyes. Black drool sizzled out of a gaping maw.

"Finally," Mercy snarled, her voice low with rage. She lunged, swinging her two-handed sword as Bay spun her scythe. Their weapons hit at the same time, cleaving the demon into three uneven pieces. The creature roared once

more before exploding into hellfire and dusting them all with demon ash.

"Is everyone okay?" Neve demanded, rushing back to her friends. Miraculously, the pentagram was unbroken. The Gate was still open.

"We're okay," Puck answered. Their voice shook.

"So . . . this is what you do on your weekends?" Tameka asked unsteadily, staring at the place where the demon had evaporated.

"Pretty much." Neve looked at all of them, these unlikely friends she'd made. These impossible humans who'd given her a way to find Alexandria, who'd given her a chance. Who kept protecting her, even if they didn't know it. She didn't know how to thank them. "I'll be back soon. Don't break the pentagram until we're through."

Neve had never been good at goodbyes.

"Ready?" Bay signed when Neve joined them at the open Gate.

Neve sucked in a ragged breath. If she died now, that was the end of them. There would be no more lifetimes, nothing standing between Hell and the rest of the world. She could die. She could end everything.

But not today. Not without finding Alexandria and bringing her home.

"Yes," Neve answered. Her voice didn't shake.

Hands slipped into hers, Mercy on her right and Bay on her left. Neve held them tight as she took a step forward and plunged through the Gate.

CHAPTER TWENTY-NINE

Neve didn't have time to brace herself before pain tore through her body. It felt as if every single bone had been broken, every tendon severed, every ligament shredded into a million tiny pieces. Her nerves screamed as Neve was destroyed, ripped apart, and then, just as quickly, put back together again.

Her eyes remained closed for a few long minutes after she became aware that she wasn't, in fact, dying a gruesome and horrible death. Her breathing was shallow and shaky as she tried to force her lungs to work again.

Then she threw up. Twice.

Neve expected fire and brimstone. She expected winged demons circling through hazy orange skies. She expected Dante's Hell, the nightmarish landscape that had haunted her dreams for as long as she could remember.

She didn't expect the ocean. She especially didn't expect *her* ocean.

"Mercy?" Neve croaked when the breath returned to her lungs. Her throat burned with bile as she straightened to look for her sisters. They hadn't gone far, and both of them looked better than she felt. For the millionth time, Neve wished to be eighteen. "What is this?"

They were home. On the beach, looking out at the water as if they'd just turned around at the Hellgate. As if they hadn't gone anywhere at all.

Mercy's mouth was open, confusion plain on her features before she sucked in a deep breath and schooled her expression into something more neutral. "It's a trick," she said. "It's an illusion or something." She swung her sword in a tight arc, as if she could cut through to the real Hell.

"Is it?" Bay asked softly, and despite Mercy's confident tone, Neve could sense her uncertainty. Bay knelt, bringing her fingertips to the jagged sand before standing up again. "What Aoife said . . . Maybe this—maybe this *is* Hell."

Neve didn't know what to do with that. This wasn't right. This wasn't what it was supposed to look like, and the cognitive dissonance was giving her a headache.

It was an illusion, then, a trick like Mercy said. It had to be.

Beyond the rocky shoreline, the ocean was black, froth turning the waves inky-gray where they hit the beach. The sky had been dark when she walked through the Gate, but instead of a sunrise, the world was hazy and twilit.

Aoife had said they were wrong, that the Daughters had kept things from them. But *this*? This was too much. Unease prickled along the back of Neve's neck and she shook her head.

They didn't have time for this—Alexandria didn't have time for this. They could figure out the answers later.

"We need to get moving," Neve said. She doubted that their arrival had gone unnoticed and she wasn't eager to meet the welcoming party.

"The Three Crows," Bay said, repeating Aoife's instructions.

Neve didn't even know if the Three Crows existed in this warped version of their world, but Bay sounded certain and Aoife had said it might help them get to Alexandria. She looked to Mercy, who nodded, her grip still tight on her sword.

Hang on, Alexandria, Neve thought as they began their trek from the beach. *I'm here. I'm coming to get you.*

Without a car, it should have taken only an hour to get into town, but it was difficult to tell time through the haze. However similar this shadow world was to her own, it seemed to have forgone technology entirely. There were no electric lights dotting the roadside, no telephone wires strung parallel to the streets. Cars didn't line the roadways, and the roads themselves seemed paved as an afterthought, more rough stone than concrete. It was all so strange, and the farther they walked without the world giving way to brimstone and hell-fire, the twitchier Mercy became.

Things got even weirder the closer they came to town. Neve recognized everything: Main Street, Hawthorne Lane, the little hobby shop on Chestnut. Structurally, it was all there.

The roads led where they'd always led, and the buildings were the same as they'd been her entire life. Even the Dunkin' was in its rightful place.

It was a mirror, a reflection distorted just enough to make Neve's skin crawl. The colors were wrong. Everything was muted or too bright without any shades in between. Garish neon battled against the dull grays and dingy browns surrounding her. The haze kept everything half-lit. In many places, nature had taken over. Roots burst out of the street in random intervals, and creeping vines had claimed several buildings as their own. Neve had no idea how vines managed to look threatening, but she had the feeling that they weren't quite the vegetation she was used to. She had a vivid mental image of being swallowed up, encircled and crushed if she got too close.

Note to self: stay away from the shrubbery.

Neve took a surreptitious peek at her phone. The screen was black, and it wouldn't rouse no matter how hard she jammed the power button. "Hell *would* be pre–Industrial Revolution," Neve complained, mostly to break the festering silence. Neither of her sisters answered.

Before Neve could take another step, Bay's outstretched forearm stopped her in her tracks. Her eyes were pitch black. Neve froze. Bay's sudden silence could only mean demons, and the three of them crept forward, hands on their weapons.

All at once, the streets weren't empty. They were filled with . . . Neve didn't know what. Given Bay's reaction, they had to be demons, but none of them looked like the monstrosities that broke through the Gate. They looked *human*. Nearly. Like Neve was seeing them through an altered reflection. Their skin was slightly too bright, as if suffused with light, their eyes too pigmented. They were oversaturated. Human-adjacent.

"What the shit?" Mercy murmured. She pressed close, muscles tensed in preparation to attack. Neve followed suit, gripping the hilts of her weapons tight enough that it hurt.

"Wait," Bay signed before either of them could move. "Look."

None of the demons had noticed them. None of them even looked at them sideways. They just kept moving, some alone, some in pairs or bigger groups. Like . . . like *people*. Like they weren't monsters made of pure malice, hell-bent on ripping into the world and destroying everything in their path. Like they just *lived* here.

Mercy swore under her breath, but there was a strange, wild look in her eyes. Neve felt it echo in her chest, churning confusion that shattered through the three of them, shaking the triad to its core. These demons weren't trying to get out. They weren't making for the Hellgate. *Why?*

"We need to keep moving," Neve insisted, extricating herself from the icy swirl of emotion pinning them in place. They could have a collective identity crisis when Alexandria was home, not before.

They almost made it. Bay led the way to the Three Crows, skirting crowds who never looked at them twice. Mercy brought up the rear, so tense that she was a breath away from snapping. Neve wanted to ask if she was okay, but she bit the inside of her cheek and swallowed the question. Of course she wasn't okay. None of them was okay right now. They were in Hell. But also not. Maybe. Neve's head hurt.

Then, for the second time, Neve bumped into Bay as she froze. Neve's breath hissed through her teeth and she went for her weapons again, expecting trouble.

"Brigid?" Bay whispered, her voice raspy but undeniable as she stared at a little girl in their path. Bay's horror thrummed in Neve's chest.

The girl turned to them, and for a moment she looked like the rest of the creatures milling about. She was young, elementary-school age. Doe-brown eyes found them, and Neve suddenly felt like the world was tilting under the terrible weight of this strange girl's gaze. Bay was wrong; she had to be wrong. This couldn't be Brigid. Brigid was missing. She was one of them, was *family*.

Then everything went sideways. The girl's eyes turned flat black, and all the life leached out of her skin. *"You."*

"Brigid," Bay said again, her voice even fainter.

"Morrigan," Brigid hissed, and Neve's blood turned cold at the sound of her family's true name spat like a curse. The girl demon stalked forward, half-feral with rage, and Neve's ears popped as the barometric pressure plummeted. "Morrigan!" she shrieked.

Their name rippled through the crowd, and all the demons who'd ignored them started looking all around. It was like they were electrified, mobilized and scrambling where they'd been peaceful just a moment before.

"Morrigan! Morrigan!" Faster than Neve could unsheathe her weapons, the crowd of demons started screaming. They were out for blood.

Their blood.

CHAPTER THIRTY

Y ou've got to be kidding me," Mercy snarled. Her sword was out in earnest this time, blessed steel glinting wickedly in the half light.

The street was in chaos. Everywhere Neve looked, demons streamed about, some wielding weapons, some only fists. Above the din of stamping footsteps and the clamor of voices, one word rang like a clarion cry:

"Morrigan! Morrigan! Morrigan!"

"Traitors," Brigid snarled in a voice much too deep to come out of such a young mouth. She stalked through the churning crowd with deadly intent.

"Wait—" Bay started as Mercy moved to charge the tiny demon, but her voice was gone again and Mercy was beyond stopping. So was Neve, for that matter. She couldn't take this anymore—the strangeness and uncertainty. She needed something familiar, and the hatred in Brigid's eyes was the same as in every demon who'd ever come through the Gate. Neve could deal with hatred.

"Come get some!" Mercy roared. Neve ducked around Bay's still-outstretched hand and darted forward to follow before a stampede of demons rushed between them, a mass of bodies so thick that it obscured her vision of her sisters.

They weren't attacking. They were running, scurrying over the cracked pavement and disappearing into the shadowy versions of buildings Neve had known all her life. They were *scared*.

"Where do you think you're going?"

Neve pulled up short as the single biggest person—demon, *whatever*—she'd ever seen stepped into her path. He loomed over her by more than a foot, and most of his face was concealed by a monstrously bushy beard almost as red as Neve's hair.

The hammer in his hands pulled most of her focus. Not just because it could crack her skull like an egg, but because of the sense of déjà vu that nearly bowled her over. Pain flashed behind her eyes, as if her mind was trying to correct what she was seeing by force. It felt like the moment just after a camera flash, when the too-bright afterimage hasn't settled.

Metal clanging and snarled obscenities dragged her attention back. Neve adjusted her grip on her weapons, shifting from foot to foot as she sized up the obstacle that stood between her and her sisters.

"Morrigan," he rumbled darkly, spitting her name like Brigid had, like it was a curse.

Gritting her teeth, Neve didn't answer before she darted into his guard, managing one clean strike before he moved on her. She was hysterically outmatched, but she wasn't going to let it stop her. Her sisters couldn't afford for her to let it stop her.

He was too fast for something his size, pursuing Neve with relentless determination no matter how she tried to dance out of his way. After her surprise attack, she couldn't get close enough for another, and a single hit from that hammer would be enough to end this rescue mission before it began.

The hammer strikes left craters where they fell, getting closer and closer to Neve with every blow. Despite the Daughters' complaints, sparring with Mercy had taught Neve to recognize when she was in a no-win scenario. This was one of those times. She couldn't beat him; right now the best she could hope for was to escape.

"Enough!" The haze was so dense that Neve could see her voice ripple through the air as the word shifted into a scream.

Her power hit him as he held the hammer aloft, preparing for another devastating blow, and Neve took advantage of his momentary stillness to rush past. She ducked underneath his arms, sword flinging out desperately to slice at his ankle.

Neve didn't know if, or for how long, her little trick would incapacitate him, but she heard his roar of pain and felt the road vibrate as he collapsed onto the street.

Bay and Mercy were in a battle of their own by the time Neve got to them, spinning and slashing so fast that their limbs blurred, but Brigid was everywhere, tearing at any bit of exposed skin, too fast for either of them to get a hit on her. They were losing.

Neve's fists tightened around her weapons, fury coloring her vision scarlet. This time the air rippled more violently as she screamed, like the sound might tear through the very fabric of this world.

Brigid should have been frozen by the force of Neve's scream, but it only slowed her. She turned to Neve, her eyes narrowing.

"Nema—"

Neve's name was barely halfway out of Brigid's mouth when the curved silver tip of Bay's scythe burst from the center of her chest. Brigid fell to her knees, making a horrible, wet sound as Bay ripped her scythe free.

It took a moment for Neve to realize that Brigid was *laughing*.

"We knew . . ." Brigid hacked. Dark liquid dribbled out of her mouth. "We knew you'd come back. He promised you would."

"Who?" Neve demanded, taking a step closer to Brigid's crumpled form. Bay moved as well, stepping in front of Neve to keep her from getting too close. Neve fought the urge to shove past.

"You really have no clue, do you?" Brigid spat a glob of

blood onto the pavement. "He knew you'd come back. He knew." Her voice cracked, but she managed one more hacking laugh that scraped down Neve's spine. "You're not getting away from us again. Never again."

Her breath gurgled in her throat and Neve saw the exact moment she died, the hateful light leaving her eyes wide and glassy. Her mouth tugged up in a pained, victorious smile, and Neve flinched away from an explosion of burning ash that didn't come. Brigid's body simply lay there, crumpled in the place it had fallen.

"Bay . . ." Mercy started, turning to Bay with wide eyes. Bay was still eerily silent, but tears flowed down her face, cutting clean streaks through the blue-gold speckles of blood on her cheeks.

Neve's stomach swooped again. The blood on her face wasn't Bay's. This time she dodged her sister's attempt to stop her as she inched closer to Brigid's still-intact body. It wasn't an illusion or a trick or a mistake. It was *real*.

The blood already drying on her mouth and staining her middle where Bay had slashed her stomach to ribbons was wrong. It was too dark to be human, but not black like Neve had first thought. It was blue. A very particular shade of blue that caught the dim light and flashed gold. Just like hers.

"No." Mercy shook her head, backing away from the body as if Brigid was going to get up and start fighting them all over again. Her eyes were on the demon's blood—*their* blood. Bay didn't move, still as a statue save for the tears still carving trails down her cheeks. "This is wrong," Mercy said, shaking her head again like she was trying to dislodge something behind her eyes. "I can't—Bay, this is wrong."

"I see it too," Bay signed, shaking off the stillness for a moment. "I . . ." Her fingers twitched, hesitating. "I see it. It's really her."

"See what?" Neve demanded. She was already shaken from the fight, from Brigid and everything that was wrong with this place, but what scared her the most were the looks her sisters exchanged. Neve sensed their confusion, their fear, and some kind of horrible understanding as they looked around this hellish mirror world.

Before either of them could answer, the ground shook and Neve saw the hammer-wielding man limping toward them. Part of her wanted to stay and fight now that it was three-on-one, but one look at Bay and Mercy told her that whatever they were seeing—whatever Neve couldn't remember—they weren't going to be much help.

Run, instinct urged. *Run and hide. Live to fight again.*

"Come on," Neve whispered, stowing her weapons despite the part of her that keened for more bloodshed. Bloodshed was simple and reliable. It was *easy*. "Come on, we've got to go." She grabbed her sisters' hands and hauled them away. It took some doing to get them to move, but eventually Mercy broke into a sprint, taking the lead. As Bay picked up speed, Neve took a single glance backward.

Brigid had known them. She'd known Neve, known her name—her true name. *He knew you'd come back.* It didn't make any sense. How could they come *back*, unless—

Unless they'd been here before.

The thought hit her like a blow, and Neve wrenched her eyes away from Brigid's body. No. Mercy was right; that was impossible. It was a trick.

But if your blood is the same, whispered the voice from her nightmares, *what does that make you and your sisters?*

Neve followed Mercy blindly, and by the time she blinked the grit from her eyes, they were in front of the Three Crows. It wasn't theirs and it wasn't home, but it was something, and Neve plunged through the front door. Her throat was hot, a scream building behind her teeth, but there was no one to fight, no monster to take the brunt of her anger and fear.

The shop was barren, stripped of the books, the homemade remedies, the decorative geodes that Mercy loved and Aoife hated. It was all gone, or maybe it had never been there in the first place. Only the bones remained, the ancient wood and mortar that held the place together.

Mercy and Bay were still silent as Neve barred the door behind them—not Bay's battle-born silence but something startled and awful, like they couldn't bring themselves to speak the truth of what they'd seen. They looked unmoored, gazing around the Three Crows like they weren't seeing it at all. Like something else was occupying their vision.

"Mercy," Neve started. Her stomach turned at the glassy look in Mercy's eyes. "Merce, what's going on?"

"I . . ." Mercy started, her voice smaller than Neve had ever heard it. "I *remember*."

CHAPTER THIRTY-ONE

How? How could Mercy possibly remember this place? How could she remember Hell?

It's not Hell and you know it, hissed the boy's voice in the back of her head. It was louder now, humming out of time with her jackrabbit heart.

"Mercy," Bay said gently, laying a hand on Mercy's shoulder. "It's—"

"It's *bullshit,*" Mercy snarled, lashing out at the wall and putting a hole through it. "This isn't *right!*"

"You know that it is," Bay said softly.

"No." Mercy roared, slamming both fists against the remains of the wooden countertop and reducing it to splinters. She paced like a caged animal, her frenzy making Neve's blood race. It didn't make any sense. How could they have been here before? And if the Daughters knew—

If the Daughters knew, then they'd been lying to them for as long as Neve had been alive. Longer. Since the cycles of death and rebirth had begun.

"I think . . ." Bay said softly. "We *made* this place." Her eyes were far away, clouded by memories. "It's an echo, just separate enough from our world not to be able to interact with it, but they're still connected. I think we wanted to make someplace new entirely, but it didn't . . . it didn't work. So we dropped a veil over the whole world and left to guard the only way through. We left them all behind."

Neve blinked, her breathing shallow as she tried to absorb it all. Echoes and veils and—

"How is that *possible*? What does that make us?" Neve asked. Not gods, surely. Her headache pounded behind her eyes. It felt like she was coming undone. "If we *did* this . . . what are we?"

Bay shook her head. "I . . . I—"

"Isn't it obvious?" Mercy said when Bay faltered. Her voice dropped, low and soft and so much worse than shouting. "We're the same as them. This is where the pantheon went. We've been killing our *family*."

Neve reeled, trying to piece it all together, trying to force it to make sense. Something in her relaxed into the explanation even while her heart screamed that it couldn't be true. "But what *are* we?"

"Old," Bay murmured. "I think we're very . . . very old." It wasn't a good enough answer, but Bay's eyes closed, her mouth trembling before she spoke again. "Aoife knew. They all knew. I think she wanted to tell us, but there wasn't enough time."

Aoife had sent them to the Three Crows for a reason; she must have known this would happen, that this place's connection to them in both worlds would trigger whatever latent memories they'd left behind. Was that what Aoife had meant by sending them here? It couldn't be. Mercy and Bay were devastated. They had answers, but they were in no shape to fight.

You're mostly human. That's what Aoife had said, and it was the human part that was slowing her down, putting them all at risk.

Which meant it was the human part that had to go in order for Neve to survive long enough to bring Alexandria home. She sucked in a breath, half-expecting to be flattened by memories now that she'd figured it out, but nothing happened. Her headache persisted, the humming building to a scream as Neve realized that Aoife hadn't just sent them here for the truth; she'd sent them here to force Neve's abilities to manifest early.

Only, it hadn't worked. Aoife's gamble had failed.

A glance out the window revealed the dimming sky. They were wasting time.

Remember why you're here. Neve sucked in a breath, inhaling panic and forcing it back out. Aoife thought they all needed to be fully manifested to face whatever was waiting for them. Neve's hands shook and she clenched her fists to keep them still. They would have to be enough as is.

"We have to keep moving," she said. "Alexandria—"

Neve's voice was drowned out by a howl from outside. The single note pierced the air like the low bray of a hunting horn, and Neve knew without a doubt that they were what was being hunted.

"Where do we go?" Neve asked, turning to Bay desperately. Bay would know what to do. Bay always knew what to do. She could get them through this. "Aoife said to come here, but I don't—Bay, I don't know where to go."

Bay's mouth opened and closed before she shook her head. "I don't know," she signed, her voice disappearing again in anticipation of the fight coming to their doorstep. "I don't know."

"I do," Mercy growled. "You've got to go home."

"What?"

Mercy huffed, scraping her bangs back over her sweaty forehead. "This whole thing—all of it—started at the convent. It's the only other place with the strongest connection to us."

"*We* have to go home," Neve said. "We all have to go." It was obvious, now that she thought about it. Neve ground her teeth; she should have realized sooner.

Mercy smiled, and in an instant, all her rage gave way to grief. Neve choked on her mourning—mourning *them*, who they'd been and who they'd thought they were before all this.

Neve wanted to shake her, to snap her out of this. There

was a hunted, haunted look in her eyes that Neve couldn't read. The howl rang out again and Neve could hear the pounding of dozens of feet—too many for them to fight, not now.

"Take her home, Badb," Mercy said, straightening. For a second she looked like a soldier, before Neve saw how close she was to coming apart. She was traumatized and angry, so grief-stricken that Neve didn't know how she was still standing, and just about the bravest person Neve had ever seen. "I'll give you time."

"No," Bay signed, her fingers punctuating the air furiously. "We go together."

"They'll run us down," Mercy said. She pulled out her broadsword, holding it with both hands. Her eyes found Neve's, pinning her in place. "You have to save Alexandria. That's the point of us, right? And I have to save you." She smiled again, tearful. "That's the point of me."

Mercy thought she was going to die. Neve could feel it. She thought this was her last stand, and she didn't care. She was going to do it anyway, to give Neve a chance.

"Mercy—"

"I love you," Mercy said. Her lips curled into a snarl and before Neve or Bay could stop her, she burst out of the Three Crows.

"No!" Neve shouted, moving to go after her, but Bay grabbed her by the arm and held her fast. "Let me *go*."

Bay's grip didn't relent. Beyond the walls, Mercy's shouts and taunts carried over the noise of the demons hunting them.

"Stay quiet," Bay ordered before dragging Neve out of the shop. They hugged the wall, and Neve's breath caught in her throat at the massive crowd of creatures that had been about to descend on them. There were too many. Mercy couldn't fight them all.

"We have to help her," Neve hissed. Bay's hand clapped over her mouth and Neve fought the urge to bite her.

"She's giving us a chance," Bay signed shakily. "She made her choice. We have to keep moving."

Neve wanted to scream. She wanted to demand how Bay could even suggest that they leave Mercy behind, and she would've done it if she didn't feel Bay's despair thundering through her. Bay was barely keeping it together, and Neve knew that if she kept fighting, her sister would shatter.

"She's going to make it," Neve declared when Bay released her. Like if she said it out loud she could force it to be true. She refused to believe that she'd led her sisters here to die.

Emulating Bay's silence, Neve crept away from the Three Crows, away from the crowd that wanted to rip them limb from limb. She only looked back once, to see Mercy staying just ahead of the horde, her teeth flashing as bright as her sword as she hacked at anything that came too close.

Please, Neve prayed. She prayed to Mercy. Her sister, her protector, one-third of her soul. *Please come back to us.* Mercy would live. She would find a way. She would survive this— they would all survive this. They had to.

CHAPTER THIRTY-TWO

Neve and Bay moved quickly, picking through ruined streets as the gray half-light turned into true darkness. Neve braced for an ambush around every corner, seeing eyes that glowed with predatory malice in every twisted shell of the buildings she'd known. Neve flipped Alexandria's hood over her hair, as if it could protect her from the watchful eyes of the creatures hunting them.

Nothing attacked. She could hear movement in some of the structures, but whatever manner of creatures hid within, they weren't the warlike sort. Not like the horde hunting Mercy.

Not like Neve and her sisters.

The thought made her stomach turn. How could they have gotten it all so wrong? If they were the same creatures they'd killed for millennia, why did they leave? Neve couldn't fathom it—couldn't wrap her head around the fact that they'd been living a lie for a thousand years. She was still disconnected from her memories, but Mercy and Bay hadn't known either. Whatever they'd done, for whatever reason, they never intended to come back.

Bay tapped her, dragging Neve's attention back to the

present. "You okay?" she asked. Her voice still hadn't returned as they made their way back home.

Home. Where the Daughters had raised them, knowing that they were the same monsters they'd been fighting for centuries. Where their caregivers, their guardians, the closest thing they had to parents, had been lying to them since the day they'd been reborn and every cycle since the whole damn thing started.

"Fine," Neve lied.

Bay's thumb touched her temple before coming together with her other thumb by her chin. "Memories?" she asked, as if they still might turn up at any moment.

Maybe they would, Neve didn't know. The rule book she'd followed her entire life had been doused with gasoline and set alight in front of her, and now it was all she could do not to get burned.

Neve shook her head. She didn't want to talk about any of this.

She *wanted* to get Alexandria back. She wanted to go back home to the lie she'd known her entire life. The lie that was her identity and her purpose. She wanted to forget all this.

You already did, remember? hissed the voice in the back of her head. She felt like she was being torn in half. A battle for her soul, her heart. Neve clenched her fists around the hilts of her weapons, too tight. Her grip slipped and Neve hissed under her breath as a line of blue-gold opened up on her palm. The pain was a distraction and a reminder. None of this mattered. *Alexandria* was her heart, and whatever they'd done to this place, Neve would do it all over again to keep Alexandria safe.

Somehow they made it to the convent without being spotted, and for the first time, Neve really noticed what an imposing figure the Gothic structure cut against the sky. Looking at it looming on the cliffside, she could understand why so many people in town thought that they were witches. Neve used to think that the truth was better, but it was actually so much worse.

"Wait," Bay signed, holding out a hand to stop Neve before she got too close. "It's warded."

Neve didn't know how Bay knew, but she didn't question it, even though the thought of stopping when she was so close made her want to tear her hair out. What the hell were they supposed to do now?

The air swished as Bay swung her scythe in an experimental circle. The steel flashed against something invisible that Neve hadn't sensed and Bay frowned.

"I can get through it." Bay swung her scythe again. "It's going to take a moment. Cover me."

Neve nodded, holding her weapons tight to her chest and pressing herself against Bay's back. No doubt whatever had put up the ward was sending scouts to find out who was trying to break through.

It wasn't long until heavy footfalls pounded against the broken path that surrounded the convent. Six demons rounded the corner in tight formation, all bristling with weapons.

Neve couldn't take that many. Not even close. With her full strength, maybe, but not as she was. Not alone, and Bay needed time to get them through the wards around the convent. Fear thrilled her blood, coursing like poison, and for a second Neve wanted to throw down her weapons and run.

Neve ground her teeth, hating herself for her own weakness. She was too close, and she'd already lost too much. Her childhood, her identity—Mercy. She wasn't giving up now.

Neve didn't let them get close before she sucked in a breath and screamed. Her voice was hoarse and she was terrified and exhausted, but it was enough. The demons stopped in their tracks. One dropped his weapons in his attempt to get away from her as quickly as possible.

Hurry, Bay, she thought, darting between the paralyzed guards, slashing and stabbing with her sword and dagger before skipping out of their reach. Her scream died in her throat and Neve knew that their fear would wear out quickly. The guard who'd dropped his weapons went down first as Neve stuck her dagger through his ribs and then slashed his throat open when he staggered.

She managed glancing blows off the others' weapons as they began to move, shaking off the paralysis and advancing again. *Shit.* Neve snarled as a fist clipped her in the chin. She was quickly surrounded, still focused on keeping the guards away from Bay, when something slammed into her left shoulder. Neve felt the pressure first, before pain made her vision white out, and she staggered. She blinked back to herself to see a dagger buried in her flesh up to the hilt.

"Morrigan bitch," the demon snarled. Her bloody-red eyes burned. Neve tried to move, to scramble away, but she couldn't risk opening Bay up to an attack. "Not so superior now, are you?"

Neve braced for a killing blow, closing her eyes in anticipation of pain that never came. She opened her eyes to see Bay moving like a lightning strike, twirling her scythe so fast that it was just a metallic blur.

The guards staggered away, unprepared for such a furious assault, but instead of tearing them down, Bay turned. Her scythe stopped moving for a single second as she reached for Neve and shoved with all her considerable strength. Neve stumbled back, falling through a field of static before she managed to right herself.

"No!" Neve shouted, springing forward to grab Bay's hand, to bring her through too, but whatever hole Bay had cut through the convent's protections sealed as soon as Neve was through. Neve slammed her fists against the intangible barrier, pain lighting up her nerves as magic sparked against her skin.

Bay's mouth flicked up and she nodded, satisfied, before turning back to the advancing creatures. She didn't fight, just ran, blowing past them faster than they could keep up, her scythe swinging on either side of her body like a deadly twirler's baton. Leading them away from Neve. Giving her a chance before reinforcements came.

Neve screamed, a human scream this time, and slammed her fists against the barrier one more time as Bay vanished out of her sight. She was gone. Her sisters were gone. And Neve was back where she'd started. Alone.

CHAPTER THIRTY-THREE

She was wasting time. It took Neve too long to turn around and face the shadowy facsimile of her home. The black stone sucked in any light, and Neve could feel it pulling at her like a dying star before supernova.

Neve inhaled through her nose, trying to steady herself before slipping in a first-floor window. She couldn't afford a frontal assault, not with the way her muscles ached with exhaustion. Her left arm hung limply by her side. She wasn't going to be fighting with it anytime soon. The thought made her stomach clench. She was going into this alone and one-handed.

There was something very wrong with the air inside. The convent was drafty at the best of times, but it had never been hollow. This place was a husk. It was a tomb. Neve and Mercy had never run through these halls, careening into walls and roughhousing with their muted strength. Bay had never filled the air with absentminded singing. Clara and Aoife had never walked hand in hand; Maeve had never read them bedtime stories in her drawling Irish brogue. This convent was desolate, but more than that, it was angry. It *hated*. Neve could feel the hate in it, oily and noxious.

Whatever was waiting for her, whatever had been haunting her for so long, it was here. It had always been here.

Neve prowled the empty halls, passing rooms that leered at her, mocking with how they resembled the place she'd grown up. She was braced and tense, anticipating attacks around every corner.

"Where are you?" Neve murmured as she hunted, holding her sword across her body. She wanted to call out, to scream, and draw attention. She wanted to get this over with already. The waiting was murder. Her nerves were fried. Neve wasn't built for this, and patience had never been her strong suit.

The library was the heart of the convent and Neve circled toward it, wound tighter and tighter with every step. She felt like something was pulling her forward, guiding her. Something she couldn't place but that had a viselike grip on her heart.

When she finally—*finally*—heard voices around a corner, Neve didn't bother with subtlety.

Fighting through the pain, she rounded the corner screaming. The guards staggered away from her, reaching for weapons, but she had the element of surprise. Neve slashed at the first, her blade slicing through his windpipe. He crumpled without a sound. Neve cut the other's legs out from under him and stabbed clean through his chest once he was on the ground.

They didn't disappear, and Neve wrenched her gaze away from the bodies, focusing on the massive double doors leading into the library instead. Whatever was beyond those doors, it had been waiting for a thousand years. Neve was by herself. She was injured and could barely muster the energy to scream.

But Alexandria was in there. Alexandria was in there, and Neve wasn't leaving this terrible place without her. It wasn't the smart thing to do—it wasn't even the *right* thing—but it was human, and in this moment, Neve was more human than she'd ever been.

She inhaled deeply through her nose before throwing the doors open hard enough that they collided against the walls with a loud bang.

Floating lanterns were barely enough to stave off the darkness, casting deep shadows around the gutted room. The bookshelves that Maeve had spent her life maintaining, the books the Daughters had collected for a thousand years, were all gone. Only the structure remained, the Gothic arches and skyscraping ceilings. The dark was alive in here, with teeth that ripped into something deeper and more important than just skin and sinew.

There were only a handful of people waiting for her, some dressed in parodies of modern clothes. Others wore leather armor that almost looked like Neve's, and every one of them radiated power and anger.

Neve raised an eyebrow as she surveyed them, trying to sound unafraid. She wished for Mercy's ice. "Can't lie, I don't love what you did with the place."

The crowd hissed its displeasure and Neve expected them to rush her, but none of them moved. Neve gripped her sword tight, her focus drawn to a figure sitting on a high-backed throne in the very center of the room. It was an enormous, twisted monstrosity made out of shining black stone and as she got closer, Neve saw that the figure—the *boy*—looked no older than sixteen. He could've been a student at Newgrange Harbor High School.

He was perched sideways, his long legs hanging off the side of the ridiculous throne. A shock of flame-red hair fell into eyes that watched her expectantly, lazily.

"Hey there, cousin," the boy said with a smile that Neve recognized with the sudden violence of a lightning strike. "It's been a while."

CHAPTER THIRTY-FOUR

I don't know you," Neve growled, trying desperately to ignore the similarities. High cheekbones stood proud under pale skin. Mercy's sharp jaw, Bay's nose, Neve's eyes, slate gray and unyielding. They could have been *twins*. "You're not my family."

"You know," the boy said, hopping off the throne and gliding toward her, "I would have thought the same thing a thousand or so years ago. I mean, what kind of *family* would leave us behind and then seal off the gates?"

"I don't know who you are," Neve said, more desperate this time. She couldn't afford to lose her focus now. Not when she was so close.

"You really don't remember, do you?" the boy said. He cocked his head curiously, like Neve did when she was confused. She gritted her teeth at the comparison. "Makes sense. Why bother remembering the people you betrayed and abandoned? Easier to pretend that you were right about everything when you don't remember the other side. You lock us away from the world, make us into monsters when we cross over, and sleep well at night thinking that you're heroes when you've been killing your own blood."

Who are you to me? Neve didn't recognize any of the assembled crowd. None of their faces prompted anything. The kid was the only familiar one here, and something in her stomach twisted. That wasn't right either, but Neve didn't know why. She didn't care why.

"Look," Neve snapped, cutting him off. The bystanders tittered, several sucking in shocked, horrified breaths. "Clearly, you've got some childhood issues to work out. But if you want to monologue, get a therapist. I'm here for the girl you stole."

"You mean my new friend?" The boy brightened, a smile lighting up his face. It was completely, utterly hollow.

"No, dickhead—" The tittering got louder and the boy's smile dropped, replaced by something blank and ancient and terrible. "She's not *your* anything. So how about you let her go before I lose my patience."

Neve flashed a smile of her own, all sharp teeth and promised violence. She prayed he wouldn't call her bluff.

"You do not speak to me like that," the boy said, his voice wiped of all expression. A feeling like static climbed over Neve's skin and suddenly the air smelled the way it did right before a storm. Like lightning.

Neve gestured to him up and down with the tip of her sword, stalling. "You're it, huh? The big bad evil guy?"

The boy blinked. He pitched forward and Neve didn't have time to brace herself before his face reappeared only inches in front of her own. She expected him to strike out, but he just stared at her, his uncanny eyes searching her face.

"You're boring without your memories." He grinned and Neve tried to throw herself out of his reach, but she wasn't fast enough. "Let's change that."

The pressure of his fingertip against her forehead felt as though it were shattering something inside her skull, something that wasn't meant to break. Neve sucked in a deep breath as her mental defenses were flattened by a hundred different images, a hundred different memories.

Aodh—Aodh, his name was Aodh—young and grinning, whispering to servants and watching with glee as they bent themselves to his will.

Blades flashing, sparking against one another as the four of them spun around an arena that was as familiar to her as the convent back home. Bay and Mercy, Neve and Aodh laughing recklessly as they fought, hard and bloody and brutal. Blue-gold blood shone on their skin, marking them as royalty. Bay had her arm wrapped around Aodh's shoulders, ruffling his bright red hair. Their family was vast, but he had always been their favorite. They were happy. Gods, they were all so happy. A dozen others looked on, shaking their heads indulgently. The Dagda. Danu. Brigid and Lug. Her family.

Neve, watching with horror as Aodh returned from the nearby human village with a pack of his followers. Not friends. Aodh didn't have friends, he had cronies. Neve was too late to stop them. She wasn't fast enough—she could only watch as the village burned. Every single human had been slaughtered.

Screaming, begging, pleading for him to stop. Trying to make them—Aodh, those who sided with him, all of them—understand that the best thing was to leave the humans be. They were going to die out if things didn't change.

Neve, Bay, and Mercy holding hands as they slipped out of the Gate and sealed it behind them. The tears drying on their cheeks as the spell took hold and they forgot their home, their true identities—

Everything.

Neve came back to her body with a curse, her head feeling foggy from the weight of the memories. It felt as if her heart had been ripped in two. Her vision was crowded, blurry with unshed tears. She blinked furiously, seeing a shadow of a young, grinning Aodh alongside his counterpart when she finally looked up.

Gods, she'd loved him. She *remembered* loving him. He was violent, impulsive, and terrible, but he was hers. Theirs.

"We tried to explain," Neve said. Her voice was thick with loss and her eyes burned. Not for the boy who stood before her, but for the one she'd left behind. The one she'd forgotten. "We tried to make you understand. You wouldn't listen."

"No, *you* wouldn't listen," Aodh snarled, furious once more. "We're better than them, we always have been. You three were always soft, you were always *so soft.* You loved the humans more than you loved us. You abandoned us here."

You abandoned me *here.* Neve felt his grief, her mind supplying the unsaid words.

"And what?" Neve shot back. "You're in charge now?" Even if he hadn't tripped her memories, Neve would know that wasn't right. Aodh wasn't meant to rule.

"Yes," Aodh shouted, rage settling over his features like ash. "This realm is *mine.* I fought for it, I fought to rule, and it is mine by right."

"Fought *who?*"

Aodh's eyes were far away, his breathing harsh. "You were gone. You three *left us* and they wouldn't listen to me. *None of them would listen.* So I gave them a choice. Exile or battle."

Rage she didn't expect felt like it was setting Neve alight from the inside. She'd never met her extended family—she'd learned their names and their legacies in the haphazard way she could—but some part of her knew that they wouldn't have stood by and allowed this. They would have fought. They would have *died.*

"It was about *respect*—" Aodh cried.

—*it's about* respect, *Nemain!* His voice rang in her ears, from another time. *We're better than they are, we're stronger*—

343

Neve shook her head, dismissing the memory before it could drag her under. "Bullshit," she spat through her teeth. "It was about power. That's all you ever wanted."

"Stop talking," Aodh shouted over her, his voice almost cracking. Behind her, the assembled demons ducked for cover. "Stop talking, stop talking, *stop talking*!" Something tingled on the back of her neck, a whisper of compulsion that tried to force Neve to do as he said. It poked at her, more and more insistent. Neve's blood pounded in her ears and she shoved the whisper away.

Aodh took a deep breath and smiled, terrible and triumphant as if nothing had happened. "It doesn't matter. You're back."

And gods only knew how much she wished she wasn't. Neve would do anything, trade anything, to never have set foot in this place. Anything but leave Alexandria behind. "I'm back because you took someone from me."

Aodh sighed like she'd disappointed him somehow. "You're so predictable. A thousand years and you're still stupid, Nemain."

Neve had the horrible feeling that he was waiting for this. It felt like the moment in the movie where the villain revealed his grand plan, only in this movie, the villain was the familicidal cousin that she'd forgotten she'd ever had.

Aodh snapped his fingers and Neve's attention shifted to

a door behind him. Her heart jumped violently as if it were trying to leap free of her chest.

Neve moved before the door was fully opened, halving the distance between them in three strides as dim light shone on Alexandria's face. *She's alive,* Neve chanted inside her head, elation and relief making her dizzy. Alexandria was alive. There was still hope.

"That's close enough," Aodh said.

Alexandria flinched at his voice, her face still shrouded in shadow.

"Of course you would go and fall in love with a human, Nemain," Aodh sighed. "I hoped you would surprise me."

Neve ignored him, her eyes scanning Alexandria's still form. She wasn't bleeding, she looked whole, but there was something wrong. The glow of relief began to dim as Neve tried and failed again to catch Alexandria's eye. Alexandria wouldn't look at her. Why wouldn't Alexandria look at her?

"Don't be rude, cousin," Aodh said with an enormous, unsettling grin. "You two might already know each other, but your friend hasn't been properly introduced." His eyes traveled past her to the congregation assembled behind them. "Everyone, meet Alexandria Kuro, the key to our salvation."

CHAPTER THIRTY-FIVE

Neve pressed her lips together to keep from roaring her frustration. What was he *talking* about?

All around her, the crowd burst into hushed conversation, their voices high with joy. Aodh kept his eyes firmly on Neve, trying to gauge her reaction. Neve ignored him, all her focus on Alexandria.

"You look a little confused, so let me explain," Aodh began, sounding so smug that Neve had to hold herself back to keep from attacking him outright. That wouldn't end well, not for any of them. And right now, her only goal was to get Alexandria out of here in one piece. "You probably thought you were being clever, making the way to undo the spell something you thought would never exist." He made a small flourish with his hands, gesturing to Alexandria, who cowered back even farther, as if she hoped she could disappear into the dark altogether. "A human born with the ability to cross between worlds."

He smiled. "It was a good trick, but you always overestimated your abilities. You thought that the Gate would be the only way we could break free, and you dedicated your pathetic little reincarnation cycles to protecting it. None of you thought that there would be weak spots in the world where we could pass through." His smile turned cold and furious. "Having to wait for the others to kill you three over and over again has been frustrating, but I will admit, it's flattering, how much magic you spent to keep *me* from escaping in particular."

"You want someone to blame?" Neve growled, a part of her aching at the tucked-away hurt in his words. "Look in the mirror. You're the reason we did any of this in the first place."

"Neve." Alexandria's voice cut into whatever retort Aodh was about to make, and Neve nearly burst into tears. "Hell sucks."

Aodh made an impatient noise, waving his hand as his attention diverted to Alexandria. "We've tried to explain that this place isn't Hell, despite your best efforts to convince yourselves otherwise, but it seems like you chose a partner just as stubborn as you are, Nemain."

"I didn't think that demons would look like sixteen-year-old shitheads, either," Alexandria said, warming up. Her eyes blazed, simmering with anger Neve had never seen before. Like her fear was combustible, sparking and ready to burst into flame. "But my worldview is flexible."

Any hint of humor vanished from Aodh's face. Neve moved before he could open his mouth to give an order, spanning the distance between her and Alexandria in the space of a breath. Neve spun, positioning herself so she was between Alexandria and the rest of them.

"Jesus shit," Alexandria whispered, leaning her forehead against Neve's back. The fabric of her shirt dampened with tears.

We're going to be okay, Neve wanted to tell her. *We're going to get out of here.* But first, she needed to keep her cousin from killing them out of sheer spite.

"Always with the drama." Aodh rolled his eyes, as if he hadn't had a temper tantrum ten seconds ago. "Really, Nemain, there's no need for bloodshed. I was going to give her back to you. In fact, you can both go right now."

One of the demons waved its hands and a black ripple appeared in the air, looking like the Hellgate had when the demons opened it from the outside. Weak spots, Aodh had said. Like the ones he'd used to terrorize Alexandria by proxy for years. Neve's chest tightened again.

It was a trap. Of course it was; it had to be. There was no point in letting them go so easily, not after everything he'd done to get Alexandria here. The rippling portal widened, and Neve could almost hear the ocean and the sound of ravensong. Home.

"I'm serious," Aodh said, waving them toward the rip in reality. "You're both free."

Alexandria's hands clenched around the fabric of Neve's shirt. "You need to go," she whispered. "But you have to leave me behind."

"What?" How could she even suggest something like that? "I'm not leaving without you."

"If I go through, the spell breaks," Alexandria explained in a broken whisper. "I'm not supposed to exist. I'm the key." She sucked in a shaky breath, nodding at the portal. "That's the lock. I'm what keeps them here, and if I go through, they follow me out. That's why they were always after me, why—why they killed my parents. They were trying to bring me here, so that I could free them."

Alexandria managed a brave smile even as tears streaked down her cheeks. "But I want you to go. Go be with your sisters and Poe and the Daughters and . . . and our friends. Tell them I say hi. And sorry and stuff. You'll come up with something."

"Tell them yourself." Neve shook her head. "You're coming home."

"No. I'm not."

Neve snarled. "Alexandria. I love you, but you are coming back with me. I will carry you if I have to."

"That's not how it works. It has to be my choice, and I choose to stay. It's safer this way."

"*I don't care.*"

Aodh yawned loudly, stretching his arms over his head. He tilted his chin at Alexandria. "This is touching, but it's time to choose, human. You can free us now or you can watch me kill Nemain, and we'll see how stubborn you really are. The result will be the same, but by all means, don't rush on my account." Aodh's smile was vicious. "I have a thousand years' worth of ideas of how to fill the time."

The threat hung in the air, crackling with violent anticipation, and it felt like the silence might stretch forever before Neve broke it. More specifically, one of her cousin's cronies broke it when he collapsed into a boneless puddle, arterial blood spraying out of his neck as Neve's knife pierced the soft place beneath his chin.

"Don't let go of me," Neve ordered, offering Alexandria her useless left hand. Alexandria grabbed hold and Neve crossed her sword over her chest. She couldn't scream, not without hurting Alexandria in the process, but Neve ducked through the churning mass, dodging and parrying instead of attacking outright, her focus squarely on the door. She needed to get Alexandria out of here; that was her priority, despite the bloody haze in her vision and how very much she wanted to kill everything in sight.

Her blade moved as fast as she could force her injured, aching muscles to go as she hacked through anything that got close enough to feel the bite of blessed steel. But there were too many of them, and she was fighting one-handed.

"Neve!" Alexandria shouted, and her hand tore out of Neve's grip.

Neve spun, reaching for her, and then the library doors exploded open from the outside, kicked with enough force that they blasted off their hinges.

"Get away from our sister!" Mercy screamed as she and Bay charged into the room, bloody and furious. Neve's heart leaped. They were here. They were alive and they were here.

The fire in her chest relit and new energy surged through Neve's body, driving her forward. Neve dodged through the crowd, never taking her eyes off Alexandria. Just a little closer, a little closer, and—

Impact. Neve heard the squelch of a blade entering her body and felt it twist inside her, turning her middle into a bloody, pulpy mess.

"Oh," she managed before the air vacated her lungs in a rush, leaving a painful vacuum behind. She blinked, her eyes tracing the violent lines of the sword protruding from her chest with detached, almost clinical, interest. Her knees buckled and she fell against a set of narrow shoulders.

Familiar gray eyes met hers. "Sorry, cousin." Aodh paused, giving her a considering look before he twisted the blade in deeper. Neve felt something break inside her. She would have collapsed if not for her grip on Aodh's shoulders and the steadiness of the blade holding her up.

Red hair brushed against her cheek as Aodh leaned in close. "I loved you the most, you know." Neve believed him, even now, even in this moment. "I hope this hurts a *fraction* of how much you hurt me."

Aodh yanked the sword out of her chest with a horrible wet scrape and Neve dropped like she was already dead. She didn't remember hitting the floor, but suddenly she was staring up at the ceiling as darkness began to creep into her vision. At least there wasn't any pain. There should have been pain.

Blood poured out of the wound in her midsection with every beat of her heart, and some absent instinct told her that her chest had been injured beyond repair. All around her, the battle raged, but it sounded as if it were moving farther and farther away with every passing second. Screams, pounding footsteps, the clang of metal against metal . . . it all faded away.

I'm sorry, Neve tried to say, but her lungs weren't working, and any sound that came out of her mouth was choked by the blue-gold blood that bubbled up in her throat. She wasn't sure who she was apologizing to. The Daughters, for taking them for granted. Her friends, for not appreciating them until it was too late. Alexandria, for not saving her.

Her sisters, for never being strong enough. For dragging them here. For failing them.

I'm sorry, she thought again. Even dying, even in her last thoughts, she didn't ask for their forgiveness. She knew that she didn't deserve it.

There was a flash of light somewhere above her, and for a single, delusional second, Neve thought that it was the after-life beckoning to her. She dismissed that thought as quickly as it had come. There was no afterlife for her, nothing on the horizon but darkness.

The light dimmed again and the cold that had started in her extremities crept through her limbs as death marched steadily toward her heart.

Gods, what a useless way to die.

Someone shouted above her, and through the haze of quiet that had descended, Neve could feel her body being moved, dragged by several pairs of hands. She wanted to swat at them, tell them not to bother. She was tired. She wanted to rest. She didn't deserve much, but maybe she deserved that.

"—not allowed to die on me, do you hear me!" Neve knew that voice. "I will never forgive you if you give up."

Maiden, Mother, and Crone, Neve just wanted to sleep. She was exhausted, and the dark was so peaceful. Everything else was too loud and too bright.

"Neve Morgan, I love you, and that means that *you are not allowed to die!*"

Alexandria. It was Alexandria. Oh. That changed things. Neve never had been able to refuse her.

"Stop yelling," she muttered. Her voice was mostly unintelligible, garbled by the blood in her mouth, but it must have been something. The sound of Alexandria's frantic laughter was almost enough to make Neve want to live.

That impulse lasted all of ten seconds, until Neve managed to pry her eyelids open to see that she was no longer inside the convent. She wasn't inside at all. The sky was iron gray above her, storm clouds threatening to break at any second, and behind, the ocean roared, beating against the sand. She was home. Somehow, impossibly, Alexandria had gotten her home.

Mercy, Bay, and Alexandria's pale, drawn faces floated above her, grimy and bloodstained. But they were *there.* They were safe, all of them. They hadn't died for her.

"It didn't work," Alexandria breathed, her gaze fixed on the Hellgate. The cliff face looked as normal and undisturbed as ever. The four of them were the only ones on the beach. They hadn't been followed. "Holy shit, it didn't work."

Even bleeding out on the sand, Neve allowed herself a moment of hazy relief. Aodh had lied. Alexandria wasn't the key after all. They were all still trapped; they couldn't get out.

Then, beside her, any remaining color drained from Mercy's face.

"*No*," she gasped.

Lightning flashed in the sky as the clouds opened, drenching them in seconds. The beach shook as if the very earth were quaking beneath them, and all at once, the cliff imploded. Alexandria swore, ducking her head to avoid the spray of debris, and Neve could only stare in horror as her nightmares came to life before her eyes.

The Hellgate was open, and her family was coming home.

ACKNOWLEDGMENTS

I always wonder what percentage of readers actually read the acknowledgments. I do. So if you've made it to the end and you're reading this, hi! I hope you liked the book. Don't tell me if you didn't; it's not my business.

First and foremost, I have to thank my agent, Patrice Caldwell, and my editor, Nicole Ellul. I couldn't have asked for a better duo of champions to help me wrangle this story into shape. Patrice, thank you for your advice and enthusiasm and for emailing me back so quickly when I queried you one million years ago in 2019. Nicole, thank you for your patience and wisdom as I stumbled through the editorial process. I couldn't have done this without either of you.

I also want to thank Pouya Shahbazian, Trinica Sampson, Katherine Curtis, and the rest of the New Leaf team for making this book a reality, as well as the amazing folks at Simon & Schuster, especially Justin Chanda, Kendra Levin, Amanda Brenner, Sarah Creech, Nicole Valdez, and Alyza Liu. Without them, this book would still be a Word file on my laptop, and I'm eternally grateful.

Writing books is a supremely weird job where I get to tell stories for a living, and I've willingly given myself homework for the rest of my life. To Erica Waters, Courtney Gould, Cat

Scully, and Eunjoo Han, thank you for being willing to sit in the proverbial library with me. I love you guys.

Thank you to Alice, Mike, Mith, Abby, Miriam, Rachel, and everyone who has supported me throughout this whole process and been the best cheerleading section a guy could ask for.

To the friends who have watched me go just a little bit insane throughout this process and who are always there with distractions or snacks, or up for impromptu walks in the rain, I love you all so much. Kristen, Kiera, Kelsey, Stasia, Addy, Diana, the Seminar, the Sparra Queen's Ensemble, and the Council of Luxu, your unending support and willingness to listen to publishing-related ramblings during D&D or when we should have been studying for finals mean the world to me.

Mom and Dad, thank you for always supporting my love of reading and being my biggest champions. Eamon and Lauren, you're my best friends in the whole world even when it feels like I'm from another one entirely. Three cheers to the Clampits.

Finally, to you, the reader: thank you. Books don't exist without someone to read them, and I hope Neve and her sisters found a place in your heart the way they did in mine.